8AB

Ryan raced up to the floor-to-ceiling barrier

The gate was made of heavy steel, ribbed vertically and horizontally for strength, and was nearly watertight. Its hinges were on the other side, inaccessible. The gate was jammed closed. He tried kicking out one of the unreinforced panels, hoping it had rusted through.

It hadn't.

"Fire blast!" he muttered, giving the gate another kick for good measure.

From the channel behind him came the sound of a terrible collision and a squeal of bending metal. There was a pause, then it sounded again. Collision. Squeal.

"Ryan!" J.B. shouted, his cry echoing down the channel.

And then the Smith boomed, and kept on booming.

Other titles in the Deathlands saga:

JAMES AXLER

DEATH LANDS®

Labyrinth

A GOLD EAGLE BOOK FROM
WORLDWIDE®

TORONTO • NEW YORK • LONDON
AMSTERDAM • PARIS • SYDNEY • HAMBURG
STOCKHOLM • ATHENS • TOKYO • MILAN
MADRID • WARSAW • BUDAPEST • AUCKLAND

First edition March 2006

ISBN 0-373-62583-9

LABYRINTH

Printed in U.S.A.

As soon as men decide that all means are permitted to fight an evil, then their good becomes indistinguishable from the evil that they set out to destroy.

—Christopher Dawson
1889–1970

THE DEATHLANDS SAGA

This world is their legacy, a world born in the violent nuclear spasm of 2001 that was the bitter outcome of a struggle for global dominance.

There is no real escape from this shockscape where life always hangs in the balance, vulnerable to newly demonic nature, barbarism, lawlessness.

But they are the warrior survivalists, and they endure—in the way of the lion, the hawk and the tiger, true to nature's heart despite its ruination.

Ryan Cawdor: The privileged son of an East Coast baron. Acquainted with betrayal from a tender age, he is a master of the hard realities.

Krysty Wroth: Harmony ville's own Titian-haired beauty, a woman with the strength of tempered steel. Her premonitions and Gaia powers have been fostered by her Mother Sonja.

J. B. Dix, the Armorer: Weapons master and Ryan's close ally, he, too, honed his skills traversing the Deathlands with the legendary Trader.

Doctor Theophilus Tanner: Torn from his family and a gentler life in 1896, Doc has been thrown into a future he couldn't have imagined.

Dr. Mildred Wyeth: Her father was killed by the Ku Klux Klan, but her fate is not much lighter. Restored from predark cryogenic suspension, she brings twentieth-century healing skills to a nightmare.

Jak Lauren: A true child of the wastelands, reared on adversity, loss and danger, the albino teenager is a fierce fighter and loyal friend.

Dean Cawdor: Ryan's young son by Sharona accepts the only world he knows, and yet he is the seedling bearing the promise of tomorrow.

In a world where all was lost, they are humanity's last hope....

Prologue

Corn Blossom choked on the first sip of the potion and her eyes filled with tears. Despite the harsh, bitter taste, she had to drink every drop. The eleven-year-old brushed aside her tears and took another, bigger swallow from the shaman's feather-decorated gourd.

From the ledge on which she stood, the far side of the canyon was a wall of black, topped by a starry sweep of sky. Trapped heat came off the distant rock in waves, pulsing through the breathless night. Her clan made its home in a broad hollow high in the canyon face, carved over millennia by wind-driven sand. Light from the communal firepit flickered over their flat-sided, mud-brick dwellings.

Hundreds of feet below, the rustling sounds grew much louder. Something crashed through the dry grass and chapparal on the canyon floor. Something huge and powerful. Drawing strength from their fear, Corn Blossom's people began to chant and beat drums with sticks, this to drown out the terrifying noises. Like her, they had painfully bloated bellies and their lips were cracked and bleeding.

The rain had stopped two winters past, rain the clan depended upon to grow squash, corn and beans in the canyon, and on the mesa directly above the cave. As the stockpiles of food in their stone-lined pits dwindled, Corn Blossom's people scavenged far and wide, but there was no game left in the canyon, and the fish had vanished along with the river. They were reduced to eating grass and insects. A world that had been lush and full of promise had become a wasteland of suffering and slow death. Dust storms divided the day, and at night the blistering air spawned hungry demons.

Neighboring settlements in the other galleries along the canyon's cliffs had already been abandoned, the long ladders discarded, the dark window openings and doorways of vacant houses like the eye sockets and drop-jawed maws of piled skulls.

The people who left the canyon were never heard from again. No trace of them was ever found. No campsites. No clothing. No bones. To spend even one night on the canyon floor meant destruction. Under the light of the full moon, Corn Blossom's own father had disappeared like a curl of smoke.

Before descending the ladder to face and fight the evil that was bedeviling them, he had given her a necklace, his most prized possession. As she drained the last of the shaman's potion, she tightly squeezed the small white shells between her fingers. In Corn Blossom's world, before the coming of Colombus, before Heisenberg, Einstein and Rutherford, all events were connected, like the string of beads around her neck. In 1300 A.D., coincidence didn't exist; everything that happened had a cause. It was a logic born of ignorance. Of desperation. Of fear.

Logic said something had brought this calamity upon her people. It said such causes could be addressed, disastrous outcomes averted by human action. Of the ten young girls in her encampment, Corn Blossom was the brightest, the happiest, the quickest. Cherished by all. Logic said only she could appease the angry gods, because it was her life, her joy, they coveted.

As the herbal concoction took effect, Corn Blossom swayed on the balls of her feet. She felt light enough to lift off and float free of the earth. Then she began to dance to the drums, her bare feet shuffling in the dust, eyes burning from the potion and the shifting pall of smoke.

After she had made a number of slow circuits around the firepit, the shaman led her to the domed rock that jutted from the lip of their ledge like a bowsprit.

Corn Blossom climbed to the crest of the rock and looked back at her mother, her sisters, brothers, aunts, uncles and grandparents. Their drumming and chanting was mixed with sobbing and shrill cries. She loved them, and she loved the world as she remembered it, before the rain stopped falling. For the return of that happy time, no sacrifice was too great. She turned away from the familiar faces, her heart aching.

Arms spread wide, Corn Blossom closed her eyes and jumped into the dark.

The shaman had promised her no pain.

He was almost right.

The wind whipping past her ears drowned out the drumbeats and the screams of sorrow. When her head hit the sloping cliff some fifty feet down, there was an

instant of sharp discomfort, then her unconscious body
started to tumble and bounce. She never felt the impact
with the canyon floor.

At daybreak when her people climbed down, they
found no body. The only footprints in the sand were
theirs.

SOME SEVEN HUNDRED YEARS later, in the spring of 1992,
a Korean war-surplus 6x6 stopped on the same canyon
floor. The river flowed cloudy and green in a deep channel along the foot of Corn Blossom's cliff. Among the
ten tourists sitting in the bench seats on the truck bed
was a stocky black woman in her late twenties. She
aimed her 35 mm camera at the high cleft. The tele-
photo zoom lens revealed a double row of deserted
structures partially hidden in shadow.

A thirteenth century high-rise, Dr. Mildred Wyeth
thought, snapping the shutter. She wished she could
have seen the view from up there. But that was impossible because the archaeological site, like the others in
the canyon, was off-limits to nonmembers of the Hopi
tribe, who owned the land.

Other shutters clicked around her, like spastic casta-
nets.

With the long lens Mildred picked out the hand- and
footholds chipped into the nearly vertical bedrock—the
commute to and from the canyon bottom had been per-
ilous, to say the least.

The canyon's vanished residents had been a vigor-
ous, athletic people with no fear of heights. A stark con-
trast to Mildred's fellow passengers, who preferred to

have their life experiences spoon-fed to them while sitting down. Her companions for the day included four Japanese men in Bermuda shorts; an impatient German couple who had brought along enough food for six, but had offered to share none of it; and three portly, middle-aged American ladies in brand-new, pastel billcaps, T-shirts, daypacks and hiking shoes.

Mildred would've much rather explored the canyon on foot or horseback, but the constraints of a week-long holiday and a lengthy itinerary made that impossible. It was her first real vacation in a long time, and she had crammed it full of interesting things to do. Perhaps too full, it turned out.

Though Mildred was a medical doctor, she didn't have a client practice. She worked for a university-affiliated, cryogenic research company. Her field of expertise was cellular crystallization, one of the major obstacles to successful reanimation of living tissue from deep cold.

The basic problem was biophysical. When the cells of most animals were frozen, their watery fluids turned to ice, which expanded to burst or crush vital, cellular components. Only a handful of species had cells that could withstand freezing, and those species revived on their own when warmed. The cells of these unique creatures contained a sugar called trehalose, which acted like antifreeze, lowering the crystallization temperature. Mildred had already verified that the transplant life of dissected, refrigerated rat hearts could be extended by many days when stored in a trehalose solution. Her ongoing research tested ways the sugar could be introduced into living bodies, and the effects of different concentrations during freezing.

Mildred was passionate about her work, which she believed would ultimately change the way all human disease was fought. Once the cryogenic process was perfected, dying patients could be safely stored until science found cures, however long that took.

While Mildred and the others snapped photos of the ruins, the sour-faced Hopi driver-tour guide probed his ear with a wooden matchstick. He wore a straw cowboy hat and his gray-streaked black hair was pulled back in a long ponytail. No cab separated him from his passengers; the 6x6 had a floorplan like a bus, only without a roof or side walls to obstruct the views.

When the shutter-clicking slowed, the driver tucked the grooming tool back in his hat band and spoke into a hand microphone. His slow drawl came out of a loudspeaker screwed to the truck bed's wooden rails. "That settlement's number eleven on your list," he informed them. "We call it the Castle because it's so high up, and because folks think it looks like one. It was first excavated in 1928, by archaeologists from the University of California at Berkeley. The buildings are from the Pueblo Three Period, from 1050 to 1300 A.D. Our ancient ones lived up there for more than five hundred years."

By "our," he meant Hopi.

From her advance reading on the subject, Mildred knew there were few hard facts about the cliff people of the canyon. They had drawn symbols on the rocks, but had left no written language to explain them. It was assumed that extended drought, which the area was prone to, had driven them away. Where they had gone and what had happened to them was anybody's guess. The Navajo, who had lived nearby for millennia, referred to the cliff people as "our ancient enemies." The Hopi and Navajo had been enemies for as long as anyone could remember, so the Hopi concluded they were related to the cliff people.

Mildred tuned out her guide. Aside from parroting terms and theories devised by social scientists to fill doctoral theses, he had nothing new to say about the missing residents, or their erased culture. Looking up at the abandoned site, Mildred felt a profound sense of loss, and of tragedy. Looking up at the ruins, she was certain that what had happened to the cliff people could never happen to her own, immensely more powerful civilization. Mildred believed in human progress and the perfectability of knowledge, a juggernaut of scientific truth rolling ever forward, ever faster.

She was dead wrong on all counts, of course.

Numbers alone didn't guarantee immunity from extinction. Nor did the weight of accumulated scientific knowledge. A century would pass before she saw the awful truth with her own eyes: That a juggernaut of progress could fly apart in an instant and take everything with it.

The final site on the tour was a half mile down-canyon, on the other side of a freestanding spire almost as tall as the mesa. Shutters snapped, but feebly this time; the pile of rocks on a low slope was hardly scenic.

"Those are the ruins of an old cabin, number twelve

on your list," the guide said. "The woman who lived in it spent her whole life in this canyon. She was born here. She never married. She died in that hut at age 109 in the 1930s. People believe she was the last of a long, unbroken line of powerful witches. They say she spoke with the spirits of our ancient ones, and that while she was alive her magic spells kept the canyon's demons sleeping. Some folks say they still do."

Mildred perked up. There was very little in the academic literature about the spiritual beliefs, or supposed beliefs, of the canyon's lost people.

"What demons?" she asked him.

"Man-eaters," he said matter-of-factly. "Folks say they've always been here. No one's sure whether the drought makes them, or whether they bring the drought with them when they come. The two are kind of a package deal. Legends say the demons are born hungry, out of the hot, still air. They only hunt at night. They love the dark. Lucky for us, we haven't had a serious drought in a long time."

"What are they supposed to look like?"

"No one knows. No one who has ever seen one has survived to talk about it."

Before the guide could elaborate further, the German couple started complaining loudly about the biting flies rising from nearby stands of scrub laurel. When the other passengers chimed in, the show was over. Smiling for the first time all day, the guide cranked up the 6x6 and drove on, crossing and recrossing the meandering stream as the canyon grew ever wider. On the other side of a broad meadow, the rutted dirt track intersected a paved road.

A mile down the two-lane highway, they reached cultivated fields and widely spaced, ramshackle trailers and cinder-block houses of riverside farms that gradually gave way to the outskirts of a small New Mexico town. Little Pueblo had an aroma all its own: part fertilizer, part Mexican spices, part grain silo.

The driver stopped the 6x6 in the parking lot of the Rest Easy Motel, where the trip had begun five hours ago. As his passengers rose to their feet, he said, "If you're looking for an authentic Native American meal tonight, try the fry bread tacos at Lupita's, off the town square. They're the real deal. And I'm not just saying that because she's my auntie."

Mildred had two more national parks to hit before her flight home on the weekend. And even though she did have time to stop and eat, dinner at Lupita's was out of the question. She'd peeked in the café window earlier, while waiting for the tour to start. The pillowy, golden brown fry bread dripped with artery-plugging grease.

When Mildred left sleepy, pungent Little Pueblo in her rental car that afternoon, she was sure she'd seen the last of the place.

She was wrong about that, too.

Chapter One

Ryan Cawdor gnawed the final, juicy gobbet of flesh from the boar rib, then tossed the bone over his shoulder to the pack of dogs prowling the rows of long tables. The resulting, savage combat was barely audible over the general din.

The stone hall's arched ceiling rang with the fiddles, squeezeboxes, trumpets and drums of a half-dozen, competing musical groups. It resounded with the clatter of knives on plates, the crash of shattering crockery, and from the far side of the room, with the scuffling, grunting chaos of a bare-knuckle brawl. The immense room was lit by bonfires roaring in massive fireplaces, torches burning in iron stanchions and candelabras spaced at intervals along the tables. Huge, faded tapestries draped the mortared walls. Dimly visible in the gloom overhead were strings of colorful pennants that hung from the high, wooden rafters.

After wiping his fingers on the table linen, Ryan paused to scratch the thick welt of scar that split the left side of his face from brow to cheek, zigzagging beneath the black patch that concealed an empty eye socket. A servant in a stained leather tunic placed a heaping platter at his elbow. Char-roasted backstraps of venison beckoned.

But first, something to cleanse the palate.

Ryan hefted a discus of sweet potato pie. The crisp, buttery crust fractured in his hands as he raised it to his mouth. In three quick bites he ate half of it. The rest he chucked over his shoulder. Drawing his panga from its leg sheath, he speared a backstrap and settled down to serious work.

It was gamy but good.

It was all good. And the courses kept coming.

Ryan ate like an animal, trying to satisfy a bottomless appetite. Though the food tasted delicious, it had no substance after he swallowed it. He had been eating for what seemed like hours, so long that his jaws ached from the chewing, and still his stomach felt hollow.

He sat in a throne chair on a dais, slightly elevated above the other diners. Beside him on a less ornate chair was his lover and battle mate, Krysty Wroth. The color of her low-cut, emerald-velvet gown matched the color of her eyes, and set off the blaze of her long sentient red hair, which had retracted into a mass of eager coils around her face. Perspiration glazed the silky cleft between her breasts and her cheeks were brightly flushed, consequences of the hall's sweltering heat.

A wave of dizziness swept over Ryan, and he nearly passed out into his plate. He was so hungry he kept forgetting to breathe between bites. He forced himself to slow down and look up from the food.

The others seated at his table had come a long way to join the party.

From the far side of the grave, to be exact.

Prince Victor Boldt, Baron Nelson Mandeville, Mashashige, Yashimoto, Captain Pyra Quadde, Baron Sean Sharpe, Cissie Torrance, Baron Tourment and Ryan's misshapen brother, Harvey, had thrown off their shrouds and were again housed in living flesh.

Despite the fact that Ryan had sealed their respective dooms, his old enemies seemed to bear him no grudge. They were in excellent spirits, gorging on the mounded banquet platters and drinking from steaming mugs of high-proof, buttered grog.

At the surrounding tables, through the shifting clouds of smoke, he glimpsed less familiar, but recognizable faces, the cannon fodder of a hundred battles, sec men and mercies who had fallen to his blaster or blade. It was among these triple stupes that the brawl had broken out.

Ryan was still pondering the puzzle of the party's guest list when Harvey Cawdor got up from his chair. Death, it appeared, had shown him no more mercy than life: Harvey still had the cruelly twisted body he'd been born with. He hoisted his mug high in salute. "Here's to Ryan Cawdor," he cried, "the glorious hero of Deathlands!"

Harvey shouted over the cheers. "Considering what he did to each of us, I think one thing's safe to say— we should have kept an eye out for him."

The tired joke drew groans and boos. Boldt and Quadde pelted the deformed man with compressed wads of bread and bits of gristle.

"And how about that panga?" Harvey crowed, undeterred. "Sure, long is good when it comes to blades, but isn't eighteen inches overcompensating for something?" He waggled his pinkie finger at Ryan.

A much better comedic effort.

Encouraged by the coarse laughter of his audience, Harvey climbed to a precarious perch on the seat of his chair. He plunged a hand into his fly and unlimbered himself. "Here's to brotherhood!" he cried, urinating in a broad arc across the banquet table, spraying and scattering the guests on the other side.

"Judging from Little Harvey there," Krysty remarked, "*your* knife must be a yard long."

Her jibe put the diners over the top. As they howled in glee, they pounded on the table with their fists and the pommels of their knives. Harvey was so amused he fell off his chair.

Penis jokes and golden showers, normally grounds for bloodshed in Ryan's world, raised no hackles this night. Everybody was having too good a time to take offense. The no-longer-dead hooted and backslapped one another as they reclaimed their places at the table.

Servants brought fresh platters of roasted meats, and long trays of cakes and pies. As everyone got busy, fiddle, squeezebox and drum started up right behind the guest of honor's throne.

Krysty pointed at a corner of Ryan's mouth. "You're dripping," she told him.

He wiped his mouth with the back of his hand, then looked down at a smear of red across his knuckles. Something tickled in the back of his throat, and he sneezed suddenly, and with great force. A gob of bloody matter shot out of his nose and landed on the tablecloth. As he stared at it, the gob fell apart, its minute components wriggling off in all directions. Ryan belched and tasted copper; his head started to spin, then his stomach convulsed. Hunching over, he vomited a shapeless, fluid mass onto his plate. Gray under their sheen of blood, like fibers of steel wool, the squirming wire worms gave off a rotten-egg stench.

Ryan shoved violently back from the table, and looking up, viewed the feast in a new light.

Literally.

The row of torches had ignited the threadbare tapestries, and the walls seethed with flame, brightly illuminating the hall—and its occupants. Seated at his table, and all the other tables were cobwebbed, moldering corpses. He turned to Krysty, and seeing her, let loose a bellow of pain.

A small, hairy-legged spider had built a home between her shriveled breasts. Her hair hung lank and lifeless to her shoulders. Her eyes were closed, and deeply sunken in their sockets, but the skin of her eyelids, face and neck twitched and rippled, animated by the still-busy parasites beneath.

As Ryan recoiled in shock, the high-pitched notes of the fiddle and squeezebox turned into a shrill, electronic whine, and the drumbeat became an intermittent whipcrack.

He came awake with a hard jerk, gasping for air.

There was none.

He lay curled on an armaglass floor, his throat scorched, a burning pain spearing deep in his lungs, and withering heat beating against his back. Gray smoke, thick with particulate matter, swirled in the small chamber, transected by wild flashes of electricity.

The jump dream had ended but his nightmare continued.

The mat-trans unit was on fire.

Beside him on the floor, he could see the slumping forms of his five companions. As he pushed up from the blistering hot armaglass, his world went dim around the edges—lack of oxygen was shutting down his brain. If he allowed himself to pass out, they would all die, and horribly. A tingling rush of adrenaline brought Ryan to full consciousness.

He had to use his shoulder to crack loose the door of the mat-trans unit, which was stuck in the jamb. It swung open, revealing an anteroom lit by a bank of flickering fluorescent bulbs. Fresh air rushed in around him, feeding the flames. Ryan sucked down a quick breath, then turned back to the blaze and his helpless friends.

He grabbed hold of the nearest arm and dragged its owner's body over to the portal. The tails of Doc Tanner's frock coat were smoking as Ryan tumbled him out of the chamber. The lanky old man didn't move. There was no time to check for a pulse—fire was starting to shoot up along the expansion seams in the armaglass floor.

Ryan gathered Krysty in his arms. Though she was unconscious, her prehensile mutie hair had retracted into the tight ringlets of mortal fear. She moaned as he unceremoniously pitched her out of the doorway.

When Ryan tried to do the same for Jak Lauren, the albino came to in his grasp. Faster than a blink, the wild child of Deathlands had the razor-sharp point of a leaf-bladed knife jammed against the front of Ryan's throat, his slitted, blood red eyes glittering.

"Jak, it's me," Ryan said, giving him a hard shake. "For nuke's sake, wake up."

The youth's eyes widened, and he immediately lowered the blade.

"Come on," Ryan said as he turned back for the others. "We've got to hurry.…"

After dragging their two remaining companions over the threshold, he and Jak did the same with all their backpacks. Crossing the chamber was like being caught on an armaglass skillet. Impervious to heat, the unit's floor plates weren't burning; it was the material beneath—circuitry, floor joists, insulation—that was on fire. Boot soles melting, Ryan retrieved his predark treasure, a scoped Steyr SSG-70 sniper rifle.

Jak staggered out of the mat-trans ahead of him, his lank white hair and ghostly skin peppered with soot. Ryan was relieved to see the rest of his crew, certainly worse for wear, but alive and awake.

Krysty sat on the floor, her long legs drawn up to her chest. She looked dazed, but she wasn't burned. In the eerie, flickering light, trapped smoke rose like steam from the shoulders and back of her fur coat.

Dr. Mildred Wyeth knelt beside her. The stocky black woman was dressed in an OD jacket, camouflage BDU pants, jungle boots and a sleeveless gray T-shirt. She wore her hair in braided, beaded plaits. On her hip was a Czech ZKR 551 revolver in a pancake holster, the same weapon she had used to win a silver medal in pistol shooting in the last-ever Olympic Games. Shortly after that victory, she had been the victim of complications during surgery, a result of reaction to anesthetic. To save her life, the medical team put her in cryogenic stasis. Less than a month later, when a massive thermonuclear exchange between the United States and the Soviet Union ended civilization, Mildred slept dreamlessly through it. She continued to sleep for another hundred years, until Ryan and the others revived her.

What had gone so terribly wrong on January 20, 2001, was anybody's guess.

Human error. Machine error. A combination of same.

And the sad truth was, it no longer mattered.

All the people who gave a damn about laying blame had been vaporized The great mistake, once made, was uncorrectable; by its very nature, it could never be repeated. It had destroyed Earth and its potential; it had derailed human history.

While Mildred attended to Krysty, Doc released the catch on his ebony sword stick and unsheathed the rapier blade. Satisfied that it wasn't damaged, he resheathed it and checked his side arm. From a tooled Mexican leather holster, he drew a massive, gold engraved revolver. The two-barreled Le Mat was a Civil War, black powder relic, and the original "room broom." Beneath a six-and-a-half-inch pistol barrel, hung a second, scattergun barrel, chambered for a single load of "blue whistlers."

Though Dr. Theophilus Algernon Tanner appeared to be a well preserved sixty, as with Mildred Wyeth, appearances were deceiving. Chronologically his age was closer to four times sixty. The Harvard- and Oxford-educated Tanner had the distinction of being the first human time traveler, albeit an unwilling one. He had been ripped from the loving bosom of his family in 1896, and drawn one hundred years into the future by the whitecoats of Operation Chronos. Doc had spent his brief time in the late 1990s as a prisoner, locked down inside the ultrasecret facility. The jubilation of the twentieth-century scientists over their success was short-lived, thanks to Tanner's ingratitude, truculence and general unpleasantness. Shortly before skydark, to rid themselves of the troublemaker, and to further test the limits of their experimental technology, they had hurled him forward in time. In so doing, they had inadvertently saved him from the nukecaust.

John Barrymore Dix, his fedora pushed way back on his head, was preoccupied, patting down his coat pockets. Ryan and J.B. had been running buddies since their convoy days with Trader, Deathlands' legendary freebooter. It was Trader who had given J.B., a weapons specialist of extraordinary talent, the nickname "Armorer." Finding nothing in his coat, with more urgency J.B. turned to his trousers. When he looked up from the fruitless search, Ryan read the expression behind the smudged, wire-rimmed glasses.

Triple red.

Dropping his Smith & Wesson M-4000, 12-gauge shotgun, J.B. jumped for the mat-trans unit. "Fire in the hole!" he shouted. "Get down!"

As J.B. grabbed the edge of the door, a string of explosions from inside the chamber rocked the room. In the same instant, a volley of buckshot ricocheted out the portal at a steep upward angle, cutting ragged furrows in the acoustic tile ceiling and shattering fluorescent bulbs.

J.B. slammed the door shut, sealing the last of the 12-gauge cook-offs behind armaglass and steel. Over the muffled explosions of the accidentally dropped shells, J.B. cursed a blue streak. He had cause to be upset with himself. In Deathlands, reliable ammo was more valuable than gold.

Even with the door closed, the adjoining walls and ceiling were starting to blister from the heat. Though there were smoke sensors and fire suppression nozzles placed at intervals along the ceiling, the century-old system was inoperative.

Still a bit dazed, Krysty got up from the floor. "What the blazes happened?" she groaned.

Ryan pointed out the deep scoring of tool marks along the door frame. Next to it, a head-size hole in the plaster revealed a mass of melted conduit and charred wiring.

The conclusion was as unmistakable as it was disheartening.

"Somebody's beaten us here," Mildred said.

"And when they saw the heavy door," Ryan added, "they must've figured to find sweet pickings on the other side. They couldn't open it with their pry bars and sledges, so they attacked the wall, looking for another way in. That was a dead end, too."

J.B. agreed with him. "After the damage was done,

the unit just sat there until we showed up," he said. "The rematerialization power surge short-circuited the system. We were lucky to come through in one piece."

"One thing is certain," Doc said as he dusted off the lapels of his frock coat, "the machine has jumped its final cargo. Once again we find ourselves reduced to more primitive means of transportation—namely, our own two feet."

"The smoke is getting worse in here," Mildred said. "No telling what kind of toxic fumes we're inhaling. There could even be a radiation leak if the containment vessel's been breached. I suggest we take this show on the road before we start glowing in the dark."

She didn't have to add that whoever had wrecked the unit could still be lying in wait.

After drawing their weapons and shouldering their packs, the six companions exited the anteroom and control room, then entered the long, doorless corridor that separated the mat-trans unit from the rest of the redoubt. Jak took point, with his lightning reflexes and .357 Magnum Colt Python revolver.

Motion sensors triggered the overhead lights as they rapidly advanced, single file. Some of the fluorescent tubes were missing, some blinked erratically, others just buzzed and snapped. Vandals had caved in the walls in places; chunks of concrete and bits of glass from broken lights crunched underfoot. The dusty floor of the hallway revealed no recent bootprints. The air was as still and stale as a crypt.

The hall ended in an open doorway. As the companions stepped through it, the light banks switched on, revealing a broad, low-ceilinged room. What had once been a communications center had been turned into a debris field of broken glass, plastic and metal, waist-high in places.

At the sight, J.B. muttered a string of obscenities.

He and Ryan had spent most of their adult lives seeking out and pillaging similar predark strongholds. The network of secret installations, complete with stores of food, ammunition, fuel and vehicles, had been built to shelter and support America's political, military and scientific elite in the case of nuclear war. But the end had come far too quickly for mass evacuations, and the installations were never occupied and used as the builders intended. The quirk of fate had left the re-doubts' caches of matériel and technology waiting, in-tact, for someone to find.

In this case, discovery was a done deal.

Here and there in the mounds of trash, individual sleeping chambers had been burrowed, then insulated and cushioned with layers of cardboard. In the middle of the room, a four-foot-high berm of trash had been pushed back, exposing an area of the floor and a wide, blackened hole chipped into the concrete. Smoke stained the ceiling above the crude firepit. Ringing the pit were a half-dozen ergonomic chairs missing their wheels and to one side of the hole lay a neat stack of fuel: gray plastic-veneered pressboard from worksta-tions and cubicle dividers hacked into kindling.

Dix knelt and picked up a chunk of charcoal, which he easily crushed to powder. "Nobody's lived here for years," he said.

The alcove they found on the far side of the room confirmed that.

Once a lounge for computer operators, its row of vending machines were torn open and gutted, spilling waterfalls of multicolored wire. Shredded candy wrappers and crushed aluminum cans littered the floor. Along the alcove's opposite wall were eight, molded plastic and tubular steel arm chairs. A large hole had been cut in each of the seats. Though the wastebaskets positioned beneath the chairs contained heaped evidence of their function, it had been so long since anyone had used the communal toilet that no odor remained.

Among the cartoons of sexual organs and acts defacing the alcove's enameled walls were scattered bits of writing. In addition to the names and erotic interests of people long gone, if not long dead, were some familiar commentaries.

"Science Blows."

"Jolt Is God."

"So many muties, so little rope."

And across the wall in a banner of rusty ink that was most likely blood: "I want to eat your liver." To Ryan the letters looked like they had been applied with a mop. Or perhaps a neck stump.

Below the graffiti was a postscript so tiny and cramped that he had to lean close to the wall to make it out. It said, "I'm right behind you."

He didn't turn and look, of course, but for an instant he thought about it, just as the writer had intended.

With a resounding *clunk* all the lights went out, plunging the companions into pitch darkness.

From Ryan's left came the scrape of a chair and shit bucket being kicked over. "By the Three Kennedys!" Doc moaned in dismay.

Heart pounding, Ryan cleared his SIG-Sauer pistol from shoulder leather. If the blackout was a prelude to an ambush, at least they were in a good defensive position, with the closed end of the alcove at their backs. Dropping into a fighting crouch, he let his eye adjust.

After a few seconds he could see the fire's faint orange glow at the doorway on the other side of the room. He smelled caustic smoke. Then a turbine started to whine on a floor far below them, and the lights came back on, only this time much weaker and with a more pronounced, almost strobelike flicker.

There was no ambush; they were alone.

"There's no point in our searching the storage levels," Ryan said as he reholstered his side arm. "This bird's been picked clean."

Successful looting of predark caches boiled down to two things: luck and timing. The luck was in finding them, as the redoubts were well-hidden, usually deep underground, often in remote areas. Though the companions' access to the mat-trans system gave them a big advantage over the competition, it didn't guarantee piles of booty at the end of the day. Booty required timing; in other words, getting there first. They had faced this disappointment many times before, and they took it in stride, now. Coming up empty-handed was part of the game.

To locate their position in the complex, and find the quickest way out, the companions started searching the adjoining rooms for a copy of the redoubt's floorplan. They found it in a ransacked office, behind a sheet of Plexiglas screwed into wall. J.B. shattered the plate with his shotgun's steel butt plate, and Krysty freed the paper map, which laid out and labeled the stronghold's levels, and all the exits.

From the other side of the room, Mildred called out to the others, "Hey, take a look at this." She stood before a three-dimensional, injection-molded, plastic relief map that covered a section of wall, almost floor-to-ceiling. Though the map had been defaced and damaged, it was still readable.

"From the lat-lon grid, that must be us," she said, indicating a small red circle nestled between a pair of desert mesas at the upper left corner. Halfway down the map was the start of a long, diagonal stripe of blue, a stripe that grew wider and wider until it necked down and abruptly stopped, blocked by a narrow white barrier.

The label on the barrier read: Pueblo Canyon Dam and Reservoir.

"I was there on vacation once, about a hundred years ago," Mildred said.

"A boating holiday?" Doc asked.

"No, it was before the dam was put in," she said. "I remember there was a big stink over its getting built. The reservoir flooded a small town on the canyon floor, and Native American prehistoric sites along the cliffs were lost. For the right to build the dam, the federal government paid reparations to the Hopi tribe, and there was a land swap, too.

"Not everyone was happy with the amount of money that changed hands, or with the relocation site. Supposedly because of the number of threats, during construction the area for hundreds of square miles was turned into a top security, no-fly zone. Military ground and air units kept out protesters and potential saboteurs. A lot of questions about the Pueblo Canyon project never got answered, such as, why it was necessary in the first place. And why approval for the funding and land trade was rushed through Congress. Once the dam was completed and the reservoir filled up, the fences came down, the military left and the controversy fell off the media radar."

"What do you make of this?" J.B. asked. He pointed at another red symbol, though smaller, in the middle of the swathe of blue, a short distance from the dam.

"Could be another redoubt," Ryan said.

"In the middle of the reservoir?" Krysty said.

"Mebbe an island?" Dix suggested.

"Then it'd have to be man-made," Mildred said. "The canyon is five hundred feet deep at that point."

"Whatever it is, it's got a name," Dix said, leaning closer to read the scratched lettering. "It looks like 'M-i-n-o-t-a-u-r.'"

"Does that mean anything to anybody?" Krysty asked the others.

A beaming Doc provided the answer, delighted at the opportunity to put his classical education to use. "The name refers to a mythical monster of ancient Greece," he said. "According to legend, it was the half-human offspring of a great bull and Pasiphae, wife of Minos, the king of Crete. The bull was a gift to the king from the sea god, Poseidon, who wanted Minos to sacrifice it to him. When the king didn't kill the animal as directed, Poseidon punished him by making his wife fall in love with it. Minos kept the monstrous product of their union, known as the minotaur, and built a maze to contain it. The king exacted tribute from conquered lands in the form of human victims, which he sacrificed to the minotaur. Ultimately, the murderous beast was defeated by the hero Theseus, with the help of Minos's daughter, Ariadne."

"Humans can't make babies with other kinds of animals," Krysty said.

"Not in the usual way," Mildred said. "And not in ancient Crete. But in a test tube, late twentieth century, with gene-splicing techniques…"

With another loud *clunk* the light banks failed again, and again the companions found themselves surrounded by blackness.

Two minutes passed, then five, while they waited with weapons drawn. This time the lights didn't come back on.

After igniting the torches they pulled from their packs, the companions followed the predark map, which turned out to be full of blind alleys. Most of the exit stairwells were blocked by floor-to-ceiling avalanches of concrete and steel. From the structural damage to the floors above, it was clear something disastrous had happened. The higher they climbed, the greater the destruction. Though they were only eight levels underground, it took them close to an hour to reach the surface. And in the end, they had to track the looters' route through the air ducts.

Standing outside in daylight, they could see why they had been beaten to the treasure trove. The redoubt's secret entrance had been uncovered by a massive landslide, which had tumbled house-sized blocks of sandstone onto the desert valley. There was no way of telling if the earthquake had been natural, or caused by the shock wave of a distant nuclear strike.

Ryan shielded his eye from the sun's brutal glare, surveying a landscape of pale brown mesa and pancake-flat plain shimmering in 120-degree, midday heat. For as far as he could see in every direction, it was just rocks and sand. Sand and rocks.

"Dear friends, I fear Judgment Day is upon us at last," Doc remarked. "Our myriad sins have finally landed us in the pit of hell."

"Or on the moon," Mildred added.

Krysty knelt in the shade cast by a fallen sandstone block. From a crevice at the base of the rock, she plucked a withered scrap of plant. The delicate white petals broke off in her fingers; the yellow center fell to fine dust on her palm. If Deathlands's brave little daisy was a testament to adaptability and survival in the most hostile of environments, it was also a canary in a coal mine. "If we stay here long, we'll die," Krysty said.

Jak squinted into the glare. "Go that way," he said, pointing south across the desolation.

"Can't miss the reservoir if we walk in that direction," J.B. agreed.

"Too hot to break trail, now," Ryan said. "We'll start after sunset. Check your canteens. Whatever water we've got, it has to last until we get there."

Chapter Two

Shielding his nose and mouth with his hand, Ewald Starr held the torch at arm's length. Firelight danced over the corpse's blackened rib stubs and caved-in breastbone, over a skull cratered from forehead to lower jaw. One leg was missing all the way to the hip. The body cavity had been plundered of its organs; the bones stripped of flesh and left mired in a sticky-looking, yellowish puddle. The fluid had splattered low across the corridor's concrete wall.

Whatever the yellow stuff was, it stank, thermonuclear.

A combination of bearpit, toxic chemical spill and rotting meat.

In the close quarters of Pueblo Dam's service hallway, the rank odor hung like an acid fog.

Ewald listened hard, but all he could hear was the chorus of hissing torches—the greasy black smoke they gave off billowed along the low, pipe-lined ceiling, driven by a steady, gentle breeze.

Three other men stood with their backs against the opposite wall, faces pale and pained, torches clutched in trembling hands. Paralyzed.

Ewald scowled at them.

Fear was the enemy.

The preamble to defeat.

Tall and dark-skinned, he wore his waist-long black hair woven into a thick braid and coiled on top of his head. This rat's nest was held in place with a pin contraption made of twists of bailing wire. A spiral of decorative branding encircled his chin, creating an angry, welted goatee. The scars of healed blade slashes and bullet wounds on his massive forearms, bare chest, and neck were lost amid larger masses of discoloration, signs of his having survived prolonged torture and punishment by burning and whipping.

Ewald hunkered down next to the body, holding his breath against the caustic fumes. The victim's clothing was a wadded mass of wet rags at the foot of the wall. Examining the jutting hip bones more carefully, he saw that when the missing right leg had been severed, a corner of the pelvis and the entire hip socket had been cut away. The clean, down-angled slice looked like a sword or ax strike. It took a hell of a sharp blade to do something like that. A hell of a powerful swordsman, too. As to what all the nasty yellow goo was, or where it had come from, he had no clue.

When he straightened, something glinted at him from the tangled rags. A single, spent, centerfire shell casing.

"Here, take this," Ewald said, passing his torch to the closest man. The whip-lean graybeard named Tolliver accepted the burden, his rheumy gaze never shifting from the mess on the floor.

"Give me your shirt," Ewald said to the big man standing on Tolliver's right.

Though they were the almost same height and weight, where Ewald was all muscle, Dunbar was all flab—a slope-shouldered blob. This morning's sudden, shocking reversal of fortune had silenced his constant, annoying chatter. Meekly obeying Ewald's command, he stripped off his tent-sized, desert camo BDU shirt. His pasty white skin hung in loose, floppy rolls around his waist, like a suit of clothes three sizes too big.

Wrapping his hand in a corner of the garment, Ewald carefully shifted the remains. The skeleton came apart at his touch, ribs and spinal column separating. As he started lifting and tossing the loose bones aside, he saw that they sat in a shallow depression in the concrete, a depression concealed by the elongated puddle that filled it. Under the broken sternum lay a stamped steel prize.

When Ewald fished out the Uzi subgun, its fixed wooden butt and forestock sloughed off the frame like so much soggy cardboard. The plastic pistol grip seemed undamaged. He shook slime from the barrel, then mopped the weapon clean with Dunbar's shirt. The blueing had been stripped from the metal, its surface left faintly pitted.

Ewald pulled back on the cocking knob. The action stuck for a second, then came free, ejecting an unfired, 9 mm cartridge that skittered across the floor. He detached the staggered row, stick mag from the butt of the grip and did a round count. Including the ejected bullet, there were twenty-nine Parabellum bullets left in the clip. He unloaded the mag, wiping down and checking each round for corrosion. Before he slapped the reloaded clip back in place, he locked the action open and looked down the barrel. In the torch light he could see pits but no obstructions or cracks. He dry-fired the Uzi, and the pin snapped crisply.

The sound startled the man on Tolliver's left, making his narrow shoulders jerk. Willjay was still in his teens, tall, gangly, with a skanky mop of brown dreadlocks. From his expression, he was on the verge of bawling for his mother. Something that Tolliver and Dunbar, preoccupied with their own self-pity, failed to notice.

The dimmie trio had been part of a convoy that had tried to cross the great desert from the south. Tried and failed. One after another, their wags had broken down. And when the last wag gave up the ghost, they'd abandoned their possessions and started walking. Two dozen of them. In a few days the food ran out, then the water. After that, the heat quickly took its toll.

Tolliver, Dunbar and Willjay, the convoy's sole survivors, thought they'd found the Promised Land when they'd accidently stumbled onto the canyon.

As had Ewald Starr, when he showed up two days later, fresh from his own ordeal to the northwest.

Ever the wolf among sheep, Ewald had wide experience in scheming and backstabbing—and in murder for profit. In this case the sheep wore ankle-length, homespun robes the color of scorched porridge. From the moment he saw the triple stupe grins of the canyon's permanent residents, he figured he'd own the place in a couple of weeks, tops. All he needed was a few like-minded individuals to help with the initial round of wet work. Once he had things well in hand, he'd make sex slaves of the suitable women and men, and field slaves of the rest.

All hail Baron Ewald Starr.

Caught up in the potential of a once-in-a-lifetime opportunity, there was no denying he had let his guard slip. Not that his customary vigilance would have guaranteed a different outcome. Pilgrim Plavik and his flock kept their plans well-concealed. Ewald had seen no weapons, other than hoes and shovels, until that morning. Rudely awakened by his hosts, he stared into their massed gunbarrels, and was relieved of his own. Escape was impossible. When they marched him outside into the street, he saw that the other three travelers had been likewise overwhelmed and disarmed.

Protests and demands for an explanation fell on deaf ears.

The entire ville turned out for the procession, men, women, children, all grinning and chanting nonsense while the pilgrim himself led the way to the top of the dam. With blaster muzzles pressed to their heads, Ewald and the others had been forced through an open manhole, and onto a series of rungs set in the wall, rungs leading down into impenetrable gloom. As they clung there for dear life, lit torches were tossed in, then the manhole cover slid shut, and the light from above went out.

Honored guests had become prisoners in a vast, concrete dungeon.

And the bad news was just beginning.

The man or woman whose bones littered the corridor had fired just one shot in self-defense—a single shot from a machine pistol capable of firing 600 rounds a minute-before being almost cut in two.

"Whatever chilled that one," Tolliver said in a shaky voice, "it was something triple-mean."

"Something mutie…" Dunbar whispered.

Ewald Starr knew all about muties. Over the years, he'd slaughtered the two-legged, homicidal freaks in face-to-face battle, in ambush, as a mercie, as a sec man. And whenever ammo was plentiful, he'd hunted them for sport. Stickies, scalies, cannies, stumpies— nukeday's genetic horrorshow—were no match for a functioning Uzi in the hands of a professional chiller.

"We're gonna die in here," Willjay moaned. "We're all gonna die!"

Before the teenager's panic could contaminate the other two, Ewald racked a round and snarled, "Dead bastard couldn't shoot straight." Weapon ready to rip, he glared at the boy. Willjay caught his meaning and shut up quick, a decision that saved his life.

"But what're we gonna do?" Tolliver asked the dark-skinned man. "How're we gonna get out of here?"

"It's simple," Ewald told him. "We work our way down to the bottom of the dam. There should be an opening on the spillway side."

"And if there isn't?" Tolliver said.

"Then we'll nukin' make one. Follow me, and make sure you all stay close."

Ewald didn't want tight ranks because he gave a radblast about their safety. The way he saw he it, the more baitfish there were in a school, the better the odds of being the one that didn't get eaten.

Halfway along the gritty, weeping hallway he found the door to a stairwell. When he opened it, the stench drove them back on their heels.

"Nuke shit!" Tolliver groaned, clapping a hand over his nose and mouth.

"More deaduns down there," Dunbar said. "Stairs could be some kind of a trap."

"Yeah, but it's the fastest way out of here," Ewald said. "Mebbe the only way out of here. You got a better idea? Mebbe you want to spend some time exploring the nooks and crannies of this place?"

Dunbar shook his head so hard his belly flab trembled. They all shook their heads.

"Then let's do it," the ex-mercie said.

With Ewald on point, they carefully descended the stairs in close formation. The light from their torches didn't penetrate far, and with every step, the odor of death grew more intense.

Two floors down they discovered its source. On the concrete landing lay the eroded remains of several corpses, their burned-out torches, and a pool of yellow bile. Tolliver scooped up a sawed-off, double-barreled shotgun that had either been dropped or thrown clear of the puddle. When he broke open the 12-gauge, its ejectors flipped out empty plastic hulls.

Ewald had already figured as much. On the facing wall were two, foot-wide, buckshot blast craters. One stood at belly height; the other was ten feet above it. There was no blood spatter in or around either of the craters. The shotgunner had missed twice at point blank range. Ewald guessed that either the second shot had been fired wild in the air, or the intended target was clinging to the wall up there. Stickies had suckers on their palms and feet; they liked to drop on unsuspecting victims. That didn't explain the sword slice—stickies didn't use weapons as a rule, preferring to tear their prey apart with their bare hands. Nor did it explain the goo.

A quick survey of the landing turned up a pair of black-powder revolvers submerged among the jumble of human bones. The Italian-made, Civil War replicas were useless; their loaded cylinders had reacted with the fluid, turning into crumbling masses of corrosion. There was no ammo for the scattergun, but Tolliver hung on to it, anyway—a club was better than no weapon at all.

On the steps below, their torches revealed still more bodies. These stripped skeletons lay on their stomachs. They'd died trying to crawl up the stairs. Without legs.

As Ewald started down, there was a distinct clicking sound. A metallic, ratcheting noise that came from the stairwell far below. At first rapidfire, it slowed, then stopped.

Though the sound lasted less than five seconds, it made a knot form in the mutie hunter's gut. Stickies sometimes made soft kissing sounds before they attacked, but they never, ever clicked.

"Wh-wh-what was that?" Willjay said.

"Shut up and listen!" Ewald growled.

But there was only silence.

After a few moments Dunbar spoke up. "Could just be a busted ventilation fan down there somewhere," he said. "Breeze might be turning the blades, making them hit something…"

The noise started again, echoing up the stairwell. Only this time, there was a definite pattern. Six quick clicks, each rising in pitch. A pause, then repeat. The hairs on the back of Ewald's neck stood upright.

It wasn't a stickie, and it wasn't a busted vent fan, either, because the sounds were getting louder by the second. Whatever it was, it was coming at them.

And fast.

At his feet lay incontrovertible proof that the stairwell was a piss-poor place to make a stand. "Run!" Ewald shouted as he turned and vaulted back to the landing.

He hit the exit door and the others followed, sprinting for their lives down the pitchdark service hallway. Over the slap of bootsoles on concrete, Ewald strained to hear the stairwell door banging open behind them.

The bang didn't come.

Ewald stopped around a bend in the corridor, and waited there for the others to catch up. If it hadn't been for the smell, he might have missed seeing the breach in the opposite wall. Yellow fluid seeped from the bottom of a gash in the concrete three feet high, and three feet wide at the middle.

"What in blazes have you got there?" Tolliver said as he and Willjay hurried up to him.

Ewald couldn't hazard a guess.

As Dunbar joined them, puffing hard, his face and folds of fat glazed with sweat, Ewald approached the opening from the side, this to avoid tracking through the puddle on the floor. He bent close with the torch. For as far as he could see, which was only five or six feet into the gash, yellow slime greased the walls. He used the butt of the torch to carefully poke at the sides of the hole. The edge of the concrete was soft, mushy even. Under pressure, it oozed like paste.

He'd never seen or heard of anything like it.

Without warning a gust of air blasted from the opening. The concussive force blew out his torch and turned the yellow fluid into mist. He felt the wetness on his fingers a split second before the pain hit. Galvanic pain, head to toe, like he'd thrust his arm into a caldron of boiling water.

As Ewald screamed and spun away, from deep inside the walls of the dam came a frantic scraping, scrabbling sound.

The burrow was a tight fit.

Chapter Three

The smooth pebble clicked against Ryan's teeth as he shifted it from one cheek to the other. The steady rasp of his breathing matched the scrape of his boot soles on the desert hardpan. He moved in an almost effortless, economical glide, the stride of a man used to walking long distances over broken terrain. Overhead the pale violet sky was cloudless, the last visible stars rapidly fading. On the horizon to his left hung an orange half-disk of sun. A dawn wind shrieked across the ancient plain in buffeting gusts that peppered his face with grit.

It was already hot.

Soon to get hotter.

For the third night in a row, he and his companions had marched, dusk until dawn, by the light of the moon. Not their standard operating procedure by any means. Under more normal circumstances, they would have stopped in a likely spot well before sunset, set up a defensive perimeter and a guard rotation, and then hunkered down with their weapons close to hand until daybreak. Travel in Deathlands was always dangerous, but the nights were the worst time to be on the move; that's when the big predators came out, the solo chillers and the pack hunters, human and otherwise. In this case, because of the heat, the distance they had to cross and their limited supply of water, they had to take the risk.

No predators had shown themselves, so far, which led Ryan to conclude that there weren't any. To survive and breed, predators needed a dependable supply of victims. There was nothing in this hell-blasted landscape for large carnivores to hunt.

The uptilted plain of beige gulleys and boulder outcrops seemed to go on forever, to the curve of the world, and beyond. There was no sign of a sizeable body of water ahead. No great crack in the earth, either. As the sun broke free of the horizon, it was like the door of a blast furnace swinging open. In seconds the air temperature jumped twenty degrees.

Ryan glanced over his shoulder. Behind him, Doc, J.B., Mildred, Krysty and Jak still appeared in good shape. Their emergency food had run out the previous day. They had shared the last, tepid sips from their canteens hours ago. Like Ryan, they were all sucking on small stones to quiet their thirsts. The companions were a battle-hardened crew, but even they had their limits. As the morning's heat increased, to conserve their strength and bodily fluids, the rest stops had to come more frequently.

The one-eyed man called a temporary halt to the march, waving the others down behind the shelter of a big boulder. Krysty, Mildred, Doc and Dix sat with their backs pressed against the base of the rock, in the lee of the wind, out of the sun for the moment. Soon they would have to stop for the day. If they couldn't find permanent shade, they'd have to create it.

Jak didn't sit down and rest with the others. He paused only long enough to nod at Ryan before he loped away, his lank white hair flying around his shoulders. He continued in the same direction they were headed, doing a recce. Ryan had known the albino youth for a very long time, but seeing him run like that after a brutal, all-night march, still brought a smile to his lips. Jak was the hardest of the hard, a true wild child of the hellscape.

"How far do you think we've come?" Mildred asked.

"Plenty far enough if you ask me," J.B. said as he wiped the caked dirt from his glasses with his shirttail. "We should be able to see it by now."

"Mebbe, mebbe not," Ryan countered. "This end of the canyon looked damned narrow on the map. The way the ground is tipped up, we might not see it until we're right on top of it."

"But we've got to be close," Krysty said. "We've got to be...."

"I find it distinctly odd that there is nothing green before us," Doc remarked. "Odd and importune."

It was an absence they'd all noticed.

Water in the desert meant an oasis, densely clustered weeds, shrubs, trees taking advantage of the scarce resource, a green stripe cutting through the panorama of sunblasted beige.

A green stripe that wasn't there.

They sat in silence in the shade, sucking on their pebbles, regathering their strength, asking themselves the same questions. How much farther could they go without water? How many more days could they last? How badly would it hurt when the end came?

When Jak returned from the recce, his bloodred eyes revealed no joy, no sadness. Nothing.

"Well?" Ryan asked him.

"Canyon ahead, quarter mile," Jak replied.

"Good work! Let's go, then," Ryan said, rising to his feet.

Jak caught his arm. "No water," he said.

A two-word death sentence.

"What do you mean no water!" Mildred exclaimed.

Jak shrugged at her. His only response was, "Come, look."

After they had advanced another hundred yards, the edge of the canyon came into view, a dark line across the ground that grew broader as they approached. It was the far wall of the fissure dropping away sheer. To the southeast, for as far as they could see, an ever-widening gash divided the hammered plain.

When they reached the canyon's near rim, they looked down a hundred-foot drop.

"Radblast!" J.B. said.

There was no reservoir. No river flowing at the canyon bottom. No plants. As Jak had said, no water.

Only dirt and rock.

"This has to be it," Ryan said. "The distance is right. The size is right. And the map only showed one canyon."

"Mebbe the water didn't back up this far," Krysty suggested.

"Or the reservoir has been drawn down considerably since Armageddon," Doc commented.

"It's also possible that the dam's been breached," Mildred said. "And that either the river's dried up, or it's running deep underground."

Tipping his hat brim to block the glare of the sun, J.B. looked down the gorge, in the direction of the dam. "The water might still be there," he said. "Below our line of sight in the canyon bottom."

"Even if the river has dried up," Mildred added, "low spots in the bed could hold standing pools. The deepest part of a reservoir is usually at the base of its dam. Even if the dam's broken, there could still be plenty of water trapped in front of it."

"Our best hope for finding water is the canyon," Ryan said. "We've got to follow it. We'd better get moving. Cover as much ground as we can before the sun gets high."

There was no discussion about whether to descend to the canyon floor; in fact the subject didn't even come up. Although walking along the rim was a much longer trek because of the short side canyons they had to skirt, it was also the high ground, and that gave them a tactical advantage. They couldn't be pinned down and ambushed on the rim.

About a half mile down-canyon, they came to a wide, flat spot that had been cleared of rocks. They would have walked right past it if Mildred hadn't spoken up. "Hey, wait a minute," she said. "We've got ourselves a field here. A cultivated field."

Doc stared at the empty patch of dirt bounded by boulders and said, "Not in recent memory, my dear."

Mildred corrected herself. "The field is a remnant of

prehistoric agriculture," she said. "A thousand years ago the local cliff dwellers grew crops on top of these canyons in plots just like that. There should be a path somewhere around here down to their cave...."

"There," Jak said, pointing out a shiny, shallow groove worn in the bedrock. It led away, to the apex of the side canyon ahead.

"This is important?" Krysty asked.

"Storage wells," Mildred told her. "All the ancient settlements had them. The residents hauled water up from the river and stored it in stone cisterns in their caves. They also built catch basins and channels that fed rainwater from the plain down to their wells. These cisterns were always covered and in shade. There could be some water left from the last rain, whenever that was." She paused, then said, "I know it's a long shot..."

"Worth a look, anyway," Ryan said.

The prehistoric path ended at the cliff edge. The companions stared down at a steep, rubble-filled chute. The scree of large rocks had been tossed from above, forming crude steps, which turned around a bend fifty feet below and vanished from sight. Ryan and the others carefully descended, as the loose rocks shifted under their weight. Around the blind corner a sandstone ledge jutted from the canyon wall. They followed the narrow walkway along the face of the overhanging cliff. It was a long, straight drop to the bottom, at least two hundred feet. The ledge led them to a broad, shallow cave with a towering, arched ceiling.

The cliff dweller ruins were barely recognizable as such. From their deteriorated condition, it was obvious that the reservoir had covered them at one time. The sun-dried bricks had melted, the two- and three-story structures had collapsed. Mud-and-stick pueblos weren't designed to be submerged and then subjected to wave action. When the dammed waters had retreated, they had done so with enough force to wash away the stone foundations of the buildings closest to the ledge.

The covered cistern lay at the back of the cave, where the ceiling sloped down to meet the floor—a wide, circular, five-foot-deep pit, lined with flat, tightly fitted stones. At the bottom of the well, spread across its lowest corner, was about a gallon of liquid.

Brown liquid.

Ryan hopped down into the pit and put a finger in it.

It was thick. Slimy between his fingers. It didn't smell bad, though.

"We're going to have to boil the hell out of that stuff before we try to drink it," Mildred said.

Ryan looked up at J.B. and said, "Better start scrounging up some wood for a fire."

J.B., Doc and Jak immediately set about kicking apart a surviving, thirteenth century mud-daub wall, this to pull out the mat of dry sticks that reinforced it. Anasazi rebar.

Mildred and Krysty joined Ryan in the bottom of the cistern. The three of them got down on their knees and sopped up the precious moisture with rags, then carefully squeezed it, drop by drop into their battered tin cookpot. Before trying to boil the mess, they filtered it through several layers of clean fabric. This removed the bigger chunks, but it was still brown, still thick.

The water of last resort.

While it bubbled and frothed in the pot, the companions moved to the edge of the ledge and took in the spectacular view.

"The people who lived up here must've thought they ruled the world," Mildred said. "They built. They farmed. They stored for hard times. They prospered. And now there's nothing left. Not even ghosts. It makes me think of that sad, sad poem…I forget the title."

"You are referring to 'Ozymandias' by Percy Bysshe Shelley, I believe," Doc said. "Words found inscribed among decaying ruins, buried in drifting sands."

"'Science Blows,'" Ryan said, quoting the ubiquitous Deathlands' craphouse graffito.

"Bravo," Doc said with a smile. "You have it precisely, dear Ryan. It is nothing less than the paradigm of human existence, forever blinded by our pride, and victims of the inexorable march of time."

"Over there!" J.B. exclaimed, pointing up at the sky.

They all turned to look.

The buzzards, perhaps thirty of them in all, were mere specs in the distance down-canyon. Circling in a slow spiral at three thousand feet, the carrion birds became visible, one by one, as they turned and were momentarily sidelit by the sun.

"Something's below them, for sure," J.B. said to Ryan.

"From the height they're flying," the one-eyed man replied, "something not quite dead enough."

His speculation was punctuated by the crack of a single gunshot, its echo rolling up the canyon.

The flat, unmistakable report of a shotgun.

"That boil is going to have to do," Ryan said. "Fill up the canteens and kick out the fire. Let's move!"

After scrambling back to the canyon rim, Ryan led the others at a full-out trot, despite the building heat and the now dead still air. Out of food, and on scant rations of barely potable water, the companions absorbed this new punishment without complaint. The buzzards weren't a good sign, but at least one person was alive. If they waited until evening to investigate, they might never catch up to whoever had fired the shot. And that could mean the difference between life and a very unpleasant death.

As Ryan ran, he kept his eye on the flock of buzzards, watching them slowly descend from altitude, then spiral down into the canyon, out of sight. He marked the spot ahead where they disappeared. There was no more gunfire. The shooter was either out of ammo, or out of luck.

It took five minutes to close the gap. The canyon beside them had grown much wider, if not deeper. It was impossible to miss the vultures against the beige of the dirt and rock—black feathers, seven-foot wingspans, angry red heads. A mob of them, fighting over the spoils. Ryan flipped up the lens covers on his telescopic sight and scanned the crude campsite. He counted four sets of human legs half-hidden under the flapping wings and snapping beaks. Legs that were kicking, shuddering amid the frenzy.

"All dead?" Mildred asked.

"Let's find out," Ryan said. He tucked the Steyr tight to his shoulder and squeezed off a 7.62 mm round.

The bolt gun bucked hard and downrange, a lone buzzard exploded in a puff of blood and dark feathers. As the loose bag of bones tumbled to the ground, the other birds abandoned their feeding positions. Squawking, flapping, they hopped to the safety of nearby rocks.

Ryan surveyed the now-still human forms through the scope, then said, "Yep, they're all dead."

"Shooter must've taken off," J.B. said.

"Can't tell from up here," Ryan said. He handed the Steyr to his friend. "Jak and me are going to go have a look-see. Watch our backs."

They found and followed a narrow chimney of rock that led to the canyon floor and the gruesome campsite. Four of the bodies were clustered together; the fifth lay a short distance away.

"Been dead awhile," Jak remarked of the four.

Because of the heat, it was hard to say how long. The torsos and limbs were swollen up like balloons with the gases of decay. Two of the bodies that lay on their backs had actually burst open, exposing sun-shriveled, sun-blackened guts. The buzzards had stripped the flesh from all four of the faces. Red, eyeless skulls poked out from fringes of hair and sagging skin. It was impossible to tell what they'd died from.

With no hint of breeze to shift the overpowering stench, it took a supreme effort of will not to turn away. That stink had ridden the canyon thermals, soaring high, spreading far and wide, attracting carrion feeders for hundreds of miles.

As Ryan and Jak moved to look at the fifth body, the big birds shifted their perches on the surrounding boulders. Brooding, watching, wary, waiting their chance to resume the feast.

"This one's fresh," Jak said.

The last dead man lay on his side in the dirt. So far he had been left alone by the vultures. They preferred their meat aged to the point of liquefaction.

It was the shooter, no doubt about it.

Ryan picked up the shotgun. It was a single shot, top break, 12-gauge with an exposed hammer. Cheap, long-barreled gun. Mass produced in the hundreds of thousands in the century before Armageddon. He tried the break lever; it moved, but the breech wouldn't open because it had been crudely welded shut. Somebody had converted the weapon from centerfire to black-powder muzzleloader. Not an unusual modification in Death-lands, where black powder was easier to find than cased ammunition. Ryan sniffed the barrel. It had been recently fired.

With devastating effect.

The dead man had put muzzle under his chin and then depressed the trigger. There was a stick on the ground beside his hand. He might have used it to get the necessary extra reach. His head was a mass of powder-scorched ruination. The front of his face gone from chin to midcranium, his brain pan emptied. The hollow glistened.

Ryan and Jak did a quick survey of the gear that lay scattered around the site. They found a few meager valuables. Battered black-powder weapons, skinning knives sharpened down to slivers, cooking utensils, empty canvas packs. The bodies hadn't been stripped of clothing and boots. There was the remains of a firepit, but no food scraps among the ashes. No food, period. Of course, they could've eaten it all before they got this far.

The one-eyed man scratched the black stubble on his chin. What's missing? he asked himself. The answer came to him at once. Canteens. There were no containers, nothing to hold water.

"Something triple ugly happened here," Ryan said. "No one tries to cross the desert without something to carry water in."

"Footprints go that way," Jak said, pointing in the direction of the dam. "One set. Big feet. Deep marks. Short steps. Heavy load."

Ryan nodded. "Blackheart son of a bitch took all their water and ran. They chased him until they dropped."

Jak knelt over the footprints in the powdery dust. The wind had eroded them. "Two, maybe three days old," he said.

"That doesn't mean he's got a full, three-day lead on us," Ryan said. "The load he's carrying had to have slowed him down. He probably stopped to rest, figuring these fools were done for."

"Catch chiller, take water," Jak said.

Ryan nodded.

The albino didn't have to add, "Leave the thieving bastard to die." That was a given. Rough justice was the only justice in Deathlands.

The dead men's gear wasn't worth the trouble to lug it away. Ryan and Jak took the time to drag the suicide over to a nearby undercut in the dry river bank. They rolled him into the shallow notch, then kicked the soil down on top of him. They didn't try to move the other bodies. The corpses would have just fallen apart, and there was always the chance of contagion from rotting flesh.

As Ryan and Jak started back up the rock chimney, the shrieking and squabbling of the vultures resumed.

Chapter Four

The extinguished torch dropped from Ewald Starr's shock-stiffened fingers. Pain squeezed him like a giant fist, making every muscle bulge, every sinew strain to the snapping point.

Unmasterable pain.

As he screamed and hopped in the dancing half light, a torrent of humid air poured from the gash, driven forth by whatever was coming. The scent that rode that evil wind triggered something deep in his brain, something primal. An unfamiliar taste, metallic and sour, flooded his mouth. The taste of panic. And of imminent, crushing defeat.

Worse suffering was on its way.

Much, much worse.

Ewald shoved Tolliver and his lit torch ahead of him. "Go!" he shrieked. "Go!!"

The direction didn't matter. To stand still was to die.

The four of them raced away, running blindly into the black maw of the corridor. Dunbar couldn't maintain the pace for more than a few yards before falling behind. Bringing up the rear, with nothing between him and whatever it was, his grunting turned frantic.

Ewald, Tolliver and Willjay didn't look back.

When the clicking started again, rattling down the hallway after them, a distant, desperate Dunbar cried out, "Help me! Help me!"

They didn't stop; in fact, they somehow found the strength to run faster. And Ewald wasn't the only one praying for it to take Dunbar. To take him and choke.

A cowardly prayer, promptly answered.

Dunbar's screech lasted only a second before it cut off. The clicking quadruple-timed, doubled that, doubled it again, climbing in volume and pitch, a triumphant roar that ended a horrible crescendo of wretching.

Ewald knew there was no guarantee that the thing would be satisfied with Dunbar, that it wouldn't pursue and chill them one by one. Like the stairwell, the hallway was a kill zone; they had to get out of it, and quick. Over Tolliver's right shoulder, Ewald saw a double doorway. "In there!" he cried.

They burst through the heavy metal doors and onto a short concrete landing that overlooked a room so broad and so cavernous they couldn't see the far side of it. Overhead, the undersides of steel I-beam trusses and buttresses were dimly visible. The network of their upper surfaces and the ceiling were beyond the reach of torch light. Smell of death was like a sledgehammer pounding inside Ewald's head.

"Man, look at your arm!" Tolliver said. "You're hurt triple bad."

Ewald's right arm had ballooned up to nearly twice its normal size and turned black, but it no longer pained him. He couldn't move his grossly swollen fingers, and he couldn't bend or raise the arm. Hanging straight down from his shoulder, it felt like it weighed a hundred pounds. When he tested his forearm with a fingertip there was no sensation, and the spongy flesh didn't spring back. The pressure left a deep dent and split the skin, like it was already dead meat. For a second Ewald thought he was going to puke.

"You better give me that blaster," Tolliver told him. "You're in no shape to use it."

Ewald grimaced at the graybeard's shaking hands. No way could Tolliver aim the Uzi. He probably couldn't even fire it. Not that the ex-mercie would have willingly surrendered his weapon, anyway.

"Don't worry about me," Ewald said. "I can shoot lefty just fine. We've got to keep moving. Got to find another way down."

The landing's short flight of steps led to a polished concrete floor. Beyond the hazy circle of light cast by the torches it was pitch black. At Ewald's direction, they turned and speedwalked in a straight line until they reached a wall. From the floor to a height of about seven feet, it was lined with narrow, sheet metal enclosures, control panel after control panel with LCD readouts, gauges, warning lights, and thousands upon thousands of exposed switches and terminals. All dead.

As they followed the wall, to their right, out on the floor, a low, hulking cylindrical shape came into view. The twenty-foot-wide, machined steel housing sat in a matching circular depression in the concrete. Ahead, there were more of the dam's generator turbines. One after another they squatted, stretching off into the darkness.

Around the silent machines were scattered bodies. A litter of corpses in random piles and puddles, in varying states of decomposition. The vast generator room was both slaughterhouse and dumping ground.

A kill zone even less defensible than the stairwell and hallway.

"Move it! Move it!" Ewald said, pushing the others to a trot.

They didn't get far.

When the clicking began, it seemed to come from everywhere at once, from the gridwork of I-beams above and the far corners of the immense room. The hall's infuriating echo made it impossible to tell how many there were, or which way to run.

"Shoot 'em!" Willjay cried. "Why don't you shoot 'em?"

Something moved out of the shadows at the edge of the torchlight. It moved past Ewald at chest height so quickly he couldn't raise the machine pistol, let alone track the target. He glimpsed a blur of brown, and got the impression of a sleek, banded body. Many legs. Powerful, jointed legs. There was a scraping sound, but the bright flash of sword he was anticipating never came. The blur bounded high in the air. He thought he saw a turned-up butt, like a deer's, an instant before it vanished into the blackness ahead.

Then something warm and wet splashed his good arm.

As Ewald turned, Tolliver's torch dropped to the floor. Sheets of blood poured out from under the man's beard. He staggered, slamming back against the control panels, and upon impact his head fell off. It didn't roll away, like the guttering torch. It flopped to one side, toppling from his cleanly sliced neck, and hung there upside down, connected to his body by a strip of skin. Tolliver's legs gave way, and a blood waterfall became a blood fountain.

Even though he couldn't see anything to shoot at, Ewald cut loose with a burst of autofire. In the strobe light of muzzle-flashes, slugs sparked off the generator housings, and the ricochets zipped around the room.

"Other way!" he shouted in Willjay's face.

Reversing course, they sprinted along the wall. Ewald didn't want to return to the hallway, but he had no choice. He had given up trying to find a quick way out. All he wanted now was cover. Some kind of cover.

They found another metal door fifty yards down the corridor. It was unlocked. Ewald and Willjay stepped into a narrow, low-ceilinged room crammed with with tall metal storage cabinets and open frame shelves. It looked safe enough. The exposed walls were free of weeping holes. They slammed the door and pushed shelves in front of it.

"What're we gonna do?" Willjay sobbed. The teenager had pissed himself. The insides of both trouser legs were dark, from crotch to cuff.

"Let me think," Ewald said. "Just shut up and let me think."

Then he made the mistake of looking down at his arm. And his brain vapor-locked. The heaviest muscles—deltoid, tricep, bicep—had begun to slough off the bones, like overcooked meat. Where his fingertips had been, red bone peeked through.

A sudden, frantic, scrabbling noise made him forget all about his ruined arm.

"Where's it coming from?" Willjay shouted, looking wildly around the room.

Walls, ceiling, floor, Ewald couldn't locate the source. But it was close. It was very close.

One of the cabinets behind Willjay shuddered, tipping forward, then crashed to the floor. Ewald blinked and the boy was gone.

Gone.

His torch lay on the floor.

Above the toppled cabinet was a gash in the wall.

Ewald lunged for the hole, the Uzi up and ready in his fist. He saw the boy's face a split second before he disappeared around a bend in the burrow. A face blanched white with fear. Elbows wedged against the slimy walls, fingers desperately, futilely clawing.

Ewald thrust the muzzle forward and pinned the trigger, firing full-auto until the weapon locked back empty. Gunsmoke filled the gash; his ears were ringing. He couldn't tell if he'd shot through Willjay and hit whatever had snatched him away. Tossing the Uzi aside, Ewald turned his full attention to the barricade. After he cleared the door and opened it, he bent to pick up the boy's torch.

As he straightened, the thing climbed out of the hole, head first, uninjured, and in no apparent hurry.

It wasn't like any mutie he had ever seen.

It had a crop of thick, bristling hairs, like spikes on top of its broad, flat skull. Its widespread eyes were solid black and huge. When it rose from a crouch, he saw the banded segments of its abdomen. It had six legs. The top pair were short, with talons at the ends; the second pair was longer, and the last two the longest of all. Standing on its back legs it was as tall as he was.

The open doorway was a foot from Ewald's back. The creature stood fifteen feet away. Before it could step closer, he made his move. A pivot started, but never completed. The thing was across the gap and in his face just as his hips started to turn.

Ewald was expecting a slash from the daggerlike horns that studded its rear legs, not a straight thrust from one of the stumpy arms.

The flesh above his right nipple dimpled around the shaft of a black thorn, a long stinger that protruded from the top of the creature's wrist. Its talons and arm flexed rhythmically, and he felt the pressure of a massive injection. At once, cold flooded his torso. Numbing cold. The small arm jerked back, withdrawing the stinger.

Ewald clutched at the wound in his chest, the numbness spreading to his legs. Before he could take a step, his knees gave way. He slumped to floor on his back and lay there, paralyzed.

As he struggled for breath, the creature leaned over him, clicking. The noise came faster and faster, becoming a single, earsplitting tone. Then the thing opened its jaws impossibly wide and, puffing its abdomen in and out, began to dry-heave in his face.

Chapter Five

While they waited for Jak to return from the canyon bottom, Ryan and the others took a rest break. With the sun almost directly overhead, there was no shade. Every surface reflected blinding light and withering heat. To keep their heads and shoulders out of the sun, they made canopies of their coats, stretching them between the tops of low rocks. As they sat on the hard ground, they tipped back their canteens and sipped at the Anasazi sludge. The thick, gritty liquid rasped down their throats. Once swallowed, it lay in their bellies like bags of wet cement.

They'd all drunk worse.

Ryan coughed to clear the mud from the back of his tongue. Through a shimmering curtain of heat waves, he took in the canyon's far rim. The valley had widened to about half a mile, and its depth was more than four hundred feet. There was no sign of a reservoir. No sign of the river that had been plugged to create it. In the low spots there were no standing pools, stagnant or otherwise. Nothing green.

There was blue, though.

A tiny clump of bright blue, visible to the naked eye in the distance below.

The plastic, antifreeze jugs stood out against the un-relenting beige of the canyon floor, flagging the water thief's abandoned campsite. The bastard had lit himself a fire down there, and tossed away his empty contain-ers before moving on, in the direction of the dam.

Jak had scaled the canyon wall, and when he reap-peared on the rim a few minutes later, his bloodless face was slick with sweat, his white hair plastered to his skull, and his breath came in ragged gasps. Even Death-lands's wild child was starting to show the effects of their ordeal. In a gravelly voice Jak said, "Fire pit cold. Nothing left in ashes."

If the chiller had food, he didn't need to cook it, Ryan thought. Maybe something dried or smoked. Something the dead travelers had brought with them. Berries and nuts pounded into a paste, then set out in the sun to harden. Or strands of jerky. One thing for sure, the bastard wasn't living off wild game. Aside from the buzzards, whose guts and body cavities were usually so packed with yard-long flat worms that even a starving man wouldn't touch their meat, the compan-ions hadn't seen anything alive. Not so much as a fly. The landscape had been scoured clean.

"Cold fire means he's still a couple days ahead of us," Krysty said. "We may never catch him."

"Could be he's running on jolt," J.B. suggested.

The potent combination of methamphetamine, nar-cotic and hallucinogen was Deathlands's recreational drug and painkiller of choice. If the thief was staying high on jolt, he could keep walking despite hunger, keep walking until his feet fell off.

"The dam isn't far, now," Ryan said. "Another five or six miles, at most. Good chance that's where our friend will have set up camp."

The dam was their only hope. The bastard had either stopped there with whatever water he had left, or there was water in the bottom of the reservoir. If neither was the case, they were all headed for the last train west. The companions gathered up their coats and packs, and trudged on.

Exhaustion, dehydration and the flat monotony of the trek made it difficult for Ryan to maintain his mental focus. His thoughts kept wandering back to the carnage they'd seen up-canyon. Dying of thirst was one of the worst ways to check out. There was terrible pain. Delirium. And a slow, lingering slide into death. The guy who'd blown off his own head had witnessed his friends' suffering, and taken a short cut. Ryan imagined that with his last breath, as he'd pressed that shotgun muzzle hard to his chin, he had cursed the thief to hell.

Betrayal wasn't unusual in the Deathlands.

It wasn't a kinder, gentler, I-feel-your-pain kind of place.

Sympathy was in shorter supply than cased ammo.

Individual survival was all that mattered in the hellscape. Survival at any cost. A brutal philosophy that Ryan Cawdor had been steeped in since birth. Over time, his friendships, his battles, and his relationship with his son, Dean, had widened his horizons. Ryan no longer dismissed out of hand the idea of risking his own skin for the sake of strangers, or in fighting for a just cause instead of a thick wad of jack from the highest bidder. And he still grieved the disappearance of his son.

After another hour of walking, as they rounded a sharp bend in the rim, the valley broadened enormously before them. Eight miles ahead, the canyon necked down again, and the sun blazed off a barrier of white concrete nearly as high as the rim. At the base of the dam, there was water; not a great predark reservoir, but a modest lake bounded on three sides by green, furrowed fields and stands of low trees.

As if that wasn't miracle enough, there was also the ville.

"Dark night!" J.B. exclaimed, thumbing his glasses back up the slippery bridge of his nose.

From a distance, it was like skydark had never happened.

Like the flooding of the canyon had never happened, either.

A mile or two from the near shore of the lake, stone and brick buildings clustered around a central square with a little park in the middle. The largest building was three stories tall with a clock tower. On the far side of the city center stood a row of grain silos. A black strip of two-lane highway paralleled that end of town. The road petered out in the middle of the plain, either buried under shifting sand or ripped away by receding waters.

"Little Pueblo," Mildred said. "Just the way I remembered it."

"'Tis indeed a wonderment," Doc prononunced. "Further evidence that the hand of the Creator works in mysterious ways."

"I'd say it was more a case of the laws of physics, working predictably," Mildred countered.

"And whose hand lies behind the laws of physics?" Doc asked with a confident grin.

"Why does there have to be a 'hand'?"

"Touché, dear Mildred. I am sure we would all like to hear your explanation."

"On nukeday, the water was five hundred feet deep over the town," she said. "All that liquid acted like a giant cushion to protect the buildings from shock and blast effects of incoming airburst missile strikes. My guess is the dam didn't get off so easy, and that's why the reservoir disappeared."

"Could have been a near-miss with an earthshaker warhead," J.B. suggested. "Those babies had an effective blast diameter of five hundred miles."

"That would explain how the entrance to that redoubt got uncovered," Ryan said. "The ground tremors brought the whole cliff down. Cracked the dam open, too."

"I don't see any people moving, anywhere," Krysty said, squinting against the glare. "And there's got to be people. Not just our water thief. Somebody's been tending those fields."

With rifle scope and binocs, Ryan and J.B. surveyed the terrain downrange.

There was something else wrong with the picture.

Unlike most other inhabited outposts in Deathlands, Little Pueblo didn't have a defensive berm of piled dirt and debris.

There were no perimeter gunposts. No fortified gates.

J.B. lowered the binocs. "I suppose there could be

snipers and spotters up here on the rim," he said. "Although they wouldn't be much use."

Ryan had to agree with that assessment. The canyon was so wide that much of it was beyond the range of even super-high-velocity, .50-caliber milspec rounds. Cap-and-ball weapons would be about as effective as chucking rocks. Snipers spaced out on the rim couldn't protect the ville from a large invading force—they couldn't concentrate enough fire to turn back attackers. The best they could do was harrass. And then only during the day. That was the problem with rim-based, spotter outposts, too. They'd be useless at night. Even if somehow they saw the invaders coming, they wouldn't be able to direct defensive ambushes in the valley.

"It's like they don't give a damn if they're overrun," J.B. said.

"Or they know it isn't going to happen," Ryan said.

"What do you mean 'they know'?" Krysty asked.

"They're sitting on an oasis in the middle of a rad-blasted desert. The nearest ville of any size must be 150 miles away. A gang of blackhearts that sets out for Little Pueblo isn't going to be in shape to rob it by the time they get here. If they get here."

"How would robbers even know it existed?" J.B. said. "After the reservoir was built, the ville's name was probably taken off all the maps. It sure wasn't on the one in the redoubt. Only way to find Little Pueblo would be to stumble onto it by accident. Then you'd have to walk out again to gather a chilling crew. And then walk in again to do the looting."

"It's a safe bet that's never happened," Ryan said. "If

it had, folks down there would know the desert wasn't enough to keep trouble out. And there'd be perimeter defenses. "

"Bastard thief got in, maybe two days ago," Krysty reminded them.

"He could be swinging from a tree right now," J.B. said. "Or else his head's on a stick in the middle of that square. No way of telling what kind of reception the folks down there give to strangers."

"We need water and food," Mildred said.

"Wait for dark, then steal," Jak suggested.

Doc didn't like that idea. "From this vantage point the valley looks bucolic and peaceable in the extreme, with ample sustenance for all," he said. "Perhaps the residents would happily share their bounty with us, if only to get news of the world beyond the hellish plain."

Jak came back with a less rosy, but much more likely possibility. "Chill us for blasters and ammo."

"We have a better chance of fighting our way out during daylight," J.B. said. "At least we can see trouble coming."

"There's another problem, whether we steal what we need or not," Ryan told them. "It's going to be a bastard long march out of this desert. It may not be possible to carry enough supplies to make it. Once we leave, there'll be no turning back."

After a pause, Krysty said, "What about Minotaur?"

"You read my mind," Ryan said. "If that three-dimensional map is right, there's a redoubt down there somewhere. And if there's a redoubt, there's a chance it has a working mat-trans unit."

"That would save us a whole lot of boot leather and blisters," J.B. said.

Before descending the cliffs and starting across the canyon floor, Ryan and J.B. each scoped the opposite rim, looking for sun flash off telesight lenses or gunbarrels, or evidence of shooters' hides built among the rocks. When they found nothing, they assumed that their side of the gorge was likewise undefended, and that it was safe to proceed. A conclusion based on battlefield experience and common sense. No way would snipers be posted on only one rim of a canyon so wide. The most effective kill zone would be created by overlapping cross fire from two sides at once.

In fighting formation the companions followed one of the large arroyos gouged out of the sand by the reservoir's violent retreat. Long before they reached the outskirts of the ville, signs of vegetation started to appear on the slopes around them. First, scattered dry weeds and brush. Then living trees, albeit stunted and scraggly. As the weeds grew thicker and green, and the trees became more sturdy, the companions saw lizards, insects, rabbits and birds. The bugs sawed and sang in the afternoon's blistering heat.

When the arroyo took a dogleg to the right, they climbed the soft bank for a recce. Just ahead was a row of rectangular, concrete pads, each sprouting rusted wires and conduit, and broken off plastic pipes.

"The remains of government-built, reservation housing," Mildred said. "Those are the foundation pads for modular prefabs and double-wide trailers. The buildings must've washed away when the water ran out."

Around the slabs were unfenced, row-crop fields bordered by irrigation ditches. The water ran clear in the ditches, shaded by tall grass and overhanging trees.

"Look at the current," J.B. said. "The river's still here, underground. They've got it working for them."

The companions then took turns laying on their bellies, washing their faces and necks, and drinking their fill of cool water. When they couldn't drink any more, they rinsed out and refilled their canteens.

"Somebody watching," Jak said softly to Ryan.

It was difficult to detect glee in those bloodred eyes of his. You had to look hard. And know what you were looking for.

There was glee in them, now.

At the edge of the field, a half-dozen, free-range chickens had stepped into view. Fat and sassy, they pecked at the soil for insects not thirty yards away.

The albino had two razor-sharp knives in his hand, one ready in his fingers, the other clasped against his palm.

Before Jak could get off a toss, the birds spooked, ducking back into the cover of the knee-high corn. He started to give chase, but Ryan stopped him. "No, Jak, let them go. Wouldn't look real good if we showed up on these folks' doorstep with their dead hens hanging on our belts. If nobody's home, we can always come back and get them later."

Refreshed, if not fed, they slid back down into the arroyo and followed it all the way to the edge of the town square. As they climbed onto the predark street, they heard muffled singing and drumming. The noise was coming from the other side of the town square and park.

"Somebody's home, after all," Ryan said. "Stay tight, now. We're on triple red."

The central area of Little Pueblo stood on an isolated crown of bedrock. Most of the runoff from the breached dam had channeled through the surrounding gridwork of streets, washing away wood frame houses and trailer homes, leaving bare concrete slabs and open air basements.

Up close, the city center wasn't in such great shape, either.

The street and sidewalks were all split to hell, with heaved-up cracks every few feet. Not one of the buildings that faced the little park had an intact window. The glass had been replaced by sheets of opaque plastic, pieces of scrap plywood and sheet metal. Ryan guessed that the repair materials that had been fished out of the lake, where all the loose debris would have ended up.

Most of the structures along the street were one-story and made of cinder block. Some still had faded signs along their facades. Lupita's Café, Little Pueblo Country Store and Bakery, Hardiman Insurance, Titterness Real Estate, Desert City Fashions.

With the muzzle of his SIG-Sauer, Ryan eased aside the sheet plastic that covered the doorway of Lupita's Café, and looked inside. Right off he got a whiff of freshly baked bread. It made his mouth water.

"Hello?" he said.

No answer.

Ryan pushed in, waving for the others to follow, with caution.

It was no longer a café. Lupita's had been gutted down to the cinder-block walls and concrete slab. The ceiling rafters and conduit pipes were exposed. It figured that none of the submerged carpet, plasterboard, subflooring, ceiling tile, and interior plywood would have been salvageable. Mildew and rot would have set in long before it ever dried out.

The main room's furniture consisted of lawnchairs, plastic milk crates and six platform beds made of scavenged interior doors propped on pairs of fifty-five gallon drums and piers of cinder blocks. From the way the straw mattresses were flattened, the beds were at least double occupied. There were no blaster racks on the walls. No blasters leaning in corners, or tucked under the beds. No ammo or lead balls or tins of black powder, either.

On the floor around the nonfunctional toilet in the café restroom were two mattresses; the adjoining storeroom had three more of the platform beds. Ryan figured that at least twenty people were sleeping in the three rooms.

The kitchen was still a kitchen. It even had some of its original, predark appliances. The doors had been removed from a commercial-sized refrigerator, and its inside turned into a storage cupboard. The stove had been converted from gas to wood, its former oven now the firebox, which was giving off considerable heat.

Cooling on a long, makeshift dining table were stacked loaves of bread-flat, round and golden brown.

J.B. pulled a heavy crockery jar from the refrigerator pantry, flipped off the lid, and stuck his finger in. It came out gooey amber. He sniffed, then he licked. "Honey," he said, eyes gleaming.

Without another word, the companions tore into the pile of fresh bread, dipping great hunks of it into the honey pot. They ate every last crumb and took turns at the jar with moistened fingers until nothing sticky remained. Start to finish, the meal took four minutes.

When they were done, Krysty said, "Traveling folks might carry corn and wheat seed with them for food, or to grow crops once they got where they were going, but bees? Chickens? No way could they survive a trip across that desert. How did they get here?"

"Might have been mat-trans-ed in, I suppose," J.B. said.

"If the people here had access to mat-trans, why would they just import seed and livestock?" Ryan said. "Why wouldn't they get the hell out if they could? What do you think, Mildred?"

The black woman didn't answer. She was staring at a square of chalkboard that hung from a nail on the wall. The board was a hundred-year-old artifact, and still in relatively good condition. It was the room's only decoration. Across the top, "Lupita's Daily Special" was painted in chipped, but legible hot pink. The dots over the *i*'s were in the shape of little flowers.

There was no special today, or tomorrow, or ever again.

"Mildred, is something wrong?" he asked.

"Just wondering what if anything that might mean,"

she said. She stepped aside so they could all see the words deeply scratched into the blackboard: "All Glory to Bob & Enid."

Nobody had a clue.

It didn't seem important at the time. Just odd.

But when they started looking through other buildings, weapons ready in case the missing owners suddenly returned, they found more references to the pair. And on the streetfront wall of Titterness Real Estate someone had charcoaled three lines of tall, crooked letters: Our love for Bob & Enid, our love for one & other makes us strong & proud.

"It would appear that paeans to 'Bob and Enid' are a recurring motif in these parts," Doc said. "I would hazard the pair were early settlers, except for the glories and huzzahs that always accompany the inscriptions. They reflect a level of adoration normally reserved for deities."

"Goddess Enid sounds okay, but a god named Bob?" Krysty said.

"That wasn't here in 1992," Mildred announced. She pointed across the street, through the line of mature trees, at the town square park.

Ryan was already staring at the windowless, one-story, gray concrete monolith that rose from the middle of the park. The roof and sides of the 50-by-80-foot structure were ribbed for strength.

Keeping low and single file, they trotted over for a closer look.

There was only one entrance, a doorway accessed down a short flight of steps. The titanium steel and pressure-locked door was blocked by a pile of stones.

The above ground structure was just the tip of the iceberg.

"We've found Minotaur," Ryan said.

"Never was an island here, then," Krysty said.

"Map was right, though," Dix stated. "Damn thing was smack in the middle of the reservoir—only on the bottom."

"Look at those reinforcing ribs," Mildred said. "The walls are massive, designed to withstand tremendous pressure. Things are finally starting to make sense to me."

"Pray tell in what regard, my dear?" Doc asked.

"The chronology," Mildred said. "It's all about the chronology. First came the rushed-through funding for the dam from Congress, then the town was condemned, and the residents relocated. A military no-fly perimeter was set up, supposedly to keep out saboteurs, but more likely to keep out prying eyes. The redoubt site was excavated and the complex installed at the same time as the dam, then hidden when the canyon was flooded. From the start, the whole Pueblo Canyon Dam project was about building Minotaur!"

"The construction and engineering you're talking about is way beyond anything I've seen before," Ryan said. "The question is, why wasn't hollowing out a mountain good enough in this case? Why the hell did they put it under all that water?"

"Mountain complexes are designed to keep out nukestrikes, radiation and uninvited guests," Mildred said. "Maybe this one was meant to keep something in."

Ryan picked up on her train of thought at once. "You mean because of the water depth?" he said.

"That's right. Without a pressurized suit or transport vehicle, no large organism could make it from the bottom to the surface alive."

"So we're not just talking concealment, then," Krysty said. "We're talking total isolation, maximum quarantine."

"Predark whitecoats left behind some triple-ugly surprises," J.B. said. "Maybe we better find out more about the place before we stick our beaks in there."

The sounds of muffled singing and drumming, which had momentarily waned, suddenly swelled.

"It's coming from the other side of the square," Krysty said. "One of those buildings in the middle of the block."

"Time we introduced ourselves to the locals," Ryan said. "See what they can tell us about Minotaur."

They followed the noise to its source, a two-story structure with a big marquee over the entrance. The marquee's frame bore the name El Mirador Theater; a row of black plastic letters spelled out the current attraction: "Prays Bob & Enid."

There were no guards on the movie house's front doors and wild festivities were in progress inside. Clapping hands, stamping feet and sticks thumping on metal kept the rolling, musical beat. The singing, now that they could clearly make it out, was more like yelling. There were no words to the tune, just nonsense syllables, joyfully shouted at top volume.

Dee-dit-deedee. Dee-dit-deedee.

"Here comes the bride?" Mildred queried.

Chapter Six

"The bride comes from where?" Krysty asked Mildred.

Ryan and J.B. wore identical puzzled looks. Jak wasn't paying any attention.

"It's just the words to an old song, 'The Wedding March,'" Mildred told them. "Written by Felix Mendelssohn in the mid-nineteenth century. Before the nukecaust it was played as the bride-to-be walked down the aisle of the church, before the wedding ceremony."

"You think people are getting married in there?" Krysty said.

"If the music means anything anymore."

"Sounds like a big crowd," J.B. said. "Maybe the whole blasted ville. If we go in all peace and love, we might not come out again."

Peace and love wasn't on Ryan Cawdor's agenda.

"Everybody got grens?" he asked.

"You want stunners, fog, or frags?" J.B. asked.

"Frags."

Mildred's eyes widened. Detonating a half-dozen antipersonnel grenades in a crowded room was some serious, undifferentiated ugly. A head-on train wreck. A plane crash. A twenty-car pile up. "They could be friendlies," she protested. "Just a bunch of butt-simple dirt farmers."

"Yeah, and we're going to give them every chance to prove that's all they are," Ryan told her. "But we've got to be ready if they aren't. There could be a couple hundred people in there, easy. If they rush us, either we lower the odds in a hurry, or we get overrun. Let them see your blasters going in. Don't let them see the grens until I show them mine."

"There's a good chance they're packing all the weapons and ammo we couldn't find," J.B. said. "They see us with our blasters drawn, things could fall apart, big-time sudden."

"If things fall apart like that, you can be sure we're going to mess up somebody's wedding night," Ryan said. "Jak, you and Doc go around the back of the building. There should be an exit or two there. The rest of us will go in through the front."

Before splitting up, they shrugged off their packs, and filled their pants pockets with extra clips and speed-loaders, and their jacket side pockets with predark grens.

While they waited for Jak and Doc to move into position, Mildred clamped a lid on the medical doctor part of her brain, the part that recoiled at mayhem and suffering, and let the battle-hardened soldier in her take command. Though they'd survived the brutal desert crossing, they were a long way from safety. And the mood of the ville folk toward strangers was a huge unknown. As Ryan said, there were way too many of them to take chances. Once the companions made contact, anything less than total committment to the frag plan was an invitation for the townsfolk to attack. In order to avoid a bloody horror show, they had to go in strong, hard, and ready to prime and toss.

On Ryan's signal, they rolled through the door, blasters up, safeties off. The noise was much louder inside. The floor shook from the stamping feet, and plaster dust fell in clouds from the ceiling.

Unless the celebrants were careful, something much worse was about to rain down.

Like the buildings on the other side of the square, the movie-house lobby had been stripped to the concrete. The candy counter was gone, as were the wallpaper and carpet. It had all the mystery and magic of a warehouse. Scavenged lumber and fifty-five-gallon drums were stacked along the facing wall, with room left for three sets of double doors, all of them closed, all of them leading into the theater.

As Ryan put a two-by-four through the handles of the middle doors, the singing and stamping stopped, and the clapping died away. They could hear a man's voice. He was talking loud, but his words were muffled by the walls.

Mildred and J.B. took the right-hand set of doors; Krysty and Ryan took the left.

"Don't go too far into the room," Ryan reminded them. "And don't let anyone get behind you until we're sure about these people."

J.B. eased through the doors with the M-4000 pump gun braced at hip height. Mildred followed with her Czech wheelgun. No one noticed their entrance, which was just as well because it took a few seconds for their eyes to adjust to the broad room's torchlight. The floor sloped down to an elevated stage. There were perhaps twenty rows of plastic seats on the slope, every one occupied. Close to the stage, people were sitting on the floor in the aisle.

The familiar music, if not its performance, had made century-old memories resurface in Mildred's head: a long, elegant white dress and veil, an exchange of vows, floral bouquets, proud parents and in-laws. What was taking place in the El Mirador was something very different.

Teenaged girls lined the bare stage, clothed in baggy, homespun robes. The man doing all the talking was tall, slope-shouldered and similarly dressed. His long black beard grew up over his cheekbones, almost to the sockets of his bulging, black eyes. Wild black hair sprouted around his head, as if he'd been struck by lightning. Beside him at the edge of the stage stood a young blond girl with her robe drawn off her shoulders.

"Just thirteen summers and look at the set of hips on her," the bearded man told the audience. "Jubilee Wicklaw will bear fifteen children, just like her mother, and her sisters."

At his command, little Jubilee, doe-eyed, a smile frozen on her face, started performing a mechanical, hip-gyrating dance more appropriate to a woman twice her age.

And a woman who wasn't six months pregnant.

In that instant, Dr. Mildred Wyeth would have shot somebody dead if she'd known who to shoot. Raised in the second half of the twentieth century, when civilization was at its peak, she found many parts of the new reality difficult if not impossible to stomach. Where there were no laws to defend the weak, the weak invariably suffered. But of course suffering was a relative term. As was exploitation. And in Deathlands, there was always something worse. Always. At least the girl looked well-nourished, and there were no obvious bruises or scars on her arms or breasts.

"Jubilee's only been married the once," the bearded man continued. "She's hardly even broken in."

"What about the one in her belly?" shouted a man down in front.

"That goes along as part of the deal," the bearded man said. "Isn't that right, Pilgrim Wicklaw?"

Someone in the center of the bank of folding seats called out, "I'm trading all my claim."

As the bearded man scanned the audience for takers, he spotted Ryan and Krysty, first, then Mildred and J.B.. He clapped his hands, threw back his head and cried, "Glory to Bob and Enid! We have guests!"

Everyone turned in their seats to see, and upon seeing, stood up.

For Mildred, staring down a couple of hundred people with just a six-shooter and a pocket full of grenades was a moment to remember.

A very long moment.

"Once again the lost are found!" the bearded man exclaimed. "Guided out of the desert by the hand of Providence. Strangers, we are bound to welcome you, even as we ourselves were welcomed. Praise Bob, praise Enid!"

The tension broke and the ville folk gave them a tumultuous welcome, with cheers and applause.

When the clamor subsided, the bearded man waved the crowd back to their seats, and gestured for the newcomers to approach the stage. "Come on up here," he said, "let's get ourselves properly introduced."

"We'll stay right where we are," Ryan said.

Where they were was in control of all the exits, with blasters in hand, but the audience seemed too excited to notice.

The bearded man didn't seem to care, either. Without pause, he proceeded with the introductions. "I'm Pilgrim Plavik," he said. "Pilgrim Wicklaw, stand up. Pilgrim Baxter. Pilgrim Dennison. Pilgrim Ardis. Pilgrim Matthews."

The men rose as he spoke each of their names. They reminded Mildred of predark, heavyweight boxers, of club fighters not contenders, their brows, ears and cheeks scarred from years of hand-to-hand combat. Like the man on stage, they were dressed in floor-length, homemade sackcloth; they all wore their beards and hair untrimmed. Pilgrim Wicklaw's hair hadn't been combed for so long that it had turned into a lopsided mass of brown felt. A single, butt-nasty dreadlock.

Seated around each of the men were lots of women, with lots of young children. Pilgrim Plavik didn't bother to introduce any of the women, and Mildred couldn't help but notice the way they beamed up at the men. In her experience, every remote population enclave in Deathlands had its own social structure. A product of isolation and grim necessity. Mildred was already getting a picture of the new Little Pueblo. A picture she didn't like.

From the seating arrangement and the adoring looks, all the females and children belonged to the half-dozen pilgrims, which left more than a hundred single men in the back rows and aisle. They didn't get introduced, either. Lean and furtive, they looked like whipped dogs. Grinning whipped dogs. From the family groupings, and the sheer size of the successful husbands, Mildred figured the single guys weren't getting any, except maybe from each other.

"I'm called Ryan," Ryan said. "This is Krysty, and Mildred and J.B. are on the other side. We're pleased to meet you."

Ryan didn't see fit to mention Doc and Jak, who were waiting for his signal in the darkness just inside the exit doors.

"Welcome to Little Pueblo, one and all," Plavik said.

The pilgrims took this as their cue to sit down, all but Wicklaw, who remained on his feet, his gaze shifting back and forth between Krysty on the left, and Mildred on the right.

His interest made Mildred's skin crawl.

Turning to Ryan, Wicklaw said, "As a gesture of respect and friendship, in the name of Bob and Enid I offer you a trade." There was neither respect nor friendship in his crafty, squint-eyed smile. "I'll swap my wife Jubilee there, for your dark one. Straight across trade. You keep the baby."

J.B. looked back at Mildred and winked. She scowled at him. It wasn't funny. Not by a long shot.

Wicklaw pointed at Mildred and said, "Come down here and sit beside me so we can get better acquainted."

Then he addressed Jubilee, "Go on, go to him, girl."

The child-mother started for the stage steps, eyes full of dread.

"Hold on right there," Ryan told her.

The girl stopped in midstep, looking to her hulking brute of a husband for direction.

But Pilgrim Wicklaw was already pushing his way out of the row of chairs. Mildred hadn't moved an inch in his direction, so he was coming to her.

Up close, he was even bigger. More like a super-heavyweight. His hair and beard looked like he'd been asleep in a cave for four or five months; from his expression he had awakened pissed off. His sweat-reek was monumental, almost stratified.

"I treat my wives good," he boasted to her. "You're never gonna do better than me. Go on, ask the others."

Over in the Wicklaw family's seats, his five spouses were smiling and nodding in eager agreement. A polygamy pep squad.

Mildred thought about telling him how old she was chronologically, but knew he'd never believe it. "Sorry, but I'm not the marrying kind," she said.

Wicklaw moved toe to toe with her, leaning over, trying to intimidate her with his size and strength. He didn't notice that she held her double-action ZKR aimed at the instep of his booted right boot. She was holding her breath to avoid taking in the big bastard's stink, all the while thinking, one in the foot, one in the balls and one between the eyes.

"You're wrong about that, Mildred," Wicklaw said. "You've just never had a real man take care of you.

You're going to love every minute of it, I swear by Bob and Enid."

When he put his callused hand heavily on her shoulder and squeezed, J.B. moved in. He jammed the barrel of his 12-gauge against the base of the man's spine, between the top of his buttocks. "Take a step back from her, pilgrim," he said, "or you'll never walk again."

It was a triple-stupe thing to do, under the circumstances.

But Mildred loved him for it.

Wicklaw backed away, his hands raised.

"Cull!" a woman's voice shrieked.

Others took up the cry. In seconds the hall rang with the chant, "Cull! Cull! Cull!"

Whatever it meant, it didn't sound like fun.

Doc and Jak stepped out of the shadows, their blasters up.

Plavik raised his arms and called out to the crowd, "Stop it, now! Stop it right now! Remember, these folks just got here. They've been through a lot. They don't understand our ways."

"Don't matter what they've been through or what they understand, and you know it," Wicklaw said. "What matters is that they follow custom from the minute they set foot here. What's right is right, praise Bob."

At the "right is right" bit, everybody in the theater stood up, purple-face outraged that newcomers had dared to challenge the rules they lived by. There were no blasters showing. Given odds of better than thirty to one, they didn't need them.

When the men, women and older children started to

push into the aisles with bloody murder in their eyes, Ryan shouted, "Wait a fireblasted minute!" He pulled a fragger from his pocket and holding the safety lever down, yanked the ring pin.

Push had come to shove.

"Shit!" Mildred hissed under her breath as she and J.B. followed Ryan's lead, holding armed explosive devices up for all to see.

With primed frags at every corner of the room, the crowd froze. And it got very quiet in the El Mirador.

Seconds passed and the stalemate stretched on and on.

No one questioned the companions' resolve to use the grens. No one dared call their bluff. But the youngest kids were already beginning to fidget and whimper. Something had to give. Good. Bad. Or ugly.

Ryan broke the awful silence. He turned to Pilgrim Wicklaw and said, "Isn't there another way for a *real man* to settle this?"

Chapter Seven

"Trade or blade!" Pilgrim Wicklaw bellowed back at Ryan. "Trade or blade!"

The crowd roared and stamped its approval, greatly relieved that the conflict might be resolved at the cost of only one life, and a life that belonged to a complete stranger, at that.

"It is the custom here," Pilgrim Plavik told Ryan as the noise died down, "to work out our trading disputes with cold steel, one on one."

Ryan knew the people of Little Pueblo might not honor the outcome of the fight if he came out on top, but it was the only chance to avoid a wholesale slaughter of the women and children. There was nothing to lose by trying.

"Until the fight's over, nobody moves," he said. "Your people stay in their seats. My people stay where they are."

Plavik nodded. "That is agreed."

Ryan slipped the ring pin back in the gren, repocketed it, then unslung his Steyr and handed it over to Krysty. As he passed her the weapon, he whispered in her ear, "If I go down, frag them."

"He's the one going down, lover," Krysty whispered

back. "Going down hard." Though there was confidence in her voice, her mutie hair had drawn up into a mass of tight, anxious ringlets. "And if the ville folk don't like it?" she asked him.

Her question only had one answer, and it was the same one he had just given her. He said it again, "Frag them."

Pilgrim Plavik quickly ushered the girls off the stage and waved for the two would-be combatants to come up and join him.

Ryan and Wicklaw mounted the stage from opposite sides and walked to its center, where Plavik waited.

"The rules are, there are no rules," said the wild-haired, robed master of ceremonies. "Last man standing is the winner, however long that takes."

Wicklaw was staring down at Ryan's black cyc-patch and scar, turning his big, blocky head this way and that to take in the view from every angle. As he did so, an ugly grin peeked through the tangle of his beard. "Looks like you already lost a knife fight, Ryan," he said. "This one's gonna last three minutes, tops, then I'm gonna take that eye you got left."

Ryan didn't rise to the bait. He stared back without expression, willing to let his panga do all the talking.

"All right, both of you step back, now," Plavik said, spreading his arms wide to separate them. When the two men were ten feet apart, he cried, "Blades out!"

Wicklaw barked a command to his cheering section.

One of his wives hurried forward, to the foot of the stage. She skittered her husband's weapon across the stage floor. Wicklaw stopped its course by stepping on it with his boot, then bent and picked it up by the wooden handle.

A farm implement.

Wicklaw slashed at the air with the cruel, two-foot-long, quarter moon of razor sharp steel. The hooklike blade of the scythe gathered in and sliced, all in one motion, using the weight and inertia of whatever was being harvested to make clean, sweeping cuts. In combat, it was no stabbing tool, but it could make deep wounds to muscle, and sever blood vessels and tendons.

Incapacitation.

Leading up to the kill stroke.

Ryan drew his own weapon from its leg sheath. The panga was eighteen inches of tempered, predark vanadium steel. Longer than a bowie knife and shorter than a short sword, it had a steel crossguard and pommel. With its heavy-backed blade, an expert knifefighter could cut through a one-inch-diameter bone with a single swipe. Although it could be used for stabbing—it had a razor point and deep blood gutters along both sides of the blade—because of its weight and balance, the panga was primarily a hacking weapon, designed to produce massive, cleaving wounds to flesh and bone.

"When I drop my arm," Plavik said, "the fight is on."

"Got any last words, One Eye?" Wicklaw asked, shifting his weight easily from one foot to the other.

Ryan had no words, last or otherwise. Nor did he have a fighting plan, a "strategy" that anyone else would have recognized as such. Knife fighting was instinctive. Reactive. Because of the speed of attack and counterattack, it bypassed thinking and logic— "if he does this, I'll do that"—and moved into a much more primitive and mysterious realm. Some blademasters visualized positive and negative energy flowing back and forth between them and their adversaries. As much as possible, Ryan visualized nothing. He emptied his mind, preparing it to receive whatever came his way.

Wicklaw on the other hand thought he had his game plan all worked out. A seasoned fighter, he had undoubtedly hamstrung dozens of inept opponents by going for the heels, right off the bat.

When Plavik dropped his arm, that's exactly what Wicklaw did. He hopped forward, squatting low, reaching out and sweeping his arm through a short arc that hooked the blade behind Ryan's feet.

Ryan jumped in the air to avoid the strike, and as he did, he lashed out with his right boot. The straight snap kick caught Wicklaw in the side of the neck as he leaned forward, a solid blow that jarred Ryan all the way to his hip. Wicklaw felt it, too. He groaned and tumbled away.

Before Ryan could close and strike with the panga, the big man had rolled to his feet. Pinkish blood oozed from his neck. The snap kick had ripped out a three-inch-square patch of his beard. The hair ball was stuck in the lugs of Ryan's boot sole, along with a strip of skin.

Wicklaw smiled as if it didn't hurt.

So it had to have.

"I eat sissy little shits like you for lunch," he said as they circled and feinted. "Don't worry, your ladies are gonna forget all about you in a week."

Ryan ignored the taunts. The stage was a blank rec-

tangle. There were no curtains. No ropes. No furniture.
Nothing to throw or fight behind. As Ryan moved
around and around, he maintained eye contact with
Wicklaw, but he wasn't just seeing the eyes. He was taking in the whole package at once, shoulders, arms, hips,
legs. Wicklaw was light on his feet for someone so big.
And with his apelike arms, he had the reach advantage,
even with Ryan's eighteen-inch blade.

The audience roared every time their pilgrim made
a lunge, but they soon tired of all the circling and testing. They wanted action. They wanted blood.

Ryan's blood.

Wicklaw tried another strategy, something that had
worked for him before, no doubt. He suddenly charged,
windmilling with the scythe, trying to knock Ryan off
balance, or back him into a corner.

Ryan pivoted away at the last second, timing the move
to duck past the downslashing blade. As the steel point
brushed his back, he hacked behind the man's knee, putting all his weight and spin-momentum into the downward blow. Under the flowing robe, it was difficult to tell
where the target was. The panga slashed through the rough
fabric and hit something solid, but it wasn't flesh or bone.

It didn't yield.

And for an instant, metal scraped on metal.

Wicklaw laughed and jumped away.

The panga had put a wide tear in the back of his robe,
which made the hem drag on the floor. There was no
blood. And from the way Wicklaw moved, no injury.
As his opponent turned, Ryan glimpsed something dull
and metallic through the hole in the fabric.

"What's wrong, One Eye? You look surprised."

With that, the big man came at him again, this time the furious charge was accompanied by waist-high, forehand-backhand slashes of the scythe, and piglike grunts of effort.

Ryan feinted a retreat, then parried and struck, bringing the panga's sweet spot down on the man's right thigh, just above and perpendicular to the knee. The heavy blade cut through the homespun cloth, then it stopped. The clash of steel on steel reverberated up his arm and the panga bounced off its target.

The blow made Wicklaw groan.

But it should have done way more than that.

It should have severed the bone in his leg, or failing that, clipped off his kneecap.

The big man sidestepped, limping slightly, keeping his blade moving to prevent a follow-up attack. Again there was no blood on the robe, no blood on the floor.

"Pil-grim! Pil-grim!" the crowd shouted, urging Wicklaw to rejoin the fight, figuring he had taken the best that the stranger could dish out.

Through the big slash in the front of the robe, Ryan could see what the problem was. He imagined Wicklaw's wives sitting around the fire of a winter's night, dutifully cutting, bending, pounding together the steel strands for their hubby's chain mail leggings.

"You're gonna have to do better than that, One Eye."

He did.

Ryan moved right, lunging toward Wicklaw. As the big man tried to cut him with a backhanded swipe, he ducked under the blow and shifted the panga to his left hand. There was a steel toe cap on Wicklaw's boot. Ryan chopped down just behind it.

Maybe there wasn't enough steel wire to make footies for the leggings.

Maybe Wicklaw liked to wiggle his toes.

The panga cleaved through the first three inches of boot, all the way through the sole, and made a gash in the floor. The toe cap and its contents bounced away. For a second there was no blood and Ryan could see the white circles of five toe stumps in the now open-ended boot. Then the blood gushed. And gushed.

Squealing in pain, his face dead white under all the whiskers and hair, Wicklaw hopped on his good foot, trying in vain to staunch the bleeding with his free hand, and keep Ryan off with the scythe. The torn hem of his robe tripped him up and he fell hard onto his back.

The crowd moaned in unison.

Ryan was on top of him a second after his head hit the floor. Straddling the man's chest, the one-eyed man brought the panga down hard with both hands. Not the point, but the knurled steel pommel.

Three hard blows.

Each punctuated by the crack of bone.

Amazingly, Wicklaw didn't pass out. He spit shattered teeth and blood from his battered mouth and tried to get up.

Before the bigger man could buck him off, Ryan flipped the blade around. With his left hand, he pressed the point over Wicklaw's heart. His right hand, clenched in a fist, he held ready to pound it in to the hilt.

A wail went up from the audience.

Realizing that all his wives were about to become widows, Wicklaw stopped fighting. His body went limp and he slumped back to the floor, coughing and blowing bubbles of blood.

As Ryan stood up and stepped away, from the rear of the room the single men booed him and catcalled. Not because he'd won, but because he hadn't properly finished the job.

It was finished, as far as Ryan was concerned. There was no point in chilling the man. He was no longer a threat.

Wicklaw's wives rushed onto the stage to tend to their man's wounds. Two of them got the boot off, while the others made a tourniquet from a strip of the hem of his robe. They bound it around his instep, and torqued it down hard with the scythe handle to stop the bleeding. There wasn't much they could do for his face.

Pilgrim Plavik remounted the stage and held up his arms for silence. When that didn't work, he let out an ear-splitting yell that quieted the crowd.

Ryan looked down at Krysty, then at Mildred and J.B. They had their grens ready.

Truth time.

"No one in this room can claim the fight wasn't fair and square," Plavik said. "Everything was by the book, praise Bob, praise Enid." He glanced back at the loser, who was sitting up on the floor with the help of his womenfolk. There were bits of teeth in his beard and the tips of the hair dripped blood.

To Ryan he said, "You thrashed him good. And as

far as I can see, he didn't even give you a scratch. Pilgrim Wicklaw shamed everyone in this ville with the piss-poor fight he put up."

Again, the single men booed.

"Because you won," Plavik shouted over the noise, "you keep your women. And you keep his trade goods, too."

Ryan frowned. It was part of the deal he hadn't foreseen.

"Come on up here, Jubilee," Plavik said.

As the pregnant girl walked across the stage, the people of Little Pueblo began to clap and sing, "Dee-dit-deedee. Dee-dit-deedee."

Chapter Eight

The sun was sinking below the horizon by the time the ville folk started filing out of the El Mirador. In all, eleven young women and girls had changed husbands, divorces and marriages accomplished in the same ceremony, a bargain sealed by a song without words.

Five of the six pilgrims appeared satisfied with their respective deals, but to Ryan it seemed an odd satisfaction under the circumstances—detached, passionless, as if they'd traded prize cows or pigs. The only celebration he'd witnessed was communal, a tribe thing. Although the pilgrims' wives welcomed the new brides with an embrace, the newlyweds themselves didn't touch.

Which was just fine with Ryan.

His pregnant, teenage bride followed on his heels as the companions set off across the town square park. Ryan shifted the Steyr on its shoulder sling to adjust the balance point. Krysty, Mildred, Doc, Jak and J.B. still had their blasters, too. That the ville folk hadn't asked them to surrender their weapons surprised Ryan. Most remote villages in Deathlands had some kind of a leave your guns at the gate policy to minimize the chance of violence. Not that the companions would have honored a request like that, anyway. They were a different breed than the unarmed, sackcloth-robed farmers. They moved in sync, triple alert, like a military unit, or chilling crew, their skins and clothing tinged with ground-in, greasy dirt from the desert crossing. Creatures from the dark side.

"You have to talk to her," Krysty told him.

He answered with a noncommittal grunt.

"She didn't ask for this any more than you did."

Ryan wasn't shocked that his long-time lover would take the side of the young girl he had supposedly just married, and was now expected to take full responsibility for. Krysty always managed to look below the surface, past the superficial, to the beating heart of things. She saw Jubilee as a tragic victim, not a threat to their relationship. That's the kind of woman she was. And one of the reasons he loved her so passionately.

Though Ryan also felt sorry for Jubilee, from experience he knew there were things he was powerless to change, and therefore had to accept. Like it or not, the hellscape was triple hard on its womenfolk. And the females who couldn't defend themselves—the young 'uns, the dimmies, the physical weaklings—got the worst of it by far.

"I know what you're thinking, Ryan," Krysty said. "This is her place, these are her people. You want to leave her here when we go."

"And you want to take her with us?"

"They've already turned her into a baby-making machine. You heard that bug-eyed bastard Plavik, bragging about how she was going to pop out fifteen kids, one after another, until she drops dead. What kind of life is that for a human being?"

"I think you're jumping to conclusions. You're mixing up what you feel and what she feels. Maybe she wants to stay in Little Pueblo. It's all the life she knows."

"That doesn't make it right."

"Staying here is her best chance to survive, and you know it," Ryan said. "If we have to walk across that desert, and she comes along, she's never going to make it. It'd be kinder to put a bullet in her head right now."

What he didn't have to say was that the weight of one more life—two, counting the baby she carried—on a desert crossing might be enough to tip the balance and get them all chilled.

"But we may not have to cross on foot," she said. "Not if we can break into the redoubt and access the mat-trans unit."

"And the mat-trans still works," he added.

"Yeah, that, too, of course."

"Look," Ryan told her, "I don't want to get this girl's hopes up, and then have to let her down. She's been hurt plenty. And she doesn't need more of that from us. If the mat-trans unit is operational and she wants to leave, we'll take her along, and at the other end find a safe place for her to have her baby. But if we can't get into the redoubt, or the unit doesn't work, she stays behind. No arguments."

That seemed to satisfy Krysty, at least for the moment.

Ryan glanced over his shoulder. His new bride had

dropped back a few yards and Mildred was walking at her side, speaking softly to her. The pregnant girl wore her blond hair pulled straight back and braided into a long, slender plait. She kept her blue eyes downcast, and her pale lips drawn tight.

Jubilee hadn't said two words to anybody since she crossed the El Mirador's stage. If she'd even looked at Ryan, he hadn't seen it. He could understand how someone so young, and in such dire straits, would be numbed by the turn of events. Expelled not only from her family group, but as things turned out, from her entire community her lot suddenly thrown in with that of strangers. But there was something else, too. Under the shock, the feeling of being abandoned, under the sadness, there was fear. It was etched in her face and the way she carried herself. A more terrible fear than circumstances warranted, Ryan thought. Like she was walking a tightrope. Or a plank. With doom all around her.

Maybe she was crazy.

Or a drama queen.

One thing was sure, she was one hundred pounds of trouble.

With his four wives and ten children in tow, Pilgrim Plavik led the way across the park. He'd promised the companions a fine, home-cooked meal to welcome them to Little Pueblo.

Though his stomach was growling again, Ryan wasn't thinking about food. He was thinking about the blackheart, water-stealing son of a bitch they'd followed to the edge of the ville. If a man wandered into a place like this, with no women to trade, nothing but his muscle and bone to offer, he was bound to end up in the theater's back rows and aisles with the other unhappy bachelors. No way would he make the rank of pilgrim overnight; in fact, the odds of him ever making pilgrim were slim. On its face, the social order of Little Pueblo appeared to be just that bottom heavy. Without blasters or squads of sec men, the few had found a way to dominate the many. Jubilee wasn't the only one who kept her eyes focused on the ground most of the time. The single men and all the other women and children lowered their heads in deference to the ville's chosen ones.

The six pilgrims controlled all the available females. And had therefore presumably sired all the ville's children. The non-alpha males hung around the fringes of the alpha-males' harems, most likely doing all the fieldwork, looking for their big chance to move up, or sneak some illicit fun when the pilgrims turned their backs. Not an unusual strategy for group survival. Ryan had seen it before, in other remote villes. What was unusual, however, there didn't appear to be any person, male or female, older than thirty years of age.

When they reached the far side of the town square, Plavik took them across the street to the three-story stone building with the tall clock tower. The clock wasn't working. At some point during the initial flooding or subsequent reemergence, one of its huge, steel hands had fallen off. Every window facing the street was either crudely boarded up or covered with sheet plastic. As Plavik and his entourage trooped up a single flight of wide stone steps to the double front doors, Ryan noted the building's cornerstone, which bore the inscription: Little Pueblo City Hall Built 1913 A.D.

Before he started up the steps, Ryan took a look back at the park. The other pilgrims and their families were crossing the street, heading for city hall. Not Wicklaw, though. He wasn't anywhere in sight. With half a right foot, it was going to be awhile before he crossed anything. Although the whole town had followed them through the square, the nonpilgrim men had stopped short of the street, and stood watching from the far side. A mob of robed ghosts.

Inside, the predark building showed considerable water damage. Most of the floor tiles were loose. The wooden trim moldings along the base of the walls, under the high ceiling, and around the doors were either missing or had warped and sprung loose from their moorings. The tan, gloss-enameled walls showed broad patches of discoloration, as did the ceiling.

A century's worth of mold from the smell of it, Ryan thought.

Short of tearing out the load-bearing walls, there had been no way to dry out the lathe and plaster after the reservoir had drained off.

Plavik moved past a set of corroded elevator doors that had been nailed shut and decorated with the words: All Glory to Bob and Enid. He started up the staircase at the end of the entry hall. The stairs were made of steel and hadn't fared so well under five hundred feet of water. The treads and railings had completely rusted out in spots, in others the metal was filigreed and paper thin. The major damage had been repaired and braced with scraps of wood, iron pipe, angle brackets and bailing wire. As Plavik and his family climbed, and the companions followed, the whole staircase began to groan and shake. Only Ryan and the companions seemed concerned by this.

Six flights up, they moved off the rickety stairs and onto the building's top floor. The town's municipal offices, preflood, had been turned into living quarters. The rooms were furnished in the same, junkyard style as the one-story businesses around the square: crude beds on concrete blocks, crude mattresses made of straw, the occasional piece of watermarked, veneer-peeling furniture; no rugs on the floors; mold spots on the walls, between hand-lettered imprecations to Bob and Enid.

The plastered ceilings had collapsed in places, exposing bare lath. One room had been turned into a kitchen. The stove, a predark Kenmore electric, had been stripped, raised a foot and a half from the floor by stacked, steel wag rims and converted to burn wood. Its makeshift vent pipe poked out through a hole in the scrap metal that covered the tall, narrow window. A huge, covered caldron and a steel, automobile hubcap half filled with what looked like vegetable oil sat on the cook top.

The brief home tour ended where it had begun, in one of the suite's living room-bedrooms. Plavik offered his guests seats on the various platform beds, then dismissed his women and children with an impatient wave of his hand. The children made themselves scarce, and the wives moved into the kitchen to prepare the feast.

When Jubilee started to follow the women, Mildred caught her by the arm and made her sit down.

Plavik seemed amused by this.

Though Ryan and the others sat, they couldn't pretend to look comfortable. It wasn't just the hard beds. Or the smell of mold. Or the subjugation of the ville's women. Plavik's body language and facial expression told them he had something up his sleeve. Something nasty. Big fun for him, the opposite of big fun for everyone else.

"Why don't you tell us something about your ville?" Ryan said.

The bug-eyed man twisted a strand of beard around his index finger. "Little Pueblo was, then it wasn't," he said with a grin. "Then it was, again. When I showed up here, it'd been risen from the ashes for nearly a century, praise Bob, praise Enid. I came over from the east, at the border of the Shens. That's where all my people lived. Wanted to see some of the world while I was young. Set off on my own. I was wild and triple stupe back then. Worked in gaudies and jolt shacks all through the western territories. I ran my own string of skanky sluts on the side, sold battery acid disguised as jolt to folks dumber than me and did some robbing when it didn't take too much effort. To make a long story short, I got myself in one big stinking mess after another. And the scrapes always ended up with blades or blasters, and blood on the floor. I'll tell you, I'm lucky to be walking around alive today."

"So you just wandered in from the desert, like us?" J.B. said.

"Started at the very bottom of the shit pile," Plavik said with pride. "Came here with nothing, and half-dead from the sun. But I got better before they could bury me, and I learned the ways of the ville. There's no place to run once you get here. You know how close the desert came to taking you out. Before you'd go through that again, you'll make do with almost anything so long as there's some shade, some water, and something to eat.

"Because I had some size to me, and I like to mix it up, I worked myself from field slave to overseer in less than a year. The men who objected to my taking their jobs got themselves drowned in the lake and turned into fertilizer.

"I'd been an overseer for mebbe six months when I chilled Pilgrim Boone and took everything he owned. Boone, he was a real big son of a bitch, even for a pilgrim. Three hundred pounds stripped naked, and all of it mean. One night I caught him on the staircase in this building, four flights up. Surprised him from the shadows with a stout rope. Had the noose around his neck and cinched tight before he knew what was happening. Then I practically ruptured myself pitching his fat ass over the stair rail. The bitter end was tied off real good, but Boone was so heavy his falling weight broke the rope in the middle. Snapped his spine at the same time."

Plavik gleefully smacked his palms together as a sound effect.

"Pilgrim Boone didn't need any more chilling after that," he went on. "When I found him laying at the bottom of the stairs, the bastard's neck was stretched two feet long." He turned to Ryan and added, "You were dumb not to chill old Wicklaw when you had the chance. You could be having his women, one after another, right now. You could be living in his rooms down on the third floor."

From the kitchen came loud sizzling sounds and the clatter of crockery. The smell of the food wafting through the doorway made Ryan's mouth water and started his stomach rumbling. "We didn't see any gaudies when we came into town," he said.

"No gaudies here. This is a dry ville. Jolt and juice don't grow food. They eat a man's strength."

"No trained sluts, either?"

"Oh, there's sluts, but none for rent, only for trade," Plavik said. "We pilgrims prize our wives above everything else. That's what Bob and Enid taught us."

Prize. Not respect. Not honor. Not cherish.

Women as livestock.

"We've never heard of Bob and Enid," Krysty said, fighting to keep the anger out of her voice. "Just who might they be?"

Plavik smiled at her. It was a question he relished answering. "Bob and Enid were the ones who came first," he said. "Right after the waters fell away. They brought with them the greatest wisdom of the world before skydark. They used it to give shape and balance to this Paradise. We praise their memories every single day."

"This great wisdom you mention," Doc said, "might I inquire as to its substance?"

It took a second or two for Plavik to sift the meaning from the old man's somewhat tortured Victorian construction. "Bob and Enid, may they abide in Glory, carried knowledge of all things on the earth," he said. "And of the inner workings of all things, down to the tiniest spec of dust."

"They were whitecoats, then?" J.B. said.

From the expression in Plavik's dark, protruding eyes, J.B.'s suggestion bordered on blasphemy. "They were seekers after truth," he said, with heavy emphasis on the last word. "They were pilgrims in a ruined land. As are we."

"Okay, Bob and Enid weren't whitecoats," J.B. conceded, "but there were whitecoats in Little Pueblo before nukeday."

Plavik gave him a blank look.

"That's one of their complexes in the middle of the square. We walked right past it. Nothing like that's been built since Armageddon."

"You're mistaken," Plavik told him. "That's the tomb of Bob and Enid. A monument to their sacred memory."

His absurd answer hung in the air for a moment before Ryan pressed the issue. "A tomb and not a temple?" he asked. "You never go down there to make your praise?"

"That would be sacrilege. The tomb is sealed for all time. It cannot be defiled."

Their interest in the redoubt was clearly starting to aggravate Plavik, so Mildred changed the subject. "We followed a man here," she said. "Picked up his trail in the canyon, tracked him almost to the outskirts of the ville. We figured he was two or three days ahead of us. Do you know who I'm talking about?"

Plavik shook his head, then smiled. "You're the first newcomers to show up in more than a month," he said. "Perhaps the man never made it? Maybe he died before he got here?"

Even if the pilgrim hadn't looked down and to the left as he spoke, the classic "tell" of a man who was lying, Ryan wouldn't have believed him. The thief had to have arrived in Little Pueblo. Why he would bother to lie about it was the mystery.

Plavik's quartet of wives swept into the room, carrying the food in a hodgepodge of serving containers. Chipped ceramic bowls, handleless mugs, and metal sauce pots brimmed with a thick, steaming soup. One of the women offered them rounds of golden fry bread from a heaping, wicker basket.

The soup was corn-based, sweetish tasting, with bits of chicken meat and flavored with chili spice. Ryan had to force himself to eat slowly to avoid scalding his mouth. As he dipped the fry bread into his pot, he looked more closely at the women and kids. Plavik's oldest wife was in her midtwenties. None of the children were older than six or seven. They all resembled their pa. Same dark thick hair, same intense dark eyes. Plavik's women didn't look at their husband straight on while they served the meal, but they weren't scared to death like Jubilee.

Maybe because they were sitting on top of the shit pile.

As more fry bread was passed around Plavik turned

to Ryan and said, "Now it's you folks' turn to talk. Tell me all about yourselves. I want to hear everything. Where did you come from? Where were you headed?"

Taking a page from his host's book, Ryan smiled and lied through his teeth.

Chapter Nine

Mildred Wyeth used the razor point of her knife to cut a slit in the sheet plastic that blocked the second story, city hall window. Outside, night had fallen on Little Pueblo. There were firelights here and there around the town square, dancing in the doorways of the occupied one-story buildings. Stars glittered overhead. No one moved in the faint moonlight. It was very hot, and the air was dead still. The smell of woodsmoke hung like a pall.

Looking out at the surround of blackness, the valley floor and the canyon walls, Mildred got a powerful, disturbing sense of Little Pueblo's precarious grip on existence. It was like a ship far out on a storm-tossed sea, floating, rudderless, at the whim of fate.

Jubilee stood at her side, mute, expressionless. Mildred had tried her best, using the gentlest possible approach, but she hadn't been able to break through to the child, or to get her to respond in any way. It wasn't catatonia, Mildred was sure of that. Jubilee knew what was going on around her. Mildred would have felt better if there'd been tears, screaming, even violence. Anything but this blankness.

When Ryan called out from the middle of the room, Mildred looked over her shoulder at him.

He waved for her to join him and the others in a circle on the floor.

She started to lead Jubilee over, too, but Ryan said, "No, not her. She can stay right there."

Mildred understood his reasoning. They didn't know if they could trust the girl yet. There was a slim chance that she wasn't as incapacitated as she looked, that she was biding her time, looking for an opportunity to get herself back in the good graces of some other pilgrim, and perhaps return to the ville's fold. If she overheard their plans, she could betray them.

"Everyone sit close," Ryan said, "and keep your voices low. We don't know who's listening."

"What do you make of all this?" J.B. asked Ryan.

"Bug-eyes was feeding us a load of bullshit," he said "The water thief got here, all right. We were following his tracks. If he'd dropped dead in them, we would've found the body. There was no reason for Plavik to lie about our chiller-friend unless something bad happened to him. Something that wasn't an accident. Something Plavik thought we wouldn't take kindly to."

"And he was lying about Minotaur, too," J.B. said. "A tomb, my ass."

"But it was sealed up like one," Krysty said. "Remember how that door was blocked?"

"Well, we'll unblock it in a little while," Ryan said. "As soon as we're sure everyone's sound asleep."

"Our host's protests notwithstanding," Doc said, "the much-revered Bob and Enid were most definitely of the whitecoat persuasion."

"Yeah," Ryan said, "they had to be. They were here

first because they walked out of that redoubt when the water level dropped."

"Atlantis becomes Eden," Doc remarked. "A veritable dog's dinner, mythologically speaking."

"Worthy of the Disney Channel," Mildred added.

No one got the joke, of course.

Of the companions, only Mildred had subscribed to cable TV, and found nothing to watch on 150 stations.

Pursuing Doc's line of thought, she said, "So, how did Eden pop up here? Sure, there's water, but look at what else these people have. Grain crops. Vegetables. Bees. Chickens."

"The seeds could have been carried across the desert," J.B. said, "but not the bees or the chickens. No way would they have survived the heat. There's only one place they could have come from, and that's Minotaur."

"The redoubt's emergency processed food supplies would have run out a long time ago," Ryan said. "Whoever designed Minotaur was looking at the big picture, at building some kind of permanent settlement here."

"But they didn't know when skydark might happen," Krysty said. "Even small livestock takes up room, requires food, makes a mess and tends to multiply. How do you store bees and chickens indefinitely?"

"Cryogenically, using liquid nitrogen," Mildred said. "Compared to defrosting and reanimating a human being, a chicken is a piece of cake. Believe me, I've done both."

J.B. had another suggestion. "Or the bees and chickens could've been mat-trans-ed in from some other location, after the nukecaust."

"I like the sound of that better," Krysty said. "Means the damn thing works."

"Or at least it worked once," Ryan said.

"It would appear that Eden is the product of much careful consideration," Doc said. "Right down to the bees necessary for proper pollination of their crops."

"They planned out the community structure here, too," Mildred said. "They knew that Little Pueblo, post-nukecaust, wasn't going to be a closed system, with a static population. Every once in a while newcomers would show up out of the desert and have to be assimiliated. There had to be a procedure for that in place. Also a procedure for removing excess people. Overpopulation would destroy everything."

"So what keeps everyone in line?" Krysty said. "There's only six pilgrims. They've got no blasters that we've seen. There aren't teams of enforcers to make the people obey. As big and mean as the pilgrims are, they couldn't turn back a mob with their bare hands."

"I think it has to do with this place," Ryan said. "About what it is, where it is, and what's all around it."

"Death all around," Jak said.

"That's right," Ryan said. "Water is life. Water is limited. Probably some years there's a lot less of it to go around. It's in everyone's interest to follow the rules. A pilgrim might get chilled and replaced, but that doesn't change anything. The system is still in place. Lots of single males at the bottom and a few pilgrims at the top."

"And there's hope built-in, even for the field slaves," J.B. said. "Plavik's an example of that."

"I agree about the stability of the pecking order," Mildred said, "but I think you're missing something important."

"What's that?" Ryan said.

"There isn't just one efficient way to organize this place. Sure, simple works best when it comes to social order, but I can think of a dozen other plans that make as much sense, given the elements we've seen here."

"Why don't the single men get together, and rearrange things so they all have wives, or at least access to them?" Krysty said.

"That's what I mean. They've got everything to gain from kicking ass. And they've got the means to do it. But they're docile as sheep. We're missing something…."

"What I want to know," Krysty said, "is what happened to Pilgrim Boone's children?"

"You're right," Ryan said. "Those kids were definitely Plavik's. They looked just like him. If this place is all about certain people making babies, what happened to Boone's?"

"It's basic Darwinism, I'm afraid," Mildred said. "In a system like this, with a handful of alpha males in charge of all the females, it isn't unusual for the new male harem-master to kill all the offspring who aren't his. This improves the chances of his kids, his genes to survive."

"And the women who mothered those kids would stand still for that?" Krysty said.

"They wouldn't have had any choice," Mildred said. "They might have even helped. In a situation like this, you can't discount the women as just being downtrodden and helpless victims. They can be as determined and deadly as the dominant males. Together, the females form a kind of subclan that functions—and survives—in support of whatever male who happens to be in charge at the moment. Their real allegiance is to the subclan. To one another."

"There seems to be a dearth of graybeards on the premises," Doc said.

"Maybe they're chilling the oldies, too," J.B. suggested.

"What you mean is they're killing their own fathers and mothers," Ryan said.

"Like chilling one's offspring, that's a very difficult proposition for a human being," Mildred said. "Historically speaking, it's only been done in extreme circumstances, in times of starvation, disaster. Which obviously isn't what's going on here. There's plenty of everything."

"Why haven't they tried to chill us?" Krysty asked. "Because we've got blasters and grens?"

"Or mebbe because we have you and Mildred," Ryan suggested. "Women are status here. They're treating us like we're not-quite pilgrims."

He looked over at Jubilee. She stood by the window, staring out at the night.

"That one could tell us a lot," Ryan said.

"If she was talking," Mildred said.

Chapter Ten

Because her back was to the newcomers, Jubilee couldn't make out their words. She wasn't really trying to hear what they were saying, anyway. It was all wasted effort. There was nothing they could do, or plan to do that would change anything. And there was nothing she could do to go back to the way things were.

She breathed in the familiar smells of the night. Woodsmoke. Chili spice. Wet earth from the lake. And as she did the aching pain in her throat became almost unbearable. No tears came, though. She had no more tears left. She had every reason to believe that this was her last night on Earth. That she would die without ever seeing her baby's face.

Like the one-eyed man and his male friends, she was the walking dead.

Their two women companions still had a few good years left, by Little Pueblo standards. Unless they proved difficult.

Jubilee knew all about the consequences of being difficult. That's what got her put on the trading block. She wasn't submissive enough to suit Wicklaw. She asked him questions. It was automatic, in her nature.

And when she didn't like the answers he gave her, she asked him more questions. It was a recipe for disaster.

Her sister Wicklaw-wives had taken her aside numerous times and tried to explain to her that despite the way things looked on the surface, the women of the ville really controlled everything. They said they all just pretended to be weak in order to rule behind the scenes. The idea rang false to her, as it had when her own mother had first told her the same thing, years ago—her mother, who had been culled at age twenty-nine, after birthing fifteen children for four pilgrims. The power over life and death wasn't in the hands of the womenfolk. The way Jubilee saw it, no one in Little Pueblo was in control. They were all prisoners. All condemned, all awaiting execution.

Before the afternoon's assembly, the word on her prickly attitude had gotten around to the other pilgrims, through the wives' grapevine. She knew in advance that no one was going to trade for her.

Not today, not ever.

In Little Pueblo, not fit to trade meant not fit to live.

For a moment in the movie house, when the strangers had their grens out, and were threatening the entire ville with destruction, she wanted to scream out "Do it! Chill them all before they chill you!" The words had died in her throat. She was thirteen years old, she was pregnant and she had no faith in grens. Or the threats of strangers. Calling out for blood would have only sped up her own end. Keeping quiet meant few more minutes of agony-free life for her and her unborn baby.

Jubliee Wicklaw felt the one-eyed man approach her

from behind. She couldn't escape him any more than she could escape her own fate, so she didn't try.

He came close, but he didn't touch her. He spoke in a low, soothing voice. He promised that he wouldn't harm her or her baby. He had questions for her, he said. He wanted to know what was in store for him and his friends. He wanted to understand the way Little Pueblo worked.

Jubilee had seen strangers wander in from the desert many times before, but never any quite like these. Dangerous people. Skilled fighters. Arriving in a squad, not in ones or twos. And the women were as hard as the men, and in the same way. All of them had been kind to her.

In their ignorance, they still had hope.

"What do the pilgrims do to strangers?" he said, his voice no longer soothing. "We need to be ready, understand? For better or worse, you're in this with us. If we go down, you go down."

She had no answers for Ryan. Already staring at her feet, Jubilee turned her head away.

He caught her by the chin and made her face him.

For a second she looked helplessly into that sky-blue eye of his. It seemed to probe her very soul. Unable to break free, she clamped her eyes shut, hoping he hadn't seen the truth.

Chapter Eleven

Three hours after the moon had set, Ryan walked over to the straw mattress where Jubilee lay. It was dark in the room and he couldn't tell if she was asleep or not. When he touched her shoulder, she stiffened, but she didn't jerk away, so he guessed she had to have been awake.

If the girl was afraid her new husband wanted to exercise his marital rights, she had nothing to worry about.

"Get up," Ryan said softly, but firmly. "We're going for a walk and you're coming with us."

When she sat up, he said, "If you make any noise, or try to warn the pilgrims , we will tie you up and gag you, and drag you along. Do you understand?"

If she nodded, he couldn't see it in the dark.

"Say yes, or we'll tie you up right now," he said.

In a voice barely above a whisper she said, "Yes."

Behind him the door opened a crack and a shaft of light from the hall cut through the gloom. From the looks of her face, she'd been curled up on the straw pallet, crying.

Ryan took her by the arm and led her to the door, where the companions waited. With their packs strapped on and rattle-proofed, they were ready to put

Little Pueblo behind them, forever. The light in the hall came from torches burning in makeshift stanchions. Except for the hissing of the flames there was no sound. And there was no one on guard in the corridor. They moved single file out the door and along the hall to the staircase. Jubilee was sandwiched in the middle of the line, between Mildred and Krysty.

The stairs creaked and quivered as they descended. Jak and Ryan took the lead and J.B. brought up the rear. They only had a short way to go, just one floor to pass before they reached the foyer and the city hall entrance. The rickety staircase was a necessary evil. If it hadn't been for the pregnant girl, they would have used a rope from one of their packs to rappel out the window and onto the street.

Jak and Ryan paused on the first-floor landing, listening hard. Again, they heard no sounds except for the sizzling of the torches. There was no way to know whether the pilgrims had put guards on them or not. Or how close the guards would be stationed. To be safe, the companions had to assume that they were under some kind of surveillance. It made the early morning recce more challenging. Their plan was to break into the redoubt, and if possible jump out of the gateway mat-trans. If that wasn't possible, to return to city hall unseen and before they were missed.

Ryan had no illusions about what would happen to them if they were caught in the act of breaking into Minotaur. The ville folk weren't going to take kindly to the desecration of Bob and Enid's "tomb." But staying in Little Pueblo wasn't an option. Compared to what surrounded it, the place was paradise, all right, but it was also a prison for people who valued their freedom. The companions weren't field hands, and had no aspirations to becoming same. On principle, they refused to live off the forced labor of others. And none of them was willing to go along with the Darwin-harem thing.

When they reached the foyer, they found the long corridor lit by torches at either end. They had to pass by four doorways, including the elevator, which Ryan discounted because it had been nailed shut. No light leaked out from under the other doors. Before they began to advance, Ryan made sure Jak was aware of the potential threat.

As they proceeded, he and the albino started opening the doors and clearing each of the rooms. The idea was to get out of the building without alerting anyone. Poking their heads and weapons in the rooms increased the chances of a firefight, and discovery, but it was the only way to prevent the worst case scenario—a crossfire ambush in the corridor.

When Ryan and Jak approached the third and last door, everything went to hell. Three men burst out of the doorway carrying cut-down, predark pump shotguns on shoulder slings, hip-braced to fire. They weren't pilgrims. They were field slaves with blasters.

One half of the companions' plan was down the crapper. There would be no sneaking back to the second floor.

The man standing in front of Ryan swung the muzzle of his 12-gauge back and forth at waist height. "Don't move," he warned.

As he spoke, something *whooshed*. With a thunk, a shiny steel blade slammed into his right eye socket. The man's head snapped back, and his knees buckled. The knife point had driven through the thin bone behind the eye and deep into his brain.

As he fell, dead on his feet, the other two guards looked on in astonishment. The lapse of attention lasted less than a second, just long enough. Ryan pivoted from his hips, bringing the butt of the Steyr around in a tight, precise arc. It was sacrilege to use a finely tuned sniper rifle as a bludgeon, but under the circumstances there was no alternative. The steel-shod butt crunched into the nearer man's temple, poleaxing him. The tremendous force of the blow sent him sprawling into the guard beside him.

Before that man could recover his balance and fire, a leaf-bladed knife pinned his beard to the front of his throat, burrowing deep, its point cutting his windpipe and his carotid artery. He let the shotgun fall on its sling and clutched at his neck with both hands. As blood sheeted down the front of his robe, his mouth opened and closed, like fish out of water.

Jak ripped the blaster away from him, and Ryan shoved him against the wall. Goggle-eyed, his mouth still moving, he slid to the floor. It took him about a minute to bleed out. The homespun robe soaked up the gore like a sponge.

"This one's dead, too," Mildred said, leaning over the guy who'd taken the blow to the temple. "You caved in his head."

Krysty had her left hand clamped on Jubilee's shoulder. In her right hand she held her Smith & Wesson Model 640. The girl was trembling, her face blanched by shock.

Ryan surveyed the mess they'd made. Even if they could find a place to hide the bodies, there were puddles of blood all over the floor. Way too much to clean up.

"I think we just wore out our welcome," J.B. observed.

"Permanently, I fear," Doc said

"Do you think there'll be more waiting for us outside?" Mildred queried.

"If the pilgrims posted three guards in here," Ryan said, "it means they don't trust us. And if they don't trust us, you can bet there're more."

"They could be set up to defend Minotaur," Krysty said. "They could have an ambush set up in the park, figuring we'd try to loot it."

"They could be anywhere," Mildred said.

"Word isn't out, yet," Ryan said. "We've got to break into Minotaur before they realize we're on the move."

"And if the mat-trans unit doesn't work when we get there?" Krysty said.

The companions all looked at Ryan.

"Let's hope there's a ton of ammo inside," he said, "because we're going to need it."

Outside the city hall's front doors, the only light on the street was from the blanket of stars. The town square was bathed in deep shadow, its bordering row of trees cast wide pools of impenetrable darkness, their trunks and branches obscured the view of the redoubt. The companions filed down the steps, keeping low and moving at a trot.

The street to the corner was deserted.

No sentries in sight.

With J.B. and Ryan covering the rear, backstepping with weapons up, they crossed over to the park. Jak and Doc led them to the cover of the nearest trees, which were fifty feet from the corner of the square. They took up kneeling positions around the trunks, covering all directions.

Up and down the line of trees nothing moved. Not a twig. Not a leaf. Between them and the low, concrete oblong of the redoubt was seventy-five yards of tightly cropped grass. Ninety yards of open space to cross in the scorching, breathless night.

"If we have to retreat, we're going to need covering fire," Ryan said. "Doc, you stay here and watch our backs. Jak, cross over to the trees on the other side, and do the same from there. Keep an eye on the redoubt's entrance, too. We'll signal when we've got the door open. And when we do, you come running."

"Be assured that we will do just that, my dear Ryan," Doc said.

The albino slipped into the shadows of the line of trees, and promptly vanished. After a minute or two, starlight reflected off something white near the base of a tree trunk directly across the sward. Jak was in position.

Before they set off, Ryan leaned close to Krysty and whispered in her ear, "Watch the girl close. When she realizes what we're up to, she may make a fuss. Can't have that."

Krysty nodded.

With Ryan in the lead, J.B., Krysty, Jubilee and Mildred ran for the redoubt. If anybody was watching them from the trees, they kept quiet and out of sight. When Ryan reached the front wall, he hurried along it to the steps leading down to the entrance.

Jubilee stopped short when he waved the others down the steps ahead of him. Her eyes grew wide, and with a whimper she broke free. She got three steps before Krysty caught her by the back of her robe and jerked her back, hard.

"No!" the girl gasped. "You can't! You must not!"

Krysty clamped a hand over her mouth and held her still. "Stop it," she said into the girl's ear. "I don't want to hurt you. Don't make me hurt you."

Jubilee stopped struggling at once. She looked at Ryan with pleading eyes.

In vain as far as he was concerned.

The child knew nothing about the inner workings of redoubts and the network of mat-trans units that connected them. She knew only superstition and myth.

Bob and Enid.

He helped Krysty pull Jubilee to the bottom of the stairs, where they forced her to sit. The concrete pad was stacked with smooth boulders, a steeply angled slope that leaned against, and blocked the vanadium door, top to bottom. The entrance's keypad lock was just visible on the outside edge of the pile, on the right. Unlocking the door was pointless at this stage; with all the rocks in the way it wouldn't open.

Mildred took a look-out post near the top of the

steps while J.B. and Ryan ditched their packs, then started moving the stones to clear the way. The rocks were so heavy they could only manage to carry one at a time. They staggered up the steps with their burdens, and when they got to the top, they rolled the stones out onto the neatly trimmed grass.

As JAK WATCHED his friends disappear down the stairwell, his heart did a little flip in his chest. He'd had the same bad feeling many times before. The sense that everything was on the verge of falling apart. In a way, and on a scale that would boggle his radblasted, mutie mind.

This wasn't the doomie sight.

Jak couldn't read the future like the pages of a book already written. His unease came as his brain digested the facts of the present. They'd gotten themselves into a box for real, this time. There was only one possible safe way out, and there was a good chance that was a dead end.

Mildred would have said he was calculating probabilities. Whatever it was, Jak just did it, like breathing in and out.

And while he did it, bad feeling and all, a smile played across his mouth. Every nerve in his body was on triple alert. In Deathlands, where most people got from here to there on foot, or on the back of some dumb animal, this was the fast lane.

When a stick softly cracked to his right, at the corner of the park, some fifty feet away, he didn't jump in surprise because he was expecting it. Bracing against the tree trunk he brought the sights of his Colt Python to bear.

His mouth tightened.

Ville folk poured through the gap in the trees. Not just on Jak's side, but on Doc's as well. Dozens of them, armed with blasters, moving quickly and with precision toward the redoubt.

Ryan Cawdor, Deathlands' warrior of warriors, had taught him that in every game, every battle, there was one move that couldn't be countered.

Checkmate.

Killshot.

That's what this was.

He squeezed the Python's combat trigger and it barked and bucked in his fist. Downrange, one of the running figures crumpled. As the man fell, he tripped up two others following closely behind. Across the park, Doc's .44 boomed. Jak caught the flare of three-foot-long muzzle-flash out of the corner of his eye.

As he lined up his sights and brought up the trigger's slack, the ville folk returned fire in a big way. Muzzles flashed at him from the grass and from the shadows below the trees. Semi- and full-auto centerfire weapons clattered and black-powder blasters unleashed thundering booms. Bullets whined past his head and thunked into the tree trunk, spraying him with bits of bark.

Jak had to throw himself belly down to avoid being torn apart.

Twisting around the base of the tree, he saw three attackers, running full tilt right at him, shoulder to shoulder.

Jak fired double action, four times, as fast as he could pull the trigger.

A pair of Magnum slugs bored through the middle man, hitting him high in the chest, sending him crashing first to his knees, then his face. The guy on the right jerked sideways as a bullet slammed his shoulder. Screaming and clutching his dead arm, he dropped his weapon and dived for the cover of the trees. The man on the left took a .357 bullet square through the bridge of his nose, and the back of his head exploded in a plume of blood mist, brains and bone that pelted the grass behind him. Rag-doll limp, he, too, went from knees to face.

His four quick shots gave the other ville folk something to aim at. From three sides they poured a fusillade of fire at his muzzle-flashes. And the air was full of screaming slugs and pistol balls. Under the onslaught, the tree before him started to shake and fall apart. Leaves, limbs, hunks of bark rained on him. Dirt and grass from the low shots kicked up in his face.

To stand and fight was to die.

And for nothing.

He couldn't protect the companions from this position, and he couldn't chill enough of the enemy to improve their odds.

Jak scrambled to his feet and bolted around the tree trunk, heading for the sidewalk. As he did so, he practically collided with an oncoming robed figure. The AK-74 the person carried registered in his mind a split second before he fired from the hip. One shot straight into the gut. The Python roared and the figure was blown backward; the assault rifle went flying. Dashing on Jak saw there was no chin beard. It was a one of the pilgrims' wives, rolling on her back in the grass, clutching her stomach.

As he ran past her, he pulled a gren from his pocket and primed it. He paused to lob it over the tops of the trees, toward the massed fire. He didn't stick around for the bang. He just threw it and sprinted for the sidewalk. Blasterfire raged behind him, but not at him. It sounded like J.B. and Ryan were firing from the redoubt entrance.

Then came the rocking explosion, followed by screams.

Then more explosions, more screams. Somebody else was chucking grens, too.

The problem was, what would have worked in the confines of the theater wasn't going to work in the open square. There was too much room for the ville folk to maneuver and evade. And way too many of them.

In long strides Jak crossed the street and ducked into the front of a one-story building. It was dark inside, and no one was home. He dumped the Colt's spent casings on the floor and used a speedloader to refill the cylinder with jacketed .357 mag rounds.

Ready to resume the fight, he found the back door and a narrow alley that ran behind the row of buildings. As he stepped out, more explosions interrupted the steady crackle of blasterfire. He had to get behind the enemy, and quick. That meant coming up on the redoubt from the rear. He turned right and started to run. The alley opened onto one of the streets that ringed the square. Jak came around the edge of the last building low and fast, dashing up the sidewalk for the corner.

From that vantage point, he could see the back side

of the park. And he could see folks in robes standing in front of the trees.

Then the roar of gunfire suddenly faltered, and stopped.

If Ryan and the others weren't already dead, they were about to be.

As he raised the Python, his targets moved through the trees and out of sight into the square.

Jak cursed, then darted across the street to the tree line. Peering around a trunk he could see the ville folk sprinting for the rear wall of the redoubt. He had the bastards, now. Bracing his blaster hand against the tree, he took aim and tightened down on the trigger.

"No, my dear boy," Doc said softly beside him. "It is far too late for that."

Chapter Twelve

Lathered with sweat, his legs and back aching, Ryan lurched up the steps with yet another 120-pound boulder. He and J.B. were pushing as hard as they could, working without pause, fighting through the pain. At least they wouldn't have to replace all the rocks to cover their tracks. They wouldn't be returning to city hall, under any conditions. Not with the three corpses they'd left behind. For the companions it had come down to either the redoubt and the mat-trans unit, or risking the desert on foot.

As Ryan dumped the stone onto the grass, two blaster shots shattered the early morning stillness. The tree lines on either side of the park lit up for an instant from the muzzle-flashes, then went dark. He knew the sound of Jak's and Doc's weapons.

They weren't shooting jackrabbits.

Before he could turn, the ville folk answered fire, raining bullets down on the redoubt's entrance. Slugs sparked off the boulders scattered on the grass and slammed into the concrete wall, showering the entrance stairwell with sharp fragments.

Ryan dived down the steps, shoulder-blocking J.B. out of the line of fire. The Armorer stumbled, dropping the stone he was carrying, and it fell down the steps, nearly rolling over Krysty and Jubilee before it hit bottom.

"Dark night!" J.B. exclaimed, screwing his hat down.

They hadn't made it inside the redoubt. Their tiny force was divided. The full weight of the ville was coming down on them, and they were pinned down in a twelve-foot-deep pit.

J.B. had described the situation pretty well.

Ryan grabbed the Steyr, grimacing at the death zone a few feet above his head. Waves of bullets continued to zing off the boulders and top step. Those that missed whanged into the tempered concrete above the vanadium door. The high-powered, centerfire slugs cratered the concrete; the black-powder pistol and rifle balls flattened or shattered against it.

Returning fire was going to be a dangerous proposition.

"We've got to get in the redoubt, and quick," Mildred said. Scrambling to the bottom of the steps, she tried to lift one of the rocks out of the way by herself, but it was far too heavy for her. Though she strained, she could hardly budge it.

"Mildred," Ryan said, "let J.B. do that. Take his shotgun."

As J.B. passed the weapon over to her, Ryan told him, "If you stack the rocks on top of each other on the steps, there might be just enough room to open the door. We'll hold them off as long as we can."

Mildred and Ryan took opposite sides of the stairs,

easing up the last few steps on their butts. Right away, they could see that the rocks he and J.B. had thrown out provided some cover from the onslaught, deflecting incoming rounds and giving them something to shoot around.

Crawling forward onto the grass a yard or so, Ryan brought the Steyr tight to his shoulder. It was too dark to use the scope, but not too dark to see shadowy human forms crossing the open ground and filtering along the line of trees.

Then a frag gren detonated with a resounding boom in the middle of the grassy field. The flash lit up a sixty-foot circle and revealed a roiling plume of smoke.

In the brief flare of light, Ryan picked out a figure running right at him. He managed to snap off a shot an instant after the flash faded, but he couldn't see if he'd hit the guy. As he cycled the bolt, flipping out the spent casing, the thudding began. Bodies and body parts blown into the air started bouncing back to the grass.

Before the ville folk could resume firing, two more grens detonated, cutting off the screams of the wounded. The explosions were about thirty feet apart and tight against the tree line on Doc's side of the square. Heavy limbs cracked and crashed down, and more body parts thudded onto the grass.

The chorus of anguished shrieks and moans was drowned out by massed blasterfire from the far end of the park. Ryan aimed well below one of the muzzle-flashes and squeezed off a round. He held low because the range was way short for the Steyr's three-hundred-yard zero.

Despite Mildred's prowess with small arms, the hundred-yard distance to target was too much for her short-barreled weapons. She was forced to keep low and hold her fire, conserving her ammo until the ville folk got closer.

Which they were doing, by the second.

Ryan ignored incoming bullets thwacking the rocks in front of him and throwing dirt in his face, and methodically fired at the muzzle-flashes, giving the opposition something to think about. Behind him, J.B. was struggling with boulders. Under the clatter of bullet impacts, Ryan could hear him cursing. Krysty couldn't help him; she was holding Jubilee down, trying to keep her out of danger.

The combination of grens and Ryan's sharpshooting forced the attackers to flee the open ground. They scurried to the trees on both sides of the park, and continued to advance.

When they were forty yards away, Mildred shouldered the pump gun and opened fire. She sent blast after blast of double-aught buck sailing between the trees. With only eleven .31-caliber balls in each round, scoring a hit on moving targets was a matter of dumb luck. But the hellish rain of lead slowed them, and that was more important.

"J.B.," Ryan said over his shoulder, "is it clear, yet?"

"A few more rocks to go," he groaned.

"We've got to give it up, Ryan," Krysty shouted. "Got to make a break for it, now!"

She couldn't see, but it was already too late for that.

Ryan dug a gren from his coat pocket. He primed and chucked it.

The flash bang's paralyzing light and sound caught five or six attackers between tree trunks.

For a moment they stood like statues, caught in midstride.

Ryan and Mildred mowed them down with buckshot and .308s.

It worked so well, Ryan quickly tossed another gren, but he put a little too much on it. It landed high in the branches of a tree, then exploded. The tree burst into flames, limbs and leaves blooming in a brilliant orange ball.

In the light of the fireball, they saw what they were up against. The whole radblasted ville was coming after them.

The scattergun empty, Mildred hauled out her Czech ZKR and started picking off the running men like shooting gallery targets. The .38 didn't pack enough wallop to chill them dead. Unlike shooting gallery targets, these ducks thrashed and kicked in the grass, screaming.

The window of opportunity was rapidly slamming shut.

"J.B.?" Ryan shouted. "J.B.?"

"Almost there, almost…"

"Krysty," Ryan said, "get the keypad."

Leaving the girl at the bottom of the steps, she rushed to the door and its electronic lock.

"Now," he said. "Key in the sequence, now."

From above and behind him, Ryan heard the sound

of running feet. Before he turned, he knew what it was. And that it was something he couldn't defend against. The ville folk had flanked the redoubt and climbed onto the roof from the rear.

Rolling to his side, with the Steyr braced against his hip, he looked up at a row of blaster barrels pointing down at them.

Someone on the roof shouted, "Hold your fire! We've got 'em!"

The shooting stopped.

"Ryan, you've got nowhere to run."

Ryan recognized Plavik's voice. He was on the roof, too, but standing safely back from the edge.

Krysty stood at the redoubt keypad, her fingers poised to tap in the open command.

But a large boulder still blocked the door.

Ryan did the math, and it came up short. No way could they trigger the entrance lock, move the obstacle and get through the doorway before they were shot to pieces.

He looked at Krysty, then Mildred and shook his head. This hand had been played out. He said, "We're done."

Mildred lowered her revolver.

J.B. looked at the heap of rocks they'd moved and spit. "All for nothing," he said.

"Stand up slowly, one at a time and throw your blasters out on the ground," Plavik said.

Ryan carefully set the Steyr in the grass and rose from the dirt. As he raised his empty hands in the air, he could feel a hundred sets of blastersights aimed at his heart.

Chapter Thirteen

Krysty and the others were driven, single file, their wrists bound behind their backs, down a gauntlet of angry survivors. There was shoving, kicking and punching, but most of the abuse consisted of shouted insults and spitting. Lots of spitting.

It could have been, perhaps should have been, much worse.

Starlight revealed the carnage the companion had wrought: scorched circles in the earth where the grens had gone off; scorched bodies and parts of bodies in the grass, crumpled, unmoving figures scattered around the bases of the trees.

Krysty saw many dead on the ground, but very few wounded being tended to. Ryan and Mildred had hit what they were aiming at. Not just men, either. Several of the pilgrims' wives had been chilled. She guessed Little Pueblo had lost between twenty and thirty residents in the attack, enough to impact their ability to farm the fields. On the other hand, there were that many fewer mouths to feed.

Perhaps that's why the crowd hadn't torn them to pieces, she thought. Then another idea occurred to her. Maybe they had an even more painful punishment in mind.

Although she would have preferred a neat, quick, permanent escape via the redoubt's mat-trans unit, Krysty felt no guilt over the considerable loss of life. She and Ryan and the others hadn't come into town looking for trouble, but when it found them, backing down wasn't an option. You didn't last long in the hellscape if you weren't willing to fight to the death. There was always someone or something ready to take advantage of perceived weakness. And more often than not, an offer to negotiate a solution was seen as vulnerability, and an opening for immediate attack.

It was understandable that people didn't want to lose what little they had. Whether it was freedom in the case of the companions, or a way of life in the case of the ville folk. As always, it all came down to blasters and blades. To keeping what you had, or giving it up. And giving it up usually meant giving up breathing, because that was the only way to eliminate retaliation, with interest, at some later date.

Even though a lot of folks had died, Krysty and the others were no closer to their goal; in fact, they were farther from it. Prisoners at the mercy of their captors. Krysty knew Jak and Doc weren't among the dead. If they'd been chilled, Pilgrim Plavik would've made a point of showing them the bodies. With Jak and Doc on the loose, there was a still chance of counterattack and escape—they wouldn't leave their friends behind.

Plavik led the way across the street and up the steps of city hall. When they were inside the foyer, he directed two of the other pilgrims and a half-dozen field hands to take charge of Ryan, J.B. and Jubilee. "Escort those three to the holding cells," he said.

Ryan, J.B. and the girl went down the stairs at blasterpoint, while Krysty, Mildred, Plavik and all the pilgrims' surviving wives climbed to the second floor and entered the room they'd left twenty minutes ago.

After the torches had been lit, Krysty and Mildred were forced into chairs, and the wives retied their wrists to the chair arms, and their ankles to the legs, using turns of heavy cord.

The room was packed with people. Almost all of them were women. Looking around, Krysty counted twenty-eight wives. They weren't hiding their weapons, now. Every one of them either had a flapjack holster belted around their waist, or a handblaster hanging from a neck lanyard. The pistols were black powder. All revolvers, replica Colts and Remingtons in either .36 or .44 caliber. Some of the blasters had lost their grips, and been repaired with wraps of duct tape. Black powder was an uneven burning and inefficient propellant. From all the black-speckled hands and fingers, the women of Little Pueblo had fought at least as hard as the men.

Pilgrim Plavik looked on from the doorway, his long arms folded across his chest, until the prisoners were secured. As he approached Mildred and Krysty, his eyes seethed with cold fury.

"You've done Little Pueblo a great injury tonight," he said. "Out of ignorance and greed you have upset the balance of our lives and put us all at terrible risk."

Krysty tested her bonds. She couldn't move her arms

or her legs, and the ropes were cinched so tight around her ankles that she was already starting to lose feeling in her toes.

"Only the bravery and fighting skill of our people kept you from violating our most sacred shrine," he said. "The tomb of Bob and Enid."

"Blessed be," pronounced the assembled wives and pilgrims.

"Yeah, yeah," Mildred grumbled under her breath.

Krysty reckoned the ville folk had paid mighty dearly to protect their holy place. Unfortunately, none of the payees were pilgrims. It appeared that Plavik and his ilk had led the assault from the rear, keeping as many bodies as possible between them and the action.

"For the crime of attempted desecration," Plavik went on, "Ryan and the short man will pay the ultimate price at dawn tomorrow."

"You're going to execute them?" Krysty said, her face turning into a mask of pure hate.

Plavik shook his head. "There would be no gain in that. We will offer them to the greater glory of…"

"Bob and Enid?" Mildred suggested.

Plavik nodded.

Somehow that knowledge didn't reassure Krysty.

"And what about us?" Mildred pressed.

"You must pay for the crime as well, but unlike your male friends you have trading value. So for you there will be pain and no sacrifice. Members of your own sex will deal out the punishment." Plavik turned to the wives and said, "Remember, no scratching. No biting. No broken bones."

The women of Little Pueblo looked plenty eager to get on with it.

Pleased, Plavik and the other pilgrims left the room and shut the door behind them.

At once, one of Plavik's wives, a pudgy, freckled woman, took charge. She wore her brassy blond hair in thick, braided pigtails. Under the pudge and the baggy robe, she looked strong. She had big arms, and her callused hands were peppered with black.

"Me, first," she told the others, "then Randi, then Valerie Louise…"

When she straddled Krysty's knees, her mutie hair twisted up like a nest of crimson snakes.

"Well, lookee there," the woman said. And as she did, she reached out for the hair.

"Better watch out," Krysty warned her, "it bites."

"Might have to shave it all off, then," Plavik's wife said. "After we get done here…" With that, she started swinging and landing open-handed smacks to the sides of Krysty's face.

Krysty was ready for the blows, which came down so hard and so fast they made her see stars. She kept her jaws tightly clenched so her teeth wouldn't cut her tongue and the inside of her mouth. Even so, the rain of slaps split her lower lip.

The woman spent about four minutes on Krysty, while the other women cheered and egged her on. And when she was done with Krysty, she moved on to Mildred.

Like Krysty, the black woman absorbed the slaps without making a sound. The woman really wailed on her, too, hitting her so hard that it made her nose run and her eyes tear.

When pigtails figured she had given Mildred her best, she waved in the second woman, Randi, who was a few years younger and thirty pounds lighter. The new girl didn't know how to punch, but she sure could screech. Her roundhouse swings boxed ears and arms with little effect.

When Randi could hit no more, the one called Valerie Louise pulled her off and took her place.

"Why aren't your big, strong menfolk doing this?" Krysty said, spitting a gob of blood on the floor.

"That would be a waste of their energy," Valerie Louise said.

Her hair was coarse and brown, parted in the middle, and spread out in a dense mat across her shoulders. She had a triple hard look in her eyes that reminded Krysty of Plavik. They weren't related, though. Not if Plavik's story about his coming here a few years back was true. This wife was eighteen if she was a day.

"Besides," Valerie Louise said with a smile for her sister wives, "only a woman knows how to really hurt a woman."

A demonstration of that talent brought a scream to Krysty's lips.

"Cut us loose, bitch," Mildred said, "and we'll show you what hurts."

"That's the attitude we're trying to get rid of," Valerie Louise said. "We're doing this for your own good, believe it or not."

Not, Krysty thought.

"Because we're such valuable trade goods?" Mildred said.

"Because you're women and there aren't very many of us here. We've got to stick together to survive. There isn't any escape from this place for the likes of us. Not with a whole skin, anyhow. You're here now, and you've got to make the best of it. If you want to keep on living, you have to learn the rules and follow them like the rest of us."

Bells were ringing in Krysty's head, and not just from all the smacks. "If we don't follow the rules, we get culled."

Valerie Louise smiled.

"Just like you cull everyone else who doesn't fit in," Krysty said. "Even your own children."

"Of course. It's the only way to keep order. There's no point in feeding someone who won't obey the rules."

"I get the feeling Jubilee isn't just going to get a few slaps and be sent on her way," Mildred said.

"You're right about that. She's already had her chances. Now she's got to pay. Even the unfit serve a greater purpose in Little Pueblo, praise Bob, praise Enid."

"And what purpose is that?" Krysty asked.

"They help keep the world in balance."

"How so?" Mildred prompted.

"Bob and Enid taught us that everything has a price, and that the price must be paid by someone. If you want to know the truth, it was Enid, not Bob, who set it all down. She knew things that even the whitecoats didn't understand. She knew about the people who used to live here in olden times."

"You mean the Anasazi?" Mildred said.

"We don't have a name for them. They lived like we do, a very long time ago, right here in this place. Enid learned their secrets. Every place in the world is like a machine, that's what Enid said. The parts have to fit together for the machine to run, and when they break they have to be replaced. Either with same parts, or parts that do the same thing, more or less. Those are the rules of the world."

"And what's that have to do with the unfit?" Mildred said.

"You have to make peace with everything you can see, and everything you can't see. You have to feed the demons."

A look of surprise came over Mildred's face. "What sort of demons?" she asked.

"Hungry ones," Valerie Louise said. "Older than time."

"That's strange," Mildred said. "I heard a similar story about this place, many years ago."

"That's because it's true," Valerie Louise assured her.

"How many babies have you had?" Randi asked.

"I haven't had any," Mildred said.

"I'd say you've got three or four left in you," Randi said. "And the red head has nine or ten."

Baby machines.

For the likes of Pilgrim Plavik.

"You don't have to submit to this," Krysty told the assembled wives. "You can fight the pilgrims."

"Maybe we could," Valerie Louise said, "but we

can't fight all the men. There are too many of them. And any man can become a pilgrim with the right luck. That's the way it works in Little Pueblo. One breaks down, and another takes his place."

One woman breaks down, another takes her place, Krysty thought.

"Things have been like this since the day after Armageddon," Valerie Louise said. "Bob and Enid made it so. We can't change it. And we don't want to change it."

"Why change what works?" Mildred said.

"Exactly."

Krysty nodded as if she agreed. And the punishment came to an end without blows from Valerie Louise.

It had all been about getting them on-board with the program. Scaring them, hurting them, whatever it took. Satisfied with the progress they'd made, the wives exited the room, leaving the new converts to Bob-and-Enidism tied to their chairs.

"What about Doc and Jak?" Mildred said softly. "Do you think they got themselves chilled?"

"There's no way of knowing," Krysty said. "We can't count on their help, though, and it sounds like Ryan and J.B. are going to be in big trouble come dawn."

"To hear those wives tell it, when people get put down into that dam, they don't come out again," Mildred said.

"What was all that about feeding the demons?"

"I don't know. I got the same story from a tour guide in the early 1990s. Unkillable monsters appeared spontaneously during times of drought to prey on the people living in the canyon. He said it was a myth from the Anasazi days. It seems to have survived Armageddon. Can you get loose?"

"Only if I use my Gaia power," Krysty said. "I don't want to do that. We may need it again later, and it takes me too long to recover. We've got to find another way to get free."

Chapter Fourteen

Ryan and Dix let themselves be led down the shaky staircase. In front of them were fieldhands with torches; behind them were four more armed men, and bringing up the rear, the pilgrims in charge, Dennison and Ardis. Dennison was the bigger of the two, a wide young man with huge hands and feet. Ardis was tall, lean and hard, with wavy blond hair and a wiry mass of black chin whiskers.

The deeper they descended the stronger the mold smell got. Water stains marked the walls. Outside the limits of the torches it was very dark, and the quarters in the stairwell were tight. Tight enough so if Ryan could've freed his hands, could've made a fight of it. Even with the terrible odds, he could've grabbed a blaster from one of the lackeys and done some real damage, maybe even gotten them out of this fix. But he couldn't free his hands. And with just his feet for weapons, and the steep down angle of the steps, it was a lost cause.

He could see that J.B. was thinking the same thing and coming to the same conclusion.

The stairs ended in a long, narrow hallway lined with walls, floor and ceiling of rough-hewn stone. It was hard to breathe for all the dust they were kicking up. They were probably twenty-five feet underground, and there was no ventilation. The field hands shoved them onward.

Halfway down the corridor, Ryan saw the floor-to-ceiling bars waiting for them at the end. The heavy steel for the early twentieth century jails had survived the deluge.

After ushering Ryan, J.B. and Jubilee inside one of the cages, Pilgrim Dennison clanged the door shut and locked it with a massive iron key.

The holding cells on either side were empty.

Ryan surveyed the stone block walls and floor. The cell's lone bed was a metal rack that hung suspended from the wall by two lengths of chain. It had no mattress. In the corner was a dented lavatory bucket.

"How about cutting our hands free?" Ryan said to the pilgrims. "We aren't going anywhere."

"Not after what you did," Dennison said.

"No way," Ardis agreed. 'You stay tied."

They left an armed man to watch over them, even though they were bound and securely locked away. He pulled a white plastic lawn chair out of the adjoining cell and took seat in the hall, under the torch. After a few minutes, figuring things were well under control, he let his hairy chin fall to his chest and fell fast asleep.

Ryan and J.B. walked along the back wall and took in the graffiti scratched into the stone. It was not promising: Hell awaits; Kiss your ass goodbye, and other words to that effect.

Ryan looked over at Jubilee, who sat on the edge

of the bench, staring at her hands, which were shaking uncontrollably.

"What's going to happen to us?" Ryan asked the girl. She didn't answer.

"You know what's going to happen. Tell us."

She looked up at him, her face devoid of hope. "There'll be a ceremony tomorrow morning," she said. "We'll be taken to the crest of the dam and offered."

"I don't like the sound of that," J.B. said.

"Offered to what?" Ryan said.

"The demons."

"What are you talking about?"

"They live in the dam. As long as we give them offerings they stay inside. Those are the rules that Bob and Enid set down in the beginning. If we don't obey them, everything will fall apart."

"What do these demons look like?" J.B. asked her. Jubilee gave him a blank stare.

"Ever see one?" J.B. asked.

She shook her head. "No one has."

"Then how do you know they even exist?"

"There are screams sometimes, from the people who get put down into the dam. Terrible screams. And blasterfire inside. Not for long, though."

"How will everything fall apart?" Ryan said.

"The demons will come out into the canyon if we don't make offerings to them. They don't like it outside, they hate open space, but if they're hungry enough they will come. And when they do they will eat everybody."

"If that had ever happened you'd all be dead," J.B. said.

"It hasn't happened because folks never let it. Since the days of Bob and Enid the people have been making offerings."

"Why can't you just chill these radblasted things?" J.B. asked. 'You've got plenty of able hands, and blasters and ammo to go around."

"You don't understand," Jubilee said. "They aren't flesh and blood like us. They're spirits. They're like smoke. Bullets don't hit them. Blades don't cut them."

J.B. gave Ryan a dubious look.

They had both encountered wagloads of superstitious crap in their travels across the hellscape. Left on their own, the people of Deathlands worked out all sorts of rubbish to believe in, and organized complicated rituals to celebrate it. Separating the real dangers from the imagined ones could be a full-time job.

"Where did these things come from?" Ryan said.

"I don't know. No one knows. Where does the air come from? Or the sun? For as long as anyone can remember, they've always been here. Only now there are more of them."

"Mebbe because your triple stupes fed them and let them breed," J.B. said.

"Easy, J.B. It wasn't her doing."

"People here just followed the rules that Bob and Enid set down," Jubilee repeated. "And they've always worked to keep things safe. Bob and Enid showed us the way. They were the first to understand. They offered themselves to save the ville."

The girl wasn't helping Ryan separate the real from the bullshit. He changed the subject. "I know why J.B. and me are locked up," he said, "but what did you do?"

"I made some mistakes before you came."

"Must've been some pretty big ones," Ryan said.

"Sometimes a person can't help doing certain things, even when that person knows something bad's going to happen afterward. I don't like being told what to do. I talk back. I argue. Because of that, Pilgrim Wicklaw wanted to get rid of me, to pass me off to some other pilgrims. Only none of them would have me because of the way I am. Wives are supposed to keep quiet when a pilgrim gives an order. Wicklaw tried to trick you into trading for me because you didn't know that I'm worthless as a wife. When people are judged worthless in Little Pueblo, they get culled real quick. When they're offered to the demons in the dam, they're put to some use. People who think and act different don't live very long here. And the demons are always hungry for more."

"What will happen to Mildred and Krysty?" Ryan said.

"Some pilgrim will take them for his wives. If they don't do a good job of wifing, they'll be culled, too."

J.B. leaned close to Ryan and said, "Jak and Doc got away. Didn't see their bodies on the grass."

"If they're alive, they'll find a way to help us."

"Let's hope they do it before we get sent down into that radblasted dam," the Armorer said.

A noise on the stairs made them both turn. Not just creaking sounds. Moans. Groans. Whimpering.

"What the blazes is that?" J.B. said, moving to the bars.

At the stair end of the hall, a couple of field hands appeared, half dragging a wounded man between them. Three more wounded from the battle in the square hobbled into view behind him, bracketed by armed guards. The man in front had a broken right leg. He was making most of the racket. It looked like he'd taken a .308 round just below the knee. The slug had shattered the bone so badly that the lower part of his leg swung around like a deadweight. From knee to shoe top, the leg was drenched in blood. The guards put him on the bench in an adjoining cell. Two other men had received wounds to legs and arms, both from gunshot and gren shrapnel wounds that were bound with strips of rag. The third man was blinded, probably by a gren blast, his eyes covered with a dirty bandage.

"What's all this about?" Ryan asked Jubilee. "Why are they locking up the wounded?"

"They're the ones hurt too bad to recover. They're going to be offered tomorrow, too."

A look at the men's faces told him what she said was true.

"Well, lookee who's here," J.B. said, giving Ryan a nudge.

Limping down the hallway at blasterpoint with his hands raised was Pilgrim Wicklaw.

Chapter Fifteen

An ounce short of trigger break, with a man in his sights, Jak held his fire. He watched as the attackers climbed the redoubt's rear wall and swarmed over the roof. Doc was right. Picking off a few of them wouldn't help their friends break out. The entrance was surrounded. Ryan, J.B. and Jubilee had no place to run.

From behind the tree, he and Doc heard the call for a cease-fire, and when the shooting stopped, Plavik's demand for a surrender.

"They're still alive," Doc said. "Thank goodness for that. We need to withdraw and formulate a rescue plan."

"Trouble coming," Jak said.

Five men with blasters had just stepped from the trees onto the sidewalk, about thirty yards down. One of them pointed and yelled something and the others turned toward the newcomers.

"We go," Jak said.

Before the ville folk could get off a shot, he and Doc broke and ran, cutting across the corner of the park, putting the trees between them and pursuit. Neither of them considered making a stand in the square; there were too many enemies, too close at hand.

For an old man, Doc could still hump it pretty good,

Jak thought. And that was a good thing because the five men were running hard to catch up. There wasn't any more yelling from behind. They were saving their breath.

Jak led Doc across the street to the opposite sidewalk. He turned toward city hall, and sprinted for the one-story doorway he'd already used. Even though the sidewalk was a long straightaway, and their backs were unprotected, it was dark and he figured the men chasing them wouldn't stop and lay down bracketing fire. They didn't have clear shots, and if they stopped they risked losing their quarry altogether. He took Doc through the building and out the back door. As they cleared the rear exit, they could hear the ville folk storming in the front. This time, when he rushed into the alley, he went right, heading away from the park.

Before the hunters could close ground, they reached the mouth of the alley and got around the corner. Spread out before them was a moonscape of ruination bathed in starlight. Below the crown of the town center there were no intact buildings, just empty lots and debris from the houses that had once stood there. A hurricane or tornado would have produced much the same effect, stripping away the above-ground structures, leaving behind the concrete foundations and concrete pads, as well as a clutter of bent pipes, old water heaters, furnaces, pieces of rebar and lengths of insulated wire.

Falling down wasn't an option if they wanted to stay alive, so Jak kept to what was left of the paved streets. As he ran, he listened for the footfalls of the pursuit. He was leading them away from the square and they were following, just as he'd hoped. He and Doc had to isolate the hunters, get them as far away from backup as possible, and then quietly take them out. They had to do that before they could help Ryan and the others.

On either side of the eroded asphalt road a gridwork wasteland sloped down toward the dam. The city ground wasn't worth cleaning up to grow food on. Not when there were fertile fields already established closer to the shores of the lake.

As they neared the city limits, Jak caught a change in the sound of running footsteps behind them. He stopped, pulling Doc down into the cover of a concrete block crawlspace open to the sky.

"They split up," Jak said. He pointed off to the left. "Two that way, try to trap us."

"Shall we trap them, instead?"

Jak nodded. "No blasters. Use blades."

"I concur," Doc said. "We must dispatch the scoundrels with all due haste and return to free our companions."

"Watch feet," Jak said, jumping out of the shallow pit and cutting across the abandoned lots.

Their pursuit was still having trouble spotting them, or they would have fired a shot or two by now, either to try to pin them down, or steer them into the trap. Having split up, they were even less likely to fire for fear of hitting each other in the dark. The hunters were playing it safe, being patient, using their knowledge of the terrain. Short of some kind of lucky break, Jak figured their plan would be to tree the quarry, send back for reinforcements and wait until daylight to finish them off.

Jak would have none of that. It was a big, dark world out there.

His world.

But it wouldn't be dark very much longer.

The gridwork of streets turned into plowed fields. Jak and Doc raced over the soft, tilled earth, through waist-high corn. In the distance, the stars reflected in the placid lake. Everything was breathlessly still, as if they were moving across a painting, or a photograph.

When they reached the predark highway, Jak headed for the row of grain elevators surrounded by the fields of corn. Off to the right, about a hundred yards away, he caught movement, a pair of runners, angling in, trying to cut them off. There was no good cover before they reached the silos. And no good place to set up a countertrap. He picked up the pace, his lank white hair streaming back from his head.

With his long legs, Doc managed to keep up, but just barely. He was breathing in ragged gasps by the time they got to the silos.

The towering grain elevators hadn't fared well, what with the deluge and reemergence. The six cylinders weren't made of tempered concrete like the redoubt. They had all weathered, particularly around the metal fittings, which had rusted away, giving the elements access to the softer interior and allowing erosion to set in. The silos at either end of the row had taken the brunt of the retreating water's suction, suffering impacts from floating debris and well as the scouring action of churning rock and sand. Their external ladders had been swept away, as had their inspection doors, and domed roofs.

The storage units abutted each other, sharing common walls, so there was no way to pass between them. Which was to Jak and Doc's advantage. It bought them a little time out of sight of the hunters.

Jak and Doc rounded the end of the row and ran along the far side to a line of grain carts, dual-axeled, four-wheeled, with long yokes and multiple cross posts. Carts designed to be pulled by human beings. They stopped beside them and did a quick recce. A twenty-foot-wide ring of bare, pounded dirt surrounded the bases of the silos. More waist-high corn fields stretched off to the lake and dam. There was no decent cover that way.

To go farther meant risking getting driven against the sheer walls of the dam or the canyon. The best hope, the last hope was at their backs.

The hunters would know that, too, and expect them to make their stand at the silos.

Jak looked at the grain scattered on the ground and trampled into it. It made a light-colored path from the carts to the side of the fourth elevator.

"Ville folk using that one," he told Doc. He scanned the ladder that ran the entire length of the cylinder and disappeared over the top. "Door there." He pointed at a three-by-three-foot square of dark metal, about twenty-five feet above the ground.

"Yes, I see it. It is an inspection door, I believe. What is your idea?"

"No idea. Trick."

There wasn't time to explain further. Jak scampered, as quick as a cat, up the rusted ladder to the inspection door. It had a bolt for a lock. He slid it back and opened the door wide. It creaked on its corroded hinges. The sweet smell of grain wafted up to him from inside. The job done, he scurried back down the ladder.

"We go in field," Jak said, pulling Doc by the arm. "Two come that side, three come other way. See door. Think we're inside. maybe go up ladder to close, to lock us in. We take them from behind, from field, with blades. Won't expect that. You go that way, use carts as cover."

They split up after jumping through the first row of corn. As Doc moved away, he unsheathed his sword stick. Jak sprinted in the opposite direction, the leaves rustling softly against his legs.

As he approached the last silo, he stopped and ducked into a squat. He shook a pair of leaf-bladed knives from his sleeve. Jak had hunted small game with the wicked blades since he was a little boy. He had absolute confidence in his ability to put them exactly where he wanted them to go.

Leaning forward between the stalks, he had a view of the entire side of the grain elevators. He saw the two men come around the last silo, giving it a wide berth. They had their handblasters in both hands and aimed, looking for an immediate ambush.

Which wasn't there.

Boots crunched at the other end of the silos. Jak turned and saw three more hunters closing in. This bunch moved quickly to the cover of the carts. The first pair, meanwhile, stopped at the second silo. They were keeping distance between them, instead of bunching up, which would have made them easier targets. They weren't triple stupes.

Now would've been the time to blast the bastards. With their backs to the silos. But blasterfire would have alerted the ville and made it harder to free their companions.

Jak listened hard and heard the hunters' hushed conversation.

"Where'd they go?" one of the pair said. "Did you check under the carts?"

"Nothing there," a man on the other side said. "Nothing under them or in them."

"They gotta be here," the first man said.

"Shit, look at the inspection door," one of the trio said. "We never leave it open."

"Think we found our rabbits," the first man stated.

"Just in case we didn't, you two sweep the field. Shoot to kill."

The two men crossed the bare stretch of ground and disappeared in the corn to Jak's left.

His plan was in need of some fine-tuning.

Jak picked up a clod of earth and lobbed it into the field in the direction of the dam. It was too dark to see the track of it flying through the air, but it made a rattling sound as it landed among the leaves.

"Over there," one of the men said. "Fan out."

They moved quickly, working deeper into the field, stepping over and looking down the corn rows. They weren't trying to be stealthy. They were trying to spook their quarry into breaking cover and making a run for it.

Jak waited a few seconds, then crabwalked toward them. He couldn't see them, but he could hear them. He slipped between the rows like a ghost. They weren't looking his way, so they couldn't see the tops of the plants move. And the men by the silo were too far away from the action to see what was about to happen and shout a warning.

Even so, Jak couldn't risk chucking another dirt clod to bring them closer. He wanted to keep their backs to him. He circled around, anticipating their direction of travel, and putting himself in position to strike.

Squatting, he let the nearest man get even with him, three or four rows over. He used the man's footsteps to time his attack. When he had the rhythm, he popped up to a half crouch and sent a throwing knife whistling. The hunter had his back turned in a three-quarter view. Caught in midstride, there was no way he could whirl and fire his pistol.

The knife hit him in the side of the neck with enough force to make him stagger. Jak could see the pointed black shape sticking out below the man's ear. It was a jugular hit. The hunter automatically reached up and tore out the object. Big mistake. Blood gushed from the side of his neck.

He never got out a word.

A brain without blood is just a lump of spongy meat. His legs gave way and he sat down in the dirt.

Before his butt hit the ground, Jak was back in a squat and moving down the row, circling behind the other man.

From Jak's left came an urgent whisper. "Terry? Where the hell are you? This isn't funny."

"Here," Jak said softly, rising to his full height, his arm flying forward. He really put some mustard on it.

The leaf-bladed knife curved left to right.

The second man turned just in time to catch the steel star full in the forehead. The point penetrated bone deep enough to stun, but not deep enough to kill him outright. Jak high-hurdled the corn and threw a shoulder into the bigger man's gut, driving him to his back on the ground. Before the man could cry out, Jak clamped a hand over his mouth. Then he dragged the edge of another knife across the front of his throat from ear to ear, and held him down until he stopped kicking.

DOC HUNKERED DOWN in an uncomfortable crouch, his legs folded under him, his sword ready in his hand. Parting the leaves slightly, he peered across the open ground, at the three men standing by the grain carts. If it was difficult for him to see them in the dim light, it was infinitely harder for them to see him amid the stalks.

All to the good, he thought.

As the other two men moved into the corn, he cocked an ear, eavesdropping on the conversation of the trio that remained beside the grain elevators. They had all turned to face the fourth silo, and were looking up at the inspection door.

"One of us has to climb up there and shut that door," the tallest man said. But he made no move to do so.

"Lock the bastards in," another man muttered. "Then we can take our nuking' time chillin' them."

"That ladder don't look too sturdy," the third man

stated. "It better not be me that climbs it. Might not hold my weight."

From what Doc could see, the man had cause for concern.

"It could be some kind of trick, leaving it open like that," he went on. "They could be waiting for the first one to try the ladder. Pop out the door and shoot him dead before he gets halfway up."

"We can handle that," the tall man said. "The two that don't go up just draw a bead on the door. If something moves up there, blast it."

"So, who's going?" the second man said.

The tall man turned to the chubby one. "You're the worst shot, Fisher. So you get to do the climbing."

He took a position at the front of the line of carts. And the second man moved around to Doc's side, squatting and bracing his autopistol against the cart.

"Go on, now," the tall man said. "We've got your back."

The third man stuffed his revolver in his waistband and lumbered toward the ladder.

From behind Doc, out in the field, there was a scuffling sound. It was over so quickly they might have imagined it.

"What's that?" the man at the ladder said.

"Terry, Bill, you all right?" the tall man called. "Damn, I can't see them anymore."

There was no answer from the field.

The tall man didn't want to yell louder, as that could draw gunfire his way from the darkness.

"Shit, get it over with, Fisher," the second man said.

The third man began to climb.

Doc waited until he was almost all the way to the inspection door before he moved from the corn, his sword point held low and to the rear, his body coiled for the strike. He crossed the gap in three long strides. The man on his side of the carts sensed his approach at the last instant and turned, trying to bring his weapon to bear.

The thrust had to be perfect.

And it was.

The blade slid over the man's wrist, through the center of his chest, and skewered him, splitting his heart. The only sound was the slither of steel on bone.

Doc ripped the blade free and let the man fall.

He spun to his left and dashed for the last cart, keeping low, so the tall man couldn't see him coming.

Above them, the heavyset man on the ladder was cautiously reaching for the door.

Doc rounded the cart on a dead run, catching the tall man kneeling, with his back turned, and his weapon aimed up at the silo. Like a bullfighter, Doc knew exactly where to place the blade. Behind the right arm, five inches below the armpit, at a slight down angle. The sword hit a rib, flexing as it was designed to do, sliding around the bone, and through both lungs and the heart.

Instantaneous killstroke.

From the ladder came an anguished cry.

Doc looked up to see the man hanging on the ladder with one hand, and drawing a long-barreled revolver from the front of his pants with the other.

Doc groaned, realizing he had no choice but to return fire. Dropping to a knee beside the man he had just chilled, he hauled out his Le Mat and took aim.

Something swished through the air high overhead. The man on the ladder stiffened. His gun hand dropped. And his body fell.

He crashed to the ground, headfirst, raising a cloud of dust.

Doc stepped over, his sword ready for a coup de gráce. But the neck in question was clearly broken.

"All your trials are over, my friend," Doc said as he wiped his blade on the dead man's shirt.

"Getting light," Jak said. To the east the sky was already starting to turn lavender. "Sun up soon."

As Doc retrieved his ebony scabbard, they heard chanting and clapping from the ville.

They couldn't see what was going on from ground level, so they climbed the ladder to the top of a silo. From the domed roof they had a perfect view of the end of the square, and everything between. It looked like the entire population had turned out for the procession, which was slowly leaving the town center and heading in their direction.

"By the Three Kennedys, this bodes ill," Doc said.

Ryan and J.B. were at the head of the file, their hands tied behind their backs.

Chapter Sixteen

Ryan didn't see the man with the broken leg hang himself with his bandages. If anybody in the jail saw him, they hadn't tried to stop it. The other prisoners kept themselves busy moaning over their injuries and lamenting their fates. And blaming Ryan and J.B. for both.

Ex-Pilgrim Wicklaw was especially vocal. He who had lost too much—wives, position, teeth, toes—was now poised to lose everything else.

Ryan had tried to get more information from him about Jubilee's demons, but like her, he claimed to know very little. To hear him tell it, what the demons were and what they did were secrets sealed inside the dam. And rightfully so. The only thing Wicklaw could add was the reason why he and the other wounded were to be offered.

Demons liked their food alive, which was undoubtedly why the man with the broken leg had hanged himself.

Shortly after the other prisoners joined them, and the moaning and lamenting kicked into high gear, Jubilee had retreated into a corner and curled up like a pill bug.

There was nothing Ryan could do or say to comfort her. And comfort was misplaced effort at this point.

Ryan shut out the ranting of the other prisoners and withdrew into himself, to a place of calm. A piece of high ground to recce from. He was looking for an opportunity. And as always, he was patient. Expecting it to come. And ready to take hold of it when it did. J.B. was doing the same thing, he knew. Eyes open, brain-churning. Survival was part luck, park skill, part hard experience. They had learned that from their years backing up Trader, Deathlands's legendary convoy master.

Based on his own experience. Ryan couldn't swallow the idea that Little Pueblo's demons might be some kind of avenging eternal spirits. The hellscape was dark and twisted territory, full of nuke-spawned predators that fed upon the weak and the strong alike. Real predators, not ghosts. This wasn't the first time he'd come across people convinced that the horror-show monsters that plagued them were more than flesh and blood. It was a way for dealing with their powerlessness and fear. But in the end those predators, no matter how large, how numerous, or how terrible their weapons, were always killable. Ryan knew because he had killed them.

By the wag load.

It was also possible that the demons of Little Pueblo didn't exist at all. According to Jubilee and Wicklaw, no one had seen one of these critters and lived to tell about it. Someone locked in a concrete prison without food would surely starve to death in a couple of weeks.

And if there were no guards down there, no one went in to see what had actually happened, the chilling could be attributed to anything.

Even to demons.

The trouble with legends, Ryan thought, was that they were ninety percent bullshit and the rest was pure crap.

Less than two hours later, Pilgrim Dennison and Ardis reappeared in the corridor with the half-dozen guards who rousted the prisoners from their cells at gunpoint. All but the hanged man who lay on the floor, one end of the bandage tied around his neck, the other to the chain that held up the bed, his face the color of a plum pudding.

As he looked back over his shoulder, J.B. said, "Now that's a man who really wanted to die."

A guard pulled Jubilee to her feet and shoved her out into the hallway. She moved woodenly alongside Ryan, her eyes red from crying, her face white and drawn. She knew what was coming. She had witnessed it before. And now it was happening to her, a nightmare come to life.

"Are we going to get a last meal?" J.B. asked Pilgrim Ardis as they started up the stairs. "I'm feeling kind of hungry."

"You are the meal, dimmie."

The joke made the guards laugh out loud. Ryan didn't think it was all that funny. He was hungry, too,

With the exception of the blinded man, the wounded climbed the stairs without help from the guards. None of them struggled because they knew it was useless.

When they reached the foyer, Ryan saw light through the front doors. It was nearly sun up. A beaming Pilgrim Plavik greeted them as they stepped through the doors and onto the landing. On the street below, the entire ville had turned out for the big show, close to 150 men, women and children, dressed in their best sackcloth. They were no longer hiding their weaponry. The men and some of the older children carried blasters.

"Do you see them?" J.B. asked, scanning the throng.

"No," Ryan said.

Krysty and Mildred were nowhere in sight.

"Come's a time," Plavik bellowed to the crowd, "when each of us must go into the darkness and answer the final question. For some that time comes sooner than for others." With a sweep of his arm he indicated the assembled prisoners. "Today is their time."

"Praise Bob, praise Enid!" someone shouted.

"We will walk in solemn reverence," he continued in a shout, "as a whole and united people. We mount the noble crest, to trace the sacred line between desert and paradise, between heaven and hell, and give living offering in the name of Bob and Enid, that this place might prosper and that we might be safe forever."

The crowd began a rhythmic chant, punctuated by clapping. "Praise Bob, praise Enid. All glory to Bob and Enid. Praise Bob. Praise Enid. All glory to Bob and Enid."

Pilgrim Plavik clapped his hands in syncopated time and pranced about, dipping his shoulders this way and that, and cutting agile 360s. The ville folk did the same.

Everybody danced.

When the prisoners were forced down the steps into the street, the crowd made way for them, but continued to clap and sing. Once more Ryan noticed the conspicuous absence of oldies. The reason was clear to him, now. No one lived long enough here to grow old, even if they followed the rules. When their work slowed down or they got hurt, they got dumped in the dam. They got dumped while still alive. To serve the greater good.

Until that awful, private moment came for each of them, they were damned happy to join together as a community to celebrate the misfortune of others. Damned glad they weren't among the wounded being helped into a four-wheel car for a last tour of Little Pueblo and environs.

Ryan, J.B. and Jubilee were pushed and kicked to the front of the mob. Behind them, four men took hold of the cart's yoke and began to pull, even as the others pushed it from the rear.

Chanting their adoration of Bob and Enid, the crowd left the edge of the square and started for the dam en masse. They walked at a steady, leisurely pace, past the washed away neighborhoods, toward the silos, the lush green fields and the shining lake.

"Looks like we're going to find out firsthand what those demons are all about," Ryan said.

J.B. glanced back at the street overflowing with people, most of them armed, and said. "No way are we gonna get rescued. It would be suicide for Jak and Doc to even try. From here on we're on our own. Hands tied behind our backs and chucked into the pit."

"Just like old times," Ryan said.

It took them twenty minutes to reach the shore of the lake, and when they got there the procession turned right, walking in the lee of the enormous, sloping wall of smooth white concrete. Standing there naked in the light of the day, vast, windowless, the dam did not look like a prison.

Or a giant's tomb.

Ryan couldn't see any evidence of a crack.

Where the dam ended, an old roadbed, a remnant of the project's construction phase, angled up on the canyon's side. The crowd chanted and clapped all the way to the top.

Ryan and J.B. turned at Plavik's command and started down the paved road that ran along the dam's crest, supported by the massive concrete piers that framed the overflow gates. To their left was the verdant valley of Little Pueblo; to the right, for as far as they could see, was beige hell. Beyond the dam, the canyon grew wider and wider, opening onto a blasted plain that stretched all the way to the horizon

At the far side of the spillway, Plavik made them stop while three pilgrims used long pry bars to lever up and slide back a steel manhole cover from the middle of the road. Inside the three-foot-wide-hole, Ryan could see what looked like rungs, leading down. How far down, he couldn't tell.

Plavik stepped behind him, and he felt pressure between his wrists. Then his hands were free. Ryan turned to see the pilgrim holding his beloved panga, edge up.

"You'll need your hands to climb down," Plavik said.

At his signal, Pilgrim Dennison cut J.B.'s bonds, then Jubilee's. The others started pulling the wounded from the cart.

"I've lived with that blade for a long time," Ryan told Plavik. "Always figured on dying with it."

Plavik shrugged. "Why not?" he said. He hitched up the hem of his robe and unstrapped the leg sheath. He slipped the panga into the scabbard and handed it over.

Ten blasters held steady aim on Ryan's head as he fastened the sheath to his calf.

"It won't do you any good, you know," Plavik said. "Not down there."

Ryan looked in the hole. Standing next to it, he could see ten rungs on a flat wall before everything faded to black.

"There are blasters down there, too, if you can find them," Plavik said. "Guess what? They won't do you any good, either."

To the other pilgrims, he said, "Light the torches."

Torches were ignited and tossed down the hole.

Ryan listened for the sound as they hit bottom. It took a long time.

"Someone has to go first," Plavik said. "Do you want to choose, or shall we do it for you?"

"I'll go first," Ryan said. He looked at J.B. "Then comes Jubilee, and you come after her."

J.B. nodded.

"The hole awaits," Plavik said.

"You think this is over," Ryan told him, "but you're wrong."

"You mean you'll be back?" Plavik exclaimed,

throwing up his hands and arching his bushy eyebrows in mock surprise.

The crowd found his antics most amusing.

To the sound of their laughter, Ryan eased himself into the hole. The rungs were made of tubular steel and they hadn't corroded. As he climbed down below the level of the road, he could see that the vertical channel was much bigger than the manhole opening. A rectangular passage. Looking over his hip, he saw the dim light cast by the heaped torches far, far below him. He climbed down a few more rungs, waiting for Jubilee to get started.

"Take it slow," he told her as she stepped down into the hole. "Keep your eyes on the rungs. Don't look down. You'll be fine. I'm right here. I won't let you fall."

She didn't say anything, but she didn't freeze. She started putting one foot after another, one hand after another.

J.B. came after her.

"Watch your speed, J.B." Ryan warned him. "Don't step on her hands."

"Yeah, yeah."

As they worked their way down the sheer wall, they could hear the wounded men being forced through the manhole above them. As they descended, the light from up there got dimmer and gradually the light from below got brighter.

"Ryan, can you see anything down there?" J.B. called out.

"Nothing's moving in the light."

Outside the ring of light, there was only black.

When they were almost at the bottom, Ryan said, "Wait a minute. Hold it there."

Jumping to the floor, he pulled out his panga and crouched, ready to fight. When nothing attacked him from out of the gloom, he picked up a torch and held it high overhead. There were tunnel entrances to the right and left of the rung wall. The one of the right led back through the heart of the dam. When he turned the other way, straining to see more than ten yards down the corridor, he noticed the torch smoke was flowing along the ceiling, driven by a faint breeze to his back, from the direction of the spillway.

For the moment at least, there was no danger.

"Come on, Jubilee," he said. "Come on down." He helped her negotiate the last few rungs.

"That's one hell of a long climb," J.B. said as he dropped beside them. He bent and grabbed one of the torches.

"Must be close to two hundred feet," Ryan said.

They heard a metallic scraping sound from above and the tiny spot of light up there winked out. The ville folk had pulled the manhole cover closed. Everybody who was supposed to be inside was inside.

They couldn't see the other four prisoners descending. Their torchlight didn't penetrate that far. Wicklaw appeared out of the darkness, moving very slowly. Ryan recognized him thirty feet up by his injured, foreshortened foot. The bandages were seeping blood.

There was fear in the ex-pilgrim's eyes, fear and hate, as he stepped to the ground. Fear of his new surroundings and hate for Ryan Cawdor, who had put him there. He stooped quickly to claim a torch.

Wicklaw wasn't the only one bleeding.

The exertion of the descent had reopened the shotgun pellet wounds of the next man down. Blood streamed from holes in his right biceps and forearm, dripping from his fingertips. He picked up the last torch with his good arm.

The third man was right behind him, factoring the arm and side that had taken a load of gren shrap. "Brewster's coming," he said as he cleared the final rung. "He's moving real—"

A shrill scream from above made him look up.

Ryan lunged forward, grabbed him by the back of the collar and jerked him off his feet.

An instant later a falling body crashed to the concrete beside the rungs. It hit so hard that it bounced four feet in the air. Blood mist sprayed over them all.

Wicklaw cursed and spun away.

But not too far.

Ryan held his torch over the still form. It was the blinded man. Broken open like a watermelon from head to crotch. Either he had panicked and lost his grip on the rungs, or he had decided to go to end it all.

"Bastard got the damn thing over with, nice and quick," Wicklaw said, moping the side of his face with the cuff of his robe. "Couldn't face meeting the demons blind."

"Why'd you let him come down the wall last?" Ryan said.

"Figure it didn't matter," the gren-wounded man said. "With no eyes, he was bound to die first, anyway."

"Well, you almost came a close second."

J.B. looked up and down the identical tunnels. "What do you think, Ryan?" he said.

"We've got a little breeze coming through from that direction."

"I noticed. It could mean there's an opening of some kind outside, but the wind currents are tricky to figure. A giant honeycomb like this has temperature and humidity differences from top to bottom, and side to side, that could be pushing the air around all on their own. If there is an opening, it look like it's way the hell on the other side of the dam." He paused, then said, "The opening might be a hundred feet up."

"Could be," Ryan said. "You got a better idea?"

"Nope."

"Then we'd better get a move on."

Wicklaw blocked their path with his bulk and outstretched arms. "You two are crazy," he said. "There aren't any ways out. This place has been sealed since the days of Bob and Enid."

"If you want to stay here, that's fine," Ryan said. "J.B., me and Jubilee are going." He turned to the other men. "You can come with us or stay, it's up to you."

"We'll come," the bleeding one said.

Wicklaw moved out of the way to let them pass, his face twisted into a scowl. He stood alone with his torch for no more than two seconds before he hobbled after them, groaning each time his bad foot hit the ground.

The service corridors' ceiling was lined with pipe and bundles of electrical conduit; the walls were blank concrete and curved slightly to the left, following the bend of the dam.

As they walked into the light breeze, Ryan started to pick up an unpleasant mixture of odors. Rotten meat. Latrine. Swamp gas. Bear pit. Faint at first, it got stronger. And stronger. "Smell that?" he said to J.B.

"How could I miss it? Damn nasty."

"Mebbe we shouldn't be going this way?" the gren-wounded man said. "Mebbe we would turn back?"

"Whatever that is, partner, it's been dead awhile," J.B said.

The source of the stench was a small pile of debris that lay beside the right-hand wall. Covering their mouths and noses with their hands, they approached it. The light of four torches reflected off the pool of liquid in which the debris sat.

"Bones," Ryan said, carefully leaning over the puddle. "Those are human bones."

He and J.B. had seen corpses galore, but never quite like this. The flesh and internal organs appeared to have dissolved into the liquid. The stubs of the plundered rib cage, and the points of the hip girdle stuck up from the pool of yellow slime. The skull was missing. A wad of fluid-soaked rags, presumably the victim's clothing, lay to one side, along with a completely skeletonized leg and foot.

"Demon's work," Wicklaw announced. "Bob and Enid protect us.

"Damn that stinks," J.B. said. "Burns, too. Up inside my nose. Better not touch it barehanded, Ryan."

The one-eyed man searched the floor for an alternative. At the base of the wall, he found a foot-long scrap of heavy, insulated wire and poked it into the liquid. When he pulled it out, the fluid stuck to the end, sagging in a long, wobbly strand. He poked the wire deeper, testing the pool's depth. He felt resistance after four inches, and when he pressed harder the wire sank in another couple of inches.

"Looks like some kind of acid," he said. "Eats through the meat." When he prodded the rib cage, the bones crumbled and fell into the puddle. "It turns the bones to mush. Looks like it's eaten down into the concrete, too. There's a depression where the stuff is sitting."

"Where did it come from?" J.B. said.

"If Mildred was here, she could tell us."

"I'm glad she's not here," the Armorer said.

"It came from the demons," Wicklaw told them.

J.B. turned on him bringing the business end of his torch within singeing distance of his long beard. "What the hell have you got trapped down here, Wicklaw?"

"Things that chill, but can't be chilled, praise Bob, praise Enid."

Whatever the demons were, Ryan thought, they weren't spirits. Spirits didn't spray acid over their victims.

"Plavik told us there were blasters down here," he said.

"There are, but they won't do you any good."

"Yeah, he said that, too. Where are they?"

"Good question. The guns were left behind by Bob and Enid, and the other first pilgrims. After they forced the demons into the dam, they took weapons and ammo down to finish them off. And found it couldn't be done. When none of the fighters made it out, the rest of the ville followed Bob and Enid's instructions and sealed up the place."

"Plavik told us the building in the park was Bob and Enid's tomb," Ryan said. "Now, you're telling us they never came out of the dam. One of you is a liar."

"Not necessarily. The building in the park was Bob and Enid's tomb, but they aren't buried in it because their bodies were never recovered. The tomb is their holy shrine."

"Is there an armory or storehouse in here where they would've cached the weapons?" J.B. said.

"I don't know. Like I said, nobody came out. The blasters probably aren't in one place anymore, anyway. It's been a hundred years since the offering began. Some of the people who got put down here found the blasters, carried them around, and used the blasters to try to defend themselves. From time to time we still hear shots fired after we make an offering."

"So you're telling us the blasters and ammo could be anywhere?" J.B. said.

Wicklaw nodded.

"If there's weapons down here, let's find them," Ryan said.

As they followed the hall, they came across a few other puddles, all with floating bones. The kill sites seemed randomly scattered. Some were near the walls, some in the middle of the corridor. There were no blasters.

Ryan's torch lit up a shallow alcove set in the left-hand wall. On the floor, in the largest puddle they had seen, were four sets of stripped human remains. To Ryan, it looked like a group of prisoners had been trapped, then chilled in the blind alley. It occurred to him that four smaller puddles might have run together into one big one. Some of the victims' clothes had been ripped off and tossed aside, beyond the pool's perimeter. He lifted the corner of a pile of rags with the panga's point and discovered a prize beneath.

A steel skeleton stock.

Sheathing his blade, Ryan picked up the Galil. "J.B., take a look at this," he said.

The Armorer gave him a thumbs-up.

The predark assault rifle was Israeli-made and modeled after the Soviet AK-47, with a folding stock, select fire, open sights, detachable 30-round box magazine and shoulder sling. He dropped the mag and examined its contents. This Galil was chambered for .308 caliber, the NATO round. He counted the bullets. Nineteen, including the one in the chamber. There were no spent casings on the floor.

As he slapped the magazine back in place, J.B. said, "I got two more over here."

Ryan slipped the Galil over his shoulder and joined J.B. beside the wall. Wicklaw was holding his torch.

"Not as nice as yours," J.B. said. He showed Ryan the pair of handblasters he'd found in the back corner of the alcove—a Smith and Wesson Military and Police revolver in .38 caliber, and a 9 mm Llama semiauto pistol. The Smith looked like it had been through a couple of world wars. No blueing remained and a layer of rust coated on the barrel and cylinder.

J.B. spun the cylinder, then snapped it shut, tucking the pistol in his waistband. He quickly cleared the Llama's mag and chamber. When he worked the slide back and forth, he grimaced. "Llama's got a little hitch in getalong," he said. "Dinged up. A burr on the slide rail, mebbe."

"Will it shoot?"

"It'll shoot. Got fourteen rounds for it. Five for the Smith."

"Grand total of thirty-eight."

"Not so bad."

Ryan patted the Galil's receiver. "The poor bastard who carried this last never even got off a shot," he said.

"Does that make you feel better or worse?" Wicklaw asked him.

"Better," Ryan said."More bullets for me."

"How about letting me have one of those handblasters?" the ex-pilgrim said.

"Don't think so," Ryan told him.

"Why not? I can shoot good."

"Don't feature taking a slug in the back."

"I would never shoot you in the back, Ryan. That would be too much of a mercy."

"Forget it," Ryan said. "We keep all the blasters."

J.B. took back his torch, the Llama cocked in his right hand.

"How often have you been putting folks down here?" Ryan asked Wicklaw.

"Depends on circumstances."

"Guess."

"Mebbe a couple a month."

"How many people a year?"

"Twenty or thirty."

"For a century? That's three thousand people."

"I never gave it much thought. I suppose that must be right."

"There aren't enough bodies," Ryan said. "All those other bodies are somewhere else. Mebbe they got dragged off by whatever it is that did that." He gestured at the puddle and bones.

"There's got to be more than one," Ryan said. "Only a predator competing for food would bother finding a safe place to eat."

He made Jubilee take hold of the back of his shirt. "You're going to have to stay real close to me from here on," he told her. "Hang on tight and don't let go, no matter what happens."

Chapter Seventeen

From the vantage point of the silo dome, with the sun angling up over the horizon, Jak and Doc watched the procession snake through the corn fields below, heading for the lake.

"The people of Little Pueblo have come together for a celebration of some kind," Doc said. "With our friends as unwilling participants."

"Chill Ryan and J.B.?"

"If that's their plan, they certainly seem jubilant at the prospect."

"Can't save Ryan and J.B.," Jak said, the edge in his voice betraying anguish and frustration. "Too many blasters."

"We can only do what we can do, my boy. If our dying would free them, both of us would gladly surrender our lives. Under these circumstances, our deaths would accomplish nothing. We have to trust that our companions will endure until we can effect their escape. Mildred and Krysty are not with them."

"No. Not there."

"Then they are either already dead or being held captive back in the ville. If the good ladies are still alive, we have an excellent chance of freeing them, as the township is most certainly deserted."

"Stop talk. We go."

They climbed down the long, rusting ladder. When the procession had passed, they left the cover of the silos and ran back along the predark highway toward the city center. As usual, Jak set the pace and picked the route.

With the sun slanting above the canyon rim, they made much better time on the return trip, despite the slight uphill grade. Cutting across the abandoned lots wasn't a problem when all the ankle-twisting junk and the chest-deep, water-cut gullys were visible.

Jak led them through what in predark times had been neighborhood backyards. The wooden privacy fences that had once separated the properties had washed away, rotted, or been used as firewood. Only the metal wire fences remained, and they were largely flattened. Here and there, rusting hulks of predark wags, primarily pickup trucks, lay on their caved-in sides or roofs. Not all remnants of the previous culture had been uprooted and swept away. Tiny brick patios still bordered gutted foundations. There were driveways leading nowhere. There was even a basketball half-court, missing its backboard and stanchion. The reservoir's runoff had undermined the plate of concrete; it was crazed with settling cracks. Similar cracks marked the exposed concrete slab foundations and cinder-block basements.

The albino headed for the cover of a precariously leaning cinder-block wall.

Darting around a coil of detached metal fence, he jumped a yawning ditch and two strides later, dropped down behind the short section of wall. Doc made the jump as well. He knelt down beside Jak, breathing hard. Over a low spot in the cinder block, they could see one story down into the basement, where a rusted-out, full-sized SUV, with no seats, windows or doors, sat up to its wheel wells in fine silt.

"How much farther?" Doc said, when he stopped puffing.

"Halfway there," Jak said. "Ready?"

"By all means proceed, dear boy."

But before they could rise from cover, they heard men's voices on the far side of the wall. And footsteps running in their direction.

Jak and Doc exchanged scowls, chagrined that they hadn't seen the stragglers coming. Perhaps the men had taken a shortcut, traveling out of sight down one of the dry gullys? It was too late to second-guess the cause or the outcome. And too late to retreat. Even if Jak and Doc could have fallen back without being seen, the noise would have alerted the bastards. As was the case during the night, an exchange of gunshots was the last thing they wanted.

Doc quietly unsheathed his sword.

When in doubt, attack.

As the tramp of footfalls closed on the wall, they leaped out from behind it and came face to face with three bearded men in robes, running single file toward the dam, apparently rushing to get there before the ceremony started. The man in the lead carried a scabbarded machete on a web belt; the other two were armed with full-stock, pump shotguns on shoulder slings.

The suddenness of the assault and the proximity of their attackers took the three men completely off guard.

Jak let the machete man fly past him and hurled himself at the second man in line. His snap kick caught the shotgunner in the middle of the chest, at the low point of his sternum. Their combined momentum met head-on, producing a sickening crunch as something yielded under the ball of Jak's booted foot. He felt the jolting impact all the way to the back of his head. The shoulder-slung shotgun and its owner crashed to the dirt.

The man following was coming too fast to stop, or even dodge.

Jak had just enough time to plant his feet and sink his weight into his knees. The second shotgunner collided with Jak's lowered shoulder, his legs went out from under him, and he ended up on his back, gasping for air.

Jak grabbed the pump gun by the barrel and ripped it away from the much bigger man. Then he brought the weapon around in a tight arc, like a sledgehammer, putting all his weight behind the swing, aiming for the top of the man's head. At the last instant, his target rolled out of reach and the wooden butt stock splintered apart on a piece of concrete rubble.

"Help me! Help!" the man cried, scrambling to his feet.

Jak glanced back at the other shotgunner. The man lay on his side, a widening puddle of blood under his face; his weapon had landed five feet away from his outstretched arm. He wasn't breathing. On the broken ground of the predark backyard, the man with the machete and Doc Tanner squared off over drawn blades.

"Help me!" the shotgunner hollered.

Jak took a step toward him, winding up for another swing with the barreled action.

Realizing that all help was either dead, fully occupied, or too far away to hear, the man vaulted the wall and dropped down to the dirt of the basement floor.

Jak jumped after him.

The man rounded the nose of the marooned SUV and disappeared on the other side.

As Jak approached, he popped up with a three-foot piece of iron pipe in his hands, his eyes crazy wild, his nose leaking twin trails down his bushy mustache and beard.

Jak turned the muzzle of the shotgun on him, bracing the receiver against his side, aiming through the emptied windshield. "Give up," he said. "Give up or get chilled."

Moving behind the scant cover of the doorpost the man said, "You can't shoot me. If that blaster goes off, the whole ville will be back here."

His bluff called, Jak gripped the shotgun by the barrel and jumped onto the hood of the SUV.

The man took a hard sideways cut at his legs, but Jak saw it coming and hopped up onto the roof. The pipe slammed into the windshield frame, denting the corroded metal a good three inches. By the time the shotgunner wound up for another swing, Jak was already down on the ground beside him.

The albino brought around the shotgun action and

the two bludgeons clanged together, crossing at head height. The vibrating barrel made Jak's hands go numb for a second.

The other man staggered back, then hurled himself forward, swinging overhead, grunting from the effort.

Jak easily stepped out of the way and the blow landed harmlessly in the dirt. But before he could trap the end of the pipe with his boot, the man jerked it away and circled left. As he did so, he shoved the pipe at him like a lance, poking it in his face.

Pinned against the side of the half-sunken SUV, Jak ducked and dodged the man's jabs and slashes. He didn't have room behind him for a back swing, so he kept the barreled action at port arms, biding his time, waiting for his chance to strike.

"Where you gonna run now, mutie?" the man taunted, keeping the pipe in his face as he shifted back and forth. "You got nowhere to go. I'm gonna pound your head in."

From above the pit, Jak heard steel singing on steel.

The man with the machete hurtled past Doc before he could bring his sword to bear. Skidding to a stop, he turned and unsheathed his machete. The wide, flat blade had what looked like a razor edge. As he took the measure of his adversary's weapon, a snaggle-toothed grin appeared under the matted tangle of beard.

Thin blade against thick blade.

Long blade against short.

"En garde!" Doc said.

The man scowled.

"Come and get it," Doc translated.

Only too glad to oblige, the man charged, unleashing a flurry of backhanded and forehanded slashes at waist height, tree-felling slashes trying to drive him off his feet.

Doc jumped out of the way, attempting to parry with his sword. The effort was futile. He couldn't turn aside the strokes with his flexible weapon. The machete blade was too heavy, and the man wielding it too strong. What Doc had in his favor was speed. And a delicate touch.

He used his sword point to make the point, flicking it across the whitened knuckles that gripped the machete.

The man yelped but didn't drop his weapon. The pain and the sight of his own blood made him attack in a frenzy of slashes.

Clumsy, brutal, but effective.

Unable to deflect the blade, Doc had to give ground or be hacked to death. He backed across the littered lot, keeping the man honest with an occasional flick at his face. Doc played a stalling game, waiting for his opponent to tire, to lower his guard. To that end, he backed onto a small foundation slab that had once supported a garage or guest house. The flat surface sprouted broken off lengths of plastic, copper and galvanized pipe and long hanks of sheared wiring. Obstacles that slowed down his attacker, and in the case of the pipe gave him something to hide behind.

Not that plastic and copper pipe lasted long under the machete onslaught. But hacking it out of the way drained the man's strength.

When his blade arm dropped, Doc lunged, cutting

him again with another flick of the sword point, this time in the right shoulder, deep into the muscle. Deep enough to make the man groan.

Blood flew from the wound as he continued to swing. Red splattered the sleeve of the oatmeal-colored robe.

Doc backed up, his right leg extended to the rear, body leaning forward, sword ready to strike.

He didn't see the old water heater laying on its side behind him. When his foot hit it, he instinctively glanced back. In that instant, the man charged, chopping for his neck. Doc managed to deflect the blow with the widest part of his blade, just above the silver lion's-head handle, but the force of it drove him off balance. He sprawled backward over the rusting steel cylinder. And for a second was spread out over it, defenseless.

The machete came down in a blur. This time it was aimed to split open his chest.

As Doc rolled away, the machete clanged into the sheet steel, throwing off a shower of sparks. The blade bit deep into the metal, cleaving it. And sticking fast.

The man tried to free the machete, jerking up on the handle so hard that he lifted the heater from the concrete.

Doc lunged up from his knees and thrust, spearing the sword through his adversary's torso, just above his hipbone and out the opposite armpit. As he whipped the blade free, the man moaned and released his weapon. Clutching the wound, he staggered forward and fell face-first over the water heater.

Stone dead.

JAK SENSED HIS OPPONENT was tiring of the game. It was clear that Jak was too quick for him. Even with his back to the SUV, the albino ducked and dodged every attack the man tried. After a few minutes of fruitless, all-out effort, the idea that a counterattack was coming, and one that he probably couldn't defend against, filled the man's mind—and face—with dread.

A moment before he made his move, a light came on in his eyes.

Jak read his thoughts. The triple stupe had finally realized the obvious.

If you can't shoot, nothing's stopping me.

The man hurled the pipe at Jak's head and turned to run. Jak ducked and the pipe hit the roof and flipped away. By the time he straightened, the man was at the cinder-block wall and starting to climb. Jak stepped forward, gripping the barrel with both hands. He coiled, pivoting from his hips, and winged the shotgun at his back. The blaster flew through the air sideways, and end over end. It caught the man at the base of the neck as he reached up to grab the top of the wall and pull himself out.

Seven pounds of steel pounded his face into the cinder block. His forehead bounced off the wall, his knees buckled, and he fell to the ground.

Jak straddled him from behind, taking hold of his shoulder in one hand and his chin in the other. He gave the chin a sudden twist and the spinal column parted with a wet snap.

"Nicely turned, my dear Jack," Doc said, leaning over the wall. "I do believe we are finished here."

Jak let the man fall back to the dirt, brushed off his hands, then climbed out of the basement.

They moved with much more care through the ruined neighborhood to the edge of the city center, keeping a close watch for movement in the runoff ditches. There were no more stragglers. The one-stories that ringed the park looked deserted.

Crossing over to the square's line of trees, they peered up at the facade of city hall.

There was no sign of life there, either.

"If Mildred and Krysty are inside," Doc said, "they may well be under guard."

"Fix that." Jak unholstered his Colt Python.

"I concur, my boy," Doc said as he pulled out his Le Mat. "In the end, subtlety will only take us so far."

Side by side they rushed across the street and up the city hall steps.

Chapter Eighteen

"I can't see anything from here," Randi said from beside one of the tall windows. "They're probably almost to the dam by now."

"I wish you'd shut up," Valerie Louise said. "I'm tired of listening to your whining."

She wasn't the only one.

Krysty and Mildred, bound hand and foot to their chairs, had been a captive audience to the woman's complaining for what seemed like hours. Neither of the pilgrim wives was pleased at being assigned guard duty and thereby missing the show at the dam, but Randi was by far the most vocal. A stuck record.

"We could see the ceremony from the window at the end of the hall," she said.

"It's too far away. We wouldn't be able to see anything."

"Sure we would. maybe not the offering, but the procession across the dam. That's the second-best part."

"We're not supposed to leave them alone."

"Who'd know? Look at them. They aren't going anywhere. It'd only take a minute. You know you want to see. There might not be another offering for months."

Valerie Louise glared at the prisoners with her right

hand firmly resting on the butt of her holstered Colt Army .44.

Krysty gave her a blank, unchallenging look in return, but her stomach was churning. The women of Little Pueblo didn't just wish others misery; they wanted to cheer while watching it come to pass.

Perhaps these two had good sides. Perhaps the other women did, too. Perhaps they were kind to their children, to each other, to the chickens. But to Krysty all that had long since stopped mattering. Given the chance to free herself and her companions, she would have gladly chilled the lot of them.

Twice.

Valerie Louise clawed at her dense mat of shoulder-length hair as she considered her options. The pros and cons. And after a few moments she decided the pros had it.

"You two better not try anything," she said. "If you do, we'll make you damned sorry."

When the two wives left the room, Mildred said, "This is our chance. You've got to go for it, now."

Krysty didn't need prompting. Clearly, there was no other choice. If they were to free themselves, she had to call upon the Gaia, the invisible feminine power of the earth, using the techniques she had learned from Mother Sonja. She closed her eyes and began to breathe slowly and deeply in and out, focusing her mind on the great mystery that united all things, the warp and weave of existence.

As the connection was made and the Gaia energy started to build, she felt it as a weight pressing down upon her entire body, crushing her into the chair. When the pressure became unbearable she stopped resisting and yielded utterly to it, and in so doing felt it suddenly lift from her, leaving her weightless, floating. Up through the soles of feet, up her legs, into her hips a current of energy crackled.

Building to a towering peak.

Her face twisted in conceptration, Krysty twitched her wrists on the chair arms. The slightest of movements. They had to be precise, or the sudden application of Gaia force would have shattered both her arms. The thick ropes broke apart like they were made of silk thread.

The exertion had a price, and Krysty paid it. The terrible backwash made her black out for a split second.

She awoke to the sound of Mildred's voice. "Untie your ankles!" the doctor said. "Hurry, we don't have much time."

Though dizzy and light-headed, Krysty managed to free her legs. She moved shakily to Mildred's side and started working on her bonds.

From the hall outside they could hear the two women arguing as they returned.

"They're coming back already," Mildred said, shaking the ropes loose from her ankles. "Stand over there, out of the way."

Krysty obeyed, still too weak to be of any real help.

Mildred picked up her chair by its back and moved alongside the entry door. As the knob turned, she reared back with the chair.

When the door opened and Valerie Louise stepped

in, she was greeted by flying furniture, full in the face. Mildred caught her above the brow with the edge of the chair seat. Valerie Louise's shocked expression turned into a grimace as she jolted backward, slammed into the door frame and went down. Mildred hit her again in the head, swinging the chair so hard she broke off two of its legs when they struck the jamb.

In the doorway, Randi froze, her eyes wide. Even though she was armed with a cap and ball revolver like her sister wife, she didn't reach for it. Instead, she did what came natural. She turned and ran.

Mildred ran after her. As she ducked out the door, the doctor threw the chair at Randi's pumping legs, sweeping them out from under her, sending the woman crashing to her face. In three strides, she had hold of the chair again, and was beating Randi into the hallway floor with it. When the chair came apart, leaving her with just the back, she tossed it aside and dragged the unconscious woman into the room by her heels.

Mildred dumped Randi beside Valerie Louise, then she and Krysty stripped the bodies of their weapons.

Mildred hefted the Colt Army .44 and said, "We need more firepower than this. We've got to find our blasters." She took the torch from its wall stanchion. "Can you walk?"

Krysty could walk, but just barely, leaning on Mildred's shoulder.

The two of them started searching the adjoining rooms. They didn't have to go far. Through the next door, beside one of the platform beds, they found all their gear. Apparently intact.

Mildred picked up her ZKR 551 and passed Krysty her Smith & Wesson Model 640. They opened the cylinders and made sure the blasters were still loaded. With her favorite blaster in hand Krysty started to feel somewhat better, if not fully recovered. She sat on the edge of the bed while Mildred began sorting out the packs, collecting ammo.

A floorboard creaked in the room they had just left. As Mildred and Krysty turned and brought up their blasters, the door burst open. and they found themselves staring into the business end of a handblaster with two barrels, one over the other; the lower one as big as a cannon.

A Civil War relic.

"By the Three Kennedys, we've found you!" Doc exclaimed as he lowered the Le Mat.

Jak followed him into the room, his Colt Python in hand.

"Are you two all right?" Doc asked. "Have you been harmed in any way? The two ladies next door seem rather the worse for wear."

"We're both fine," Krysty told him, "but Ryan and J.B. are in serious trouble."

"We saw them taken away by the ville folk," Doc said.

"Where go?" Jak asked.

"They were put in the dam," Krysty said. "Locked in."

"To what end were they put there?" Doc said. "Is it a prison? The people seemed to be celebrating the event."

"More like a death house, Doc," Mildred said. "We don't understand what's involved, but it's for sure they're in great danger."

"Get them out, now," Jak said, gesturing at the door with his handblaster.

"Before we try to rescue them," Mildred said, "we have to make sure we have a way to get out of here. Chances are, when our exit comes it's going to be rushed."

"You foresee a retreat under fire," Doc said.

"I think that's likely."

"We're going back to Minotaur, then?" Krysty said.

"That's our first destination," Mildred said. "We've got to get in there. It's our best escape route. If the mattrans isn't operational, we're going to have to go to Plan B and pull together some supplies for the walk out."

"That shouldn't be a problem," Doc said. "The buildings outside are deserted. We can take whatever we need."

"We've got to get into the redoubt while the ville folk are still busy at the dam," Krysty said.

"No time to tarry, then," Doc said, reaching for a backpack.

They divided up the extra weapons and gear. Krysty couldn't carry her full share because her knees were still too wobbly. She took Ryan's sniper rifle and an ammo satchel. In addition to his own gear, Jak slung J.B.'s 12-gauge pump.

The four of them slipped out of city hall without seeing another soul. No one was moving on the sidewalk that bordered the park, or along the visible storefronts, so they crossed the cracked street to the square, slipping into the line of trees. They followed the cover of the trees, until they were directly across from the front of the redoubt. Light of day revealed the aftermath of the battle that had taken place the night before: scorch marks left by the gren detonations. Shallow craters blasted into the sward. Burned and blackened trees, bark and limbs savagely blown off.

"It looks like we won't have to move a ton of rocks this morning," Mildred said.

The area in front of the redoubt entrance was still littered with the boulders Ryan and J.B. had carried.

With Jak in the lead, they ran single file across the grass. When they reached the steps, Mildred, Krysty and Doc descended while Jak stood at the top, keeping watch.

The last rock was right where J.B. had left it, still blocking the door. Mildred and Doc took hold of either end, lifted it and swung it out of the way, onto the steps.

As they did this, Krysty moved to the keypad lock beside the door. Before she could tap in the entry code, a flurry of gunshots rang out from above.

At the head of the steps, Jak dived to his left as slugs pelted the earth and whined off the tops of the boulders. He came up on one knee with his Python blazing.

Mildred, Doc and Krysty cut loose a withering volley of fire, aiming at the edge of the roof as they backed up the stairs.

The cat was most definitely out of the bag.

Chapter Nineteen

"No, please," the blinded man moaned as he clung to the edge of the hole. His body from the armpits down was already inside; his feet were on the third set of rungs. He hung on to his last hope with every ounce of his strength. "Please, shoot me," he said.

He wasn't just begging the robed and bearded pilgrims who stood over him. He was pleading to every person on the dam, everyone he had ever befriended, everyone he had ever toiled beside, for an act of human kindness and mercy.

He was asking the wrong favor.

In the wrong place.

Of the wrong folks.

Pilgrim Plavik put the sole of his boot on top of the man's head and pressed down with all his weight, forcing him all the way into the hole. "Close it," he told the pilgrims standing by with pry bars.

Plavik kept his foot on the man's head until the very last second, pulling it away as the pilgrims dragged the heavy steel plate shut.

"Praise Bob, praise Enid, the offering is made!" he shouted to the throng. "Let us show our joy, and do them honor."

At his words, the ville folk formed two lines facing each other across the dam crest road. Plavik walked to one end of the gauntlet, clapping his hands as he did so. The people picked up the infectious beat, and by the time he turned, they were all clapping with him.

Because he was head pilgrim, it was his duty and his right to show first joy.

Plavik began to dance. He capered between the ragged rows of people, moving from one side of the road to the other, spinning around and around with his arms in the air, shaking his shoulders, extending his tongue, rolling his eyes, waggling his head.

His performance was greeted by peals of delighted laughter and shouts of "Glory to Bob and Enid!" and "All praise to Bob and Enid!"

He worked the crowd to a fever pitch as he progressed toward the manhole. By the time he got there, they were all yelling, all swaying and bobbing, and eagerly dancing in place.

It wasn't until he actually set foot on the manhole that he let loose with his best steps. A modified buck and wing with frantic shoulder shimmies and eye rolling.

The crowd roared its approval.

Then every person on the dam, starting with the pilgrims, then the wives, then the children, then the field slaves, took turns dancing down the cheering gauntlet to the manhole cover, and there performed their most spritely and energetic jig.

Dancing on someone else's grave.

Plavik melded into the slowly moving chorus line,

keeping time with his hands, and shouting encourage-
ment to the dancers and hosannas to Bob and Enid. The
ceremony was all about stalling the inevitable. Watching someone else be taken instead of you. Knowing you
dodged the bullet this time. Staying alive in the short
term was all that was possible. A philosophy subscribed
to by pilgrims and wives, and by the field hands. A philosophy created out of whole cloth by Bob and Enid,
so that the ville might survive.

The demons would surely be pleased this day. It had
been a very fruitful week when it came to offerings.

And to wives.

Plavik scanned the line on the other side of the road,
picking out Wicklaw's former mistresses and making
sexy eyes at them. The new widows gave him shy but
sexy eyes right back, whispered something to one another, then stifled giggles with their hands. Sometime
later in the day, according to the laws of Little Pueblo,
Wicklaw's women and the two newcomer females
would be divided up among the five surviving pilgrims.
As head pilgrim, Plavik would claim first and second
choice.

Two new wives.

All glory to Bob and Enid.

The crackle of blasterfire from the direction of the
ville drove all the romantic fantasies from Plavik's head
and put an equally sudden end to the dancing and cheering. Strings of blaster shots popped off, the booming
single reports and canvas-ripping autofire chatter over-
laying each other, echoing off the canyon walls.

The people of Little Pueblo rushed to the lake side

of the dam, and stood there rigid and horrorstruck, staring toward the city center, while an intense battle raged out of sight in the square park. After fifteen seconds it shut off, as if by a switch.

There was no way of telling whether the guards the pilgrims had posted had won or lost the skirmish. If they'd lost, the unthinkable might still be averted.

"They're breaking into the tomb!" Plavik cried to his flock. "We must stop them!"

"Vengeance!" someone shouted as the ville folk broke ranks and ran to defend their most hallowed shrine.

Chapter Twenty

Ryan walked with the breeze in his face, the assault rifle in one hand, the torch in the other. The flickering flame cast bizarre shadows over the corridor's windowless walls and low ceiling. The extreme limit of the light was perhaps twenty-five or thirty feet ahead; beyond that was the void.

The land of monsters.

J.B. matched him stride for stride. He, too, had a torch in one hand; in the other he carried the best of the two handblasters he'd found, the Llama semiautomatic, hammer back, safety off, finger resting outside the trigger guard. The battered Smith was tucked in his trouser waistband.

Ryan could feel Jubilee's hand twisted in the back of his shirt. She was holding on for dear life. Ryan didn't know if he could save her. He didn't know whether he could save J.B. or himself. At this point the situation was totally out of control. He and the Armorer didn't know what kind of enemy they faced, they didn't know its capabilities, or its number. Or if there was a way out of the dam. All they could do was rely on their survival instinct, their foot speed, their reaction time and their fighting skills.

In the end, that was all they ever had.

And it had carried the day before.

The wounded men drove themselves unmercifully to keep up the pace. Steeped in the superstition surrounding the dam, they were dry-mouth terrified of what lay waiting for them in the dark. Every breath they took reminded them of the proximity of death. The breeze did nothing to disperse the pall of decay, which seemed to cling to every surface. Shuffling, groaning from the effort and pain, they stayed close behind.

As they rounded the gentle curve of the hallway, the smell suddenly got much worse. Eye-watering, nose-watering worse. Like a hydrocholoric acid spill.

In the torch light, Ryan saw a crumpled shape on the floor of the corridor ahead. To the left was an open doorway.

J.B. saw it, too. "Another corpse," he said.

Like the others, it lay on its back in a puddle of yellow slime. But this one was different. There was still flesh on the bones.

To get close, Ryan had to breathe through his mouth. The fumes coming off the body burned his throat.

"Looks fresher," J.B. said, grimacing.

"The acid isn't finished doing its work," Ryan said.

Standing close to the corpse was like leaning into an open, raging furnace.

The victim was way past caring. His eyes had been melted out of their sockets, which now swam with yellow acid. His lipless mouth gaped in a silent scream, chin jutting upward. But for the branded goatee that decorated his chin, his face was stripped of skin. In some places, the flesh was entirely missing; in others it sagged like wet crepe. Both cheeks were gone, as were the ears. Below the stout neck, his torso had been split open and plundered of all its soft organs. A pool of faintly bubbling acid filled the gaping cavity, spilling over onto the concrete. The verges of the horrendous wound were bracketed by the ends of broken rib bones and showed claw or tooth marks where the flesh had been pulled to shreds.

"Your demons sure do make a mess," J.B. said to Pilgrim Wicklaw. "Now I'm glad you didn't give us breakfast."

"Got another blaster over there," Ryan said, pointing along the join of the wall and floor with the Galil.

"Now, we're talking," J.B. said as he hurried over to pick up the autopistol. He found the release and stripped out the Uzi's stick mag. "Empty," he said. He looked around on the ground for a second, then added, "No spent casings here."

There weren't any around the pool, either.

Ryan noted the dead man's trousers had been saturated with acid and ripped to tatters, but not completely torn off. He still had his boots on.

"I recognize that one," Wicklaw told them, his voice muffled by the hand that covered his nose and mouth. "He called himself Starr. He was offered to the demons two days ago."

"What do you think, Ryan?" J.B. asked. "Could that be our water thief, come to a bad end?"

"Could be," Ryan said. "His boots are the right size

for the prints we were following. Don't see many chin brandings like that."

"Yeah. Only the most hard-core, freelance mercies get themselves decorated like that. Gotta hurt like radblazes."

"Not as much as getting covered in acid."

"From the way he's laying, I'll bet he came out that door. Didn't get very far."

Ryan untwisted Jubilee's fingers from his shirt. "Stay out here with J.B.," he said. "I'm going to check the room."

With the Galil selector switch set on automatic fire, he poked his torch into the half-open doorway. He could see metal lockers along the back wall, and a row of empty metal shelves to the right. He kicked the door open wider and stepped inside. The demon stench was chokingly thick, and mixed with the odor of urine.

One of the tall cabinets had been tipped facedown on the floor. In the wall above it was a yard-long, elliptically shaped gash. Over the pounding of his heart, Ryan heard the hissing and spitting of the torch flame. Oily smoke gathered along the ceiling.

Wherever the gash led, it didn't lead to the outside. There was no air moving in the room.

Spent brass was scattered on the floor around the fallen locker. Ryan picked up one of the casings. It was a 9 mm. They were all nines. Most likely from the dead man's Uzi. He'd emptied the mag in here.

"It's clear," he said over his shoulder to J.B.

Ryan moved closer to the gash, careful not to touch any of the yellow fluid that dripped from it and smeared its edges. Holding out his torch, he peered inside.

"What do you make of that?" J.B. said to his back.

"Looks like some kind of a tunnel," he said. He stuck the end of the torch into the hole. "Can't see how deep it goes. Makes a turn or dead ends after a little ways."

J.B. peered into the gash, too. "Whatever it is," he said, "it definitely wasn't part of the original construction. This hole was dug out by something. The inside surface's coated with that yellow acid stuff. Almost like it's been lubed with it."

"The corpse was in here," Ryan said, pointing out the shell casings. "From the scatter of his empties it looks like he was firing straight into the hole. Didn't do him much good, though."

"Whatever chilled that bastard," J.B. said, "it can dig through tempered concrete."

"From the width and height of the hole it's got some size to it, too."

"Some kind of mutie gopher or mole, mebbe," J.B. suggested. "Grown giant. Turned man-eater."

"If it's a mutie, it's meaner and faster than anything we've ever come across. From the looks of all those hulls, it can outrun Parabellums fired point blank. And that doesn't explain the yellow stuff eating away the corpses. You ever hear of that before?"

J.B. shook his head.

"Whatever's doing the chilling is carrying that fluid around with it," Ryan went on. "I think it's some kind of body juice, like stomach acid. This critter likes to soften up its food before it sits down to a meal."

"You two still don't understand," Wicklaw protested from the doorway. "The demons didn't come into being because of skydark. They're not like stickies or scalies. They were here before."

"And you know this because Bob and Enid told you so?" J.B. queried.

"Yes."

The other wounded men nodded in the affirmative.

"Can you believe these triple stupes?" J.B. said to Ryan. "They're tightrope walking over hell but they won't let go of their superstition."

"Look at them," Ryan said. "It's all they've got."

"If the both of you weren't so hardheaded," Wicklaw said, "you'd let yourself see the proof that's right under your nose."

"Such as?" J.B. pressed.

"Everybody who was here before us is dead. Even though they had blasters and plenty of ammo. For more than a hundred years, those who have come in the dam haven't come out. You're up against something more powerful than any human being, or any groups of human beings, something that can't be killed."

"It's impossible to prove that something can't happen," J.B. countered.

To Ryan, he added, "Doc taught me that."

"If this thing can dig through solid walls," Ryan said, "it can pop out anywhere, at any time. I suggest we move along quick-like before it gets wind of us."

As he pushed past Wicklaw's bulk into the hallway, Jubilee reattached herself to the back of his shirt. She was as white-lipped scared as the men, and for the same reason. Deep down in her soul, she thought the critter was unchillable. Ryan wouldn't let himself consider that possibility. As long as he had rounds in his mag and his hands and feet free, he had hope. He just wished he had more solid facts to work from.

At this point it seemed like there might be more than one of the creatures, but he couldn't be sure about that. From the evidence left behind so far it was acting like a solo hunter. The bodies weren't pulled apart, which is what a pack of animals fighting over spoils would do. In fact, it appeared that each kill lay untouched except by the killer, as if the puddle of yellow bile marked the food as its and its alone. That kind of marking was only done by highly territorial and competitive predators.

This one made its kills in the halls, using the darkness and yawning open space to its advantage, attacking victims from undefended angles and unlikely hiding places. It had to be able to see or sense body heat in the dark. Maybe it even had infrared vision. It was very fast on its feet, apparently too fast to track with an auto-weapon. Some of the clean misses had to do with the element of surprise it had going for it. But certainly not all of them.

It had formidable offensive weapons, either portable or part of its body, which could incapacitate a person in seconds. It had to be triple strong to take a man out like that, and to dig through the solid walls. Its other abilities were a mystery. There was no way to tell how intelligent it was. If it could strategize. Or if it was merely an instinctive hunter, like a rattlesnake or a bear.

See it, stalk it, kill it, eat it.

Jubilee gamely kept up the fast pace Ryan set; he hardly felt her tugging on his shirt. The wounded slowed them down much more than she did. Wicklaw brought up the rear, hopping and limping on his bad foot, swinging his torch around to keep his balance.

They followed the slight breeze as the corridor continued to curve, ignoring the occasional closed metal doors they came across. After forty yards or so, they reached a crossing hallway, and stopped to recce.

Ryan watched the flame of his torch bend over to the right. The stream of air was flowing from the left, from the intersecting hallway on that side, which was the direction of the lake.

"Breeze is definitely coming from that way," J.B. said. "It could be from the crack in the dam. If there is one, it's got to be at this end."

"If it's the crack, it's going to be a dead end," Ryan said. "We're too high up."

Either way, they had to find out. Ryan and J.B. entered the much narrower corridor with Jubilee in tow. The ceiling was lower, too. It was as black as the pit of hell inside, but the wind was steady in their faces. The wounded men shuffled along behind, coughing from the torch smoke blowing back at them.

The hallway took a sharp right turn and as they rounded it, they saw a bright crack of light ahead. J.B. and Ryan's torches revealed a jagged, floor-to-ceiling fissure in the wall.

Ryan held his torch close to the two-and-a-half-foot-wide crack. There was no sign of the caustic yellow slime. This gash was man-made, and more than a century old, caused by incoming Soviet warheads on nukeday.

J.B. squeezed through opening, pistol-first; Ryan and Jubilee followed.

They found themselves in a smooth, circular, concrete channel, ten feet in diameter. To the left, it angled down into the dark.

At the end of the cylinder to the right, less than thirty feet away, was a massive screened grate.

Through which daylight streamed.

J.B. watched the other end of the channel while Ryan and Jubilee hurried to the opening. The view through the circle of heavy steel mesh was of the corn fields and lake, and the sky and canyon beyond from a height of maybe three hundred feet. Ryan could smell freedom.

It was that close.

Wicklaw and the other two men squeezed through the crack and joined them in front of the grate. At Ryan's direction, they tried to shift the screen out of its frame. No go. J.B. hurried over to help. But all of them grunting and groaning together couldn't budge the grate. On closer inspection, they saw it was secured with a couple of dozen, badly rusted four-inch-wide bolts.

Wicklaw stuck his fingers through the mesh and vented his frustration by screaming out over the canyon, "Damn you bastards! Damn you all to hell!"

Ryan could see that others had made it this far. That was clear from the words they had scratched into the channel walls. Having screamed themselves hoarse, those offered to the demons carved curses into the sides of their tomb, curses upon the people of Little Pueblo.

"From that screen, I'd say this was a water intake channel," J.B. said. He pointed into the darkness behind them. "That probably leads down into the belly of the dam."

"We could follow it out of here?" Ryan said.

"Mebbe, mebbe not. Depends on whether it's a main intake or a diversion channel. If it's a main, it'll lead right into the turbines, and we'll never get past the blades. Looks to me like it starts to angle down in a big way. Floor is smooth as a baby's butt. Nothing to grab on to, either. Without ropes we could end up freefalling two, three hundred feet."

"We gotta get lower," Ryan said. "Gotta find a way down."

"Yeah. That's our best bet."

Ryan, Jubilee and J.B. started for the fissure, but the three wounded men remained huddled by the light, their fingers and faces pressed to the inside of the grate.

"You can't stay here," Ryan told them. "Not if you want to live."

"Demons don't like the sun," Wicklaw informed him. "They won't come in here after us."

"Not until it gets dark outside," Ryan said. "And then you won't be able to stop them."

"What are you going to do when it gets dark?" Wicklaw said.

"I don't plan on being here that long."

When Ryan, J.B. and Jubilee started back to the main corridor, the wounded men followed.

"These critters have got to be faster than shit," J.B. said. "Running away doesn't seem to do any good."

"Can't tell if any of the dead stood their ground," Ryan said. "If they did, it didn't help."

"The thing that bothers me most is we haven't seen any demon corpses laying around."

Ryan shrugged. "So either there aren't any, or they make a habit of burying or eating their own."

"They don't strike me as the burying kind."

"Me, either."

When they regained the main corridor, it was decision time. They could either keep moving in the direction they were headed, or backtrack. J.B. figured they were more than halfway across the dam, and as they hadn't seen a stairwell so far, they decided to forge ahead in the hope that they'd come across one before they got to the end.

They had covered no more than a hundred feet of corridor when the clicking sounds started up.

Distant. Muffled.

"Where is that coming from?" J.B. said.

Ryan stopped short and made the others stop, too. "Quiet. Listen." he said.

There was a pattern to the noise. A pattern in the number of clicks, the space between them and their pitch. A pattern that repeated. A cycle. It seemed to come from all sides.

"They're in the walls," Ryan said. "It's coming from the walls."

"Bob and Enid protect us!" Wicklaw cried.

"Your demons are talking to you," J.B. said.

"Or to each other," Ryan suggested.

"They don't sound like four-legged animals to me," the Armorer said. "Never heard a four-legged critter make a racket like that."

"It sounds more like birds or bugs."

"Only big."

"Yeah, big."

Ryan pushed forward, holding the torch as high as he could, trying to make the light penetrate the tunnel more deeply.

"Got another gash coming up on the right wall," J.B. said.

Ryan saw it. A dark oval two feet above the level of the floor. Beneath the opening lay a pool of acid slime. He moved to the opposite side of the hall, and with his assault rifle aimed at the hole, prepared to give it the widest possible berth.

The clicking stopped.

Before he could take a step back, air exploded from the wall like a cannon shot, shaking the floor underfoot. The force of the explosion blew a mist of yellow all the way across the corridor.

Ryan's first thought was stun gren. But there was no smoke and no flash. The phenomenon wasn't thermo-chemical. It was simpler than that. Something tightly plugging the burrow had moved forward so suddenly and with enough force to blast the air from the hole. Like a gigantic plunger. The power required was almost inconceivable. Over the ringing in his ears he could hear a mad scrabbling noise.

Something was coming for them.

And they had no cover.

"Run!" Ryan snarled, pushing Jubilee ahead of him. He shouted to the others, "Back to the intake! Run!"

Wicklaw and the gren-wounded man took off with

a speed they hadn't seemed capable of before. J.B., Ryan and Jubilee ran on their heels, forcing them to go even faster. Despite the threat, the third man couldn't keep up and quickly fell behind.

As Ryan heard his footfalls drop back several very strange things happened in rapid succession.

First, there was a yelp, cut short.

The torch the third man was carrying cartwheeled overhead and landed on the floor in front of them.

And then something zoomed past so quickly it was hard to believe it was real. High and tight to the ceiling. Bounding through the air. Ryan got the impression of stripes, brown on brown. And then it was gone. If it landed ahead, it landed without making a sound.

The third man started screaming behind them.

Ryan stopped and turned. He could see the man sitting on the floor with his back to the wall. No longer screaming. He wasn't far. Ryan went back for him. When he jerked the man to his feet, a mass of slippery gray coils dropped out from under his robe and flopped around his ankles. Ryan saw the blood on the front of the robe, and the gaping, half-moon slice from hip point to hip point. He let go of the warm but dead hand and the body slumped to the ground.

"Back!" he shouted as he rejoined the others. "We've got to go back to the intake. It's the only place we can defend."

The perpendicular hallway was just around the bend. As they piled into it, they heard clicking sounds behind them. Very fast. Very close. Ryan and J.B. pushed Jubilee, Wicklaw and the other man ahead of them, through the narrow passage, then through the fissure and into the water channel.

They all backed up against the grate.

Ryan and J.B. stood shoulder to shoulder, facing the split in the wall. Ryan held the Galil braced against his hip; J.B. had both pistols raised in his hands. Torches were unnecessary. Even though the bodies blocked some of the light coming through the grate, they could still clearly see the fissure twenty-five feet away.

"At least we know where it's coming from," J.B. said.

The clicking got louder, and faster. Then it stopped.

"Are you ready for this?" Ryan said

"Ready as I'm ever going to be."

"You can't chill them," Wicklaw sobbed as he cowered beside the grate. "No one can."

Something scraped in the narrow corridor. Scraped the floor, the walls, even the ceiling. Something sharp. Something heavy. Then it, too, stopped.

The silence stretched on and on. Ryan could feel the tension building in his arms and neck until it became a burning pain. He tried not to blink as sweat ran down either side of his spine.

When it came out of the crack, it came in a single bound, crossing twenty feet in an instant. It was big, all right. As big as a man. And no part of it was human.

Chapter Twenty-One

The ambushers had been laying flat on their bellies on the roof of the redoubt, waiting for the moment when all their targets stepped down into the stairwell death-trap. With concrete walls on three sides, and the steps on the fourth, there would be no escape.

But all the targets didn't descend. The white-haired one remained at the head of the stairs, standing watch.

The seven field hands had to lay there and listen as the would-be looters and defilers moved the last rock from in front of the door. It was plain from the strangers' talk that they knew how to open the tomb. And it was likely that one or more of them would enter the sacred place before the albino left his post.

Although keeping them out of Bob and Enid's tomb was their prime directive, something they had to prevent at all costs, in the end it was an individual decision, not a group one, to open fire.

One of the men had a machine pistol and took it upon himself to spray the enemy into submission. He jumped up with the H&K and fired full-auto from the hip, sweeping a line of slugs across the top of the stairs, through the space where the white-haired stranger stood.

Like a cat, the albino dived and rolled away. The bullets spanged off the concrete and the sides of the boulders.

And the battle was joined.

The rest of the ambushers popped up and started shooting. None of the other men had automatic weapons, but the effect of six people firing semiautomatic pistols, revolvers and pump shotguns simultaneously was much the same. Had they not been so excited, so eager to score hits, had they not jostled one another's aim, the outcome of the fifteen-second fight would have been very different.

The companions were caught by surprise, but not flat-footed. They had been in similar situations many times before. And each of them knew what to do. Instead of frantically returning the wild volley of fire, just closing their eyes and hoping to hit something, they aimed their shots with deliberation, if not calm.

The exchange of blasterfire was so intense, and the range so close, it was difficult to tell who was shooting who.

As he backed up the steps, Doc touched off the Le Mat's shotgun barrel, which gave forth with a great orange flash and a deafening boom, sending a load of blue whistlers slapping into the two men standing in the middle of the rooftop firing squad. The pistol's short barrel made for a wide spread of maul shot. It stitched both men from shoulder to shoulder, staggering them back on their heels. Through the dense cloud of black-powder gunsmoke, Tanner followed up with a round from the Le Mat's pistol caliber cylinder. The head of the man on the right snapped back as he took a slug to the temple, and the other shooter grabbed at his belly and dropped to his knees, doubled over at the waist.

Flying slugs plucked at Krysty's sleeve and grazed her hair as she put two tightly spaced .38-caliber rounds into the man with the machine pistol. Jak's .357 barked in time with the second shot, and hit the same target. The force of the double impact blew the man off his feet and sent him crashing to his back. His dying hand held the trigger pinned, and the H & K chattered harmlessly into the clear blue sky until it locked back empty.

Gritting her teeth against the howling rain of lead, and the ricochets sparking and whining all around her, Mildred backed up to the top of the steps, firing two handed. Head shots were all she took. The ZKR had a butter-smooth double action, the trigger was set for combat, and the targets were stationary. Shooting gallery ducks. She emptied her weapon in short order, making sure of the kills by placing two rapidfire shots in each face. The ville men jerked backward, dropping their blasters and hitting the roof hard. One of them twisted as he fell, rolled off the edge of the roof and landed in a limp heap in front of the redoubt door.

The last ambusher was jacking another round into the chamber of his pump gun when he was struck by half a dozen bullets. Jak, Krysty and Doc had him zeroed in. And nailed. As slugs plucked at the front of his robe, his head exploded, flying into fragments.

Their ears ringing, the companions checked the roof and made sure all the attackers were dead. Smoke from the battle was still drifting over the park as they climbed back down into the stairwell.

While Doc and Mildred cleared the corpse from in front of the door, Krysty tapped the entrance code into the keypad. Something whirred in the yards-thick wall. Then there was a distinct metallic clack. And the door popped open with a whoosh of trapped air. The door was two feet thick. It swung on huge, bearing mounted hinges and its inside perimeter was gasketed with heavily greased seals.

Beyond the entry door was a vanadium steel chamber, fifteen feet long and eight feet high. There were steel benches built into the opposite walls, but no windows. The floor had a large, grated opening that looked like a drain. At the other end of the chamber was another door and keypad.

"It's an air lock," Mildred said. "When the reservoir covered this place, they used it for access. They pumped the water in or out, depending on whether someone was leaving or arriving."

Krysty tried to open the second door, but the keypad wouldn't accept the entrance code.

"Close the outer door," Mildred said.

When Krysty did that, and retried the code, the inner door opened. It, too, was massively thick and gasketed.

The banks of lights inside the redoubt began to flicker and come on automatically.

"That's a good sign," Krysty said. "At least the nuke power is still up and running."

On the other side of the door was a security station with double bulletproof glass, machine-gun firing ports, and a holding cell where incoming and outgoing personnel were confined while they were processed. The only way into the redoubt was through the holding cell. Its barred entry door was ajar, as was the one at the other end.

"One would think that five hundred feet of water would be sufficient to secure this facility," Doc said.

"Then one would think wrong," Mildred stated. "These folks were worried about uninvited guests and unauthorized exits. Look at the firing ports in the glass. Half of them aim *into* the building."

The air had a musty, slightly scorched smell. No one had been inside Minotaur in a very long time.

As they passed through the holding cell, they could see through the bars and into the adjoining security office. Loose papers were scattered all over the floor. On a gray desktop, in front of a swivel chair, stood a blackened computer monitor and drive tower.

Left on screen saver for a century, it had given up the ghost.

On the far side of the security checkpoint a wide, concrete staircase led to the redoubt's first below-ground floor—a low-ceilinged, central honeycomb of work cubicles and computer stations ringed by managers' offices, store rooms, and main frames. It was clear the place had been abandoned in haste. Spreadsheets were strewed everywhere, chairs lay where they had been overturned. Other computer terminals had burned out as well; the flare of their imploding CRTs had left black scorches on the cubicle divider walls. Personal items, family photos and oddball trinkets, were still tacked up to the work station bulletin boards.

Krysty spoke up, giving voice to what the others were thinking. "The ville folk had to have heard the shooting," she said. "They'll be coming down to investigate. When they find their dead, they'll know what happened. That we're inside Bob and Enid's tomb. At that point they'll control the only entrance with a force of more than a hundred. How are we going to fight our way out to free Ryan and J.B.?"

Jak grunted in agreement.

"It's also possible that our hosts outside are privy to the unlocking sequence," Doc said. "Part of Bob and Enid's legacy. And if that is true, they may be familiar with the lay of the land inside this redoubt. If they enter to do battle with us we would face the same kind of overwhelmingly bad odds as in the park last night. We could easily be trapped in here."

"If we aren't already," Krysty said.

"We're committed now," Mildred told them. "There's no turning back. We have to find the mat-trans unit, then locate the armory, then we figure a way out for all of us. We don't have a lot of time. First of all, we need a map of this place."

If the floorplan of every redoubt was slightly different, the location of a complete site map was invariably the same. They found the commander's office on the left side of the broad room. His name and title were emblazoned on the metal door in gold letters three inches high.

Everything was as he had left it. Neat piles of documents lay in his out-box. The leather-trimmed desk blotter was cleared and shipshape. Pens in the ornamental deskset. Paper clips out of sight. Mildred rounded the desk to examine the framed photographs lined up along the wall. One of them caught her eye at once.

"Come and have a look at this," she said to the others.

Mildred pointed at a picture of a man in a dark green military uniform shaking hands with another man in a very expensive suit in front of an American flag.

"That's our commander," she said.

The soldier had iron-gray hair trimmed in a tight crew cut and a jutting, lantern jaw. A fruit salad of medals decorated his breast. The taller man he was greeting, or being greeted by, wore an easy grin and had a practiced twinkle in his eyes.

"And that was the last President of the United States," Mildred said of the twinkler.

"Looks like a bit of a rogue," Doc said.

"Part of his charm."

Two photos to the right of the presidential shot, the same uniformed officer was smiling alongside a man and woman in buttoned up lab coats with pocket protectors. The scrawny-framed woman had a Betty Crocker hairdo dyed black, a smear of bright red lipstick and rouge spots on both cheeks. A face with all the animation of a doorknob. The lab coated man was shorter than the woman, and virtually bald. His eyes and mouth turned up at the corners giving him a vulpine look.

This photo was signed. "To Colonel Robert Townsend, Onward and Upward, Dr. Enid Mead and Dr. Bob Shumer."

"Sweet mother of God!" Mildred exclaimed. "Not *that* Bob and Enid!"

"What are you talking about?" Krysty said. "Do you actually know who they are?"

"I'm afraid so," Mildred said. "I didn't make the connection with their first names. Everybody used to call them Mead and Shumer. In the years before skydark, they were notorious. Poster children for the ethically challenged whitecoat. Academic outlaws. Their line of scientific research was internationally banned, but obviously unofficially condoned here in the States. And underwritten to the tune of this redoubt."

"What was their field of specialization?" Doc asked.

"Gene splicing," Mildred said. "Manufacturing brand-new organisms from the construction plans of existing ones."

"In other words, playing God," Doc said.

"Why was their work banned?" Krysty asked.

"There were religious conflicts, of course," Mildred replied. "All the major and minor religions went ballistic over the moral issue. But the global ban came about because of safety concerns from the scientific community. Bringing new organisms into the world is a very dangerous proposition. Theoretically, it's possible to create something that could threaten all of humankind, and that we would have no defense against.

"Think of the world as a house of cards, each card an organism that depends on all the others for support. Something designer-made could upset the balance and bring it all crashing down. It could be a more efficient component. A stronger plant. A more successful breeder. Or a new disease vector. Tinkering with species' barriers offers the chance that the diseases of one will transfer to another, jumping the normal boundaries. Which could set new and terrible plagues upon humanity."

"What did they create?" Krysty asked.

"Mead and Shumer started their work on a microscopic level. Tailoring bacteria for specific tasks, like the industrial production of pharmaceutical drugs. But when they had refined their technique sufficiently they moved up to higher life forms, and finally to vertebrates, taking a few genes from this species and a few from that. They grew DNA-conglomerate embryos in test tubes, then implanted them in host mothers who brought them to term. Bob and Enid worked with fish, chickens, cattle and pigs, supposedly trying to produce better quality livestock."

"A chicken that tastes like fish?" Doc said. "Or a fish that tastes like chicken? Some would say that it's hardly worth the trouble."

"No, Doc, it had do with increasing resistance to diseases common to particular naturally occurring species, and with increasing those species' growth and maturation rates. Bigger and faster is better."

"So what went wrong?" Krysty said.

"Murphy's law," Mildred said. "Mead and Shumer were plugging along in anonymity, nobody really understood what they were up to until a fire broke out at their main lab. After the fire was put out, it appeared that some of the transgenic creatures they had been developing had escaped the lab's quarantine. Because of the potential threat to public health the event had to be reported to the authorities, and when the news was leaked to the press, it caused a major panic in the immediate area. The escape turned out to be a false alarm, but it brought the whole matter to light. In the court of public opinion, Bob and Enid were tried and convicted of ethical misconduct. 'Playing God,' as you said, Doc. Within weeks, their university cut off their research funding and fired them. To the world's scientific community Mead and Shumer were pariahs, and their professional careers were down the toilet. It all happened a year or two before the Little Pueblo dam was put in."

"Looks like Bob and Enid took their research underground," Krysty said. "Literally."

"And the name of this labyrinthine facility takes on a new significance," Doc added.

"I need to find out more about what was going on here before nukeday," Mildred said.

"Why?" Krysty said.

"I need to find out if the demons in the dam are real. Because there's a good possibility that they are. If they do exist, we have to be prepared to fight them."

Using the map in Colonel Townsend's office, they located the position of the redoubt's laboratory floor and the mat-trans unit. The mat-trans was on the tenth floor belowground; the lab was at the next to bottom floor, number eighteen.

Back in the cubicle area, they found a service elevator, which was still operational. As the lift doors opened, from the floor above they heard a clanging noise.

Then another. And another.

Chapter Twenty-Two

Running as fast as they could, Plavik and ville folk arrived at the park a good ten minutes after the shooting had stopped. At his direction they fanned out and spread along the trees before closing on the tomb's entrance.

The body on the grass was visible to all. It had been dumped beside the boulders. It lay curled on its side. And it wasn't moving.

"Bob protect us, it's one of ours," Pilgrim Dennison said to Plavik.

There was worse news coming.

Pilgrim Ardis raced up to them, having just checked on the prisoners in city hall. "The new women are gone," he told his fellow pilgrims. "And Randi and Valerie Louise are chilled. They got themselves beat to death, looks like with a chair. The blasters we took off One Eye and the others are gone, too. And so are their packs."

"The two that got away last night must've come back for them." Plavik said. "Sprung them free."

On his signal, twenty-five men moved from the cover of the trees and took up firing positions along the front of the tomb. Kneeling, they held their weapons trained on the entrance door.

Plavik and the other pilgrims advanced to the body by the boulders and stood over it.

"One of ours," Plavik confirmed.

"Doesn't look good for the rest," Pilgrim Ardis said. "Wherever they are."

Plavik had hoped that the missing pair of strangers would try to get in the tomb again, and be slaughtered by the armed men he had placed on the roof. The opposite had occurred.

They found the dead guards on the redoubt roof in scattered pools of gore. Shot to pieces, every one.

"It's like they were stuck in a meat grinder," Ardis said.

"Look at all those shell casings," Dennison remarked.

"And not one hit, apparently," Plavik said.

Pilgrim Dennison turned to stare at the entrance door. "Do you think the strangers got in?"

Plavik grimaced. "There's no way of telling. All the rocks are moved clear. They could have done it."

"How'd they know the trick to open the door?" Ardis said.

"Damned if I know," Plavik replied. "Mebbe they didn't open it. Mebbe they shot up our men and took off across the desert. Figured to cut their losses and get clear."

"We can't go inside to find out for sure," Ardis said. "We can't open the lock. And that door won't be pried."

"And even if we could open it," Dennison reminded them, "going inside would be a sin against our faith. Bob and Enid's tomb is sacred, not to be trespassed."

"If the four of them took off across the desert," Plavik said, "we're done with them, forever. They're either gonna die of thirst out there, or they're gonna think real hard about ever coming back here."

"And if they're in the tomb?" Dennison said.

"If they went inside, we can make sure they'll never come out. We can make it their tomb, too."

Plavik waved over some of the field hands milling on the edge of the grass. "Get over here, you lot," he said. "We got some work for you." When they gathered around, he said, "We think the chillers might have got in Bob and Enid's tomb. We want you to put the rocks back. Every one of them. Make sure that door is blocked good and tight."

The men hurried to complete the task. They didn't bother lugging down the big stones. They just pushed them over the grass to the head of the stairs, tipped them over the top step, and let them bounce down the stairs and roll up against the side of the vanadium steel door.

Clang.

Clang.

And the boulders began to quickly pile up, filling the floor of the stairwell and then the steps.

Chapter Twenty-Three

For a second it stood almost toe-to-toe with Ryan.

The Galil roared thunderously in the intake channel's tight space, bucking hard in his hands as he fought the full-auto muzzle climb. Sequential starburst flashes lit up the passage, and lit up the attacking beast.

The strobe light, freeze frames burned an image into his brain.

A relatively narrow upper torso flaring to a wider bottom. Three sets of legs. The head broad and flat, with wide set, enormous black eyes.

He only saw it for an instant. The multiple, point-blank range, heavy caliber bullet impacts blew it backward, head over heels, down the channel into the darkness and the belly of the dam.

After Ryan's and J.B.'s heads cleared from the clatter of autofire, they could hear Wicklaw shouting at them.

"Did you get it?" he cried. "Did you get it?"

"Hand me back a torch," Ryan said, "and we'll have a look-see."

"Me, too," J.B. said, holding out a hand for his torch.

The floor and walls of the channel were splattered

with gobs of creamy white juice. It was what passed for the creature's blood. And there was a lot of it.

"I'd say we hit it," J.B. said.

"Don't touch that stuff," Ryan warned him. "Could be acid, or some kind of poison."

They moved down the channel, careful to step around the larger splatters, weapons ready in case it came at them again from out of the darkness. They advanced to the point where the passage started to angle down more steeply, then stopped.

"There's something down there, on the floor," J.B. said. "Over there. See it?"

Ryan held out his torch. At the extreme edge of the light, in the middle of the channel lay something that looked like a piece of wood, or a broken tree branch. He knew it couldn't be either. The intake channel's grate wouldn't admit an object that big.

"I think our demon dropped something," J.B. said, pocketing his pistol. "Cover me."

He carefully moved forward, using the left wall to keep his balance on the down-angling floor. He squatted and grabbed hold of the object, then dragged it back to the light of the grate. Wicklaw, Jubilee and the other man looked down at it with a mixture of astonishment and horror.

It was a leg.

Fully extended, it would have been close to four feet long. It had three joints—shoulder, elbow, and wrist or ankle. From the shoulder down, each section of leg was shorter than the last. The foot or hand at the end was flat-bottomed and covered with black bristle. Instead of toes or fingers, it had four black talons that appeared to be retractable. It wasn't covered with skin. Its surface was brown and hard and covered with sharp little points. Closer inspection showed the points were actually stiff hairs jutting from tiny, cone-shaped protruberances. At the shoulder, where it had been blown free of the torso hung a rag mop of sinewy white tissue.

J.B. pointed at the ridge of horns that jutted from the side of the leg, from shoulder to elbow. "That's some blade," he said.

The row of horns got smaller and smaller as they approached the elbow. It looked like a serrated sword had been welded to the limb. And it acted like one, too. A single passing swipe of the thing had opened up the other wounded man like a can of peas.

"Triple wicked," Ryan agreed.

"Is the demon dead?" Wicklaw asked.

"You mean, is the unkillable killed?" J.B. asked.

"Did you really destroy it?" the ex-pilgrim insisted.

"I'm pretty sure we did," J.B. said. "But if we didn't, at least it's gonna walk funny from here on."

Wicklaw blinked, openmouthed, as the truth sank in. His belief system had just taken a body blow. The demons weren't immortal.

Ryan nudged the severed leg with his boot. "We've never come across anything quite like this," he said. "It's in a different league than the other muties."

"Faster, you mean?"

"Not just that. Think about it. All the other mutie species are radblasted distortions of what was here before nukeday. You got your human-based mutations—

stumpies, scalies, stickies. And you got your animal-based mutations. Some are bigger than they should be, some are smaller. Size wise, this thing is at least a hundred times bigger than it should be. That armor is like a crab's or a bug's, and the leg sort of looks like that, too, but the hair on it is from an animal. Like it's part bug, part bear."

"The hair and the smell is all bear," J.B. said.

The leg reeked of funk and musk.

"Whatever the hell it is," Ryan said, "it can really move. It's nothing like a crab. More like a jumping bug. We were damned lucky to nail it. If we'd been caught in a bigger space, with more than one entrance and less firepower, if we hadn't known it was coming, it would have gotten us. It's fast and agile, and it's got a wagload of nasty weapons."

Ryan was silent for a second, then he added, "And there's more than one down here."

"If this dam is a nest," J.B. said, "we're really in for it, Ryan."

The one-eyed man dropped the Galil's magazine into his palm and checked the round counter. "I'm down to eight shells."

J.B. said, "I've got six in the Llama, still five in the Smith."

"If we stay lucky we might be able to turn back one more attack like that," Ryan said. "We've got to find more ammo for the guns we've got, or more loaded blasters."

"There's another problem, too, even if we find guns and ammo," J.B. said. "Assuming there's a way out of here, there's a whole lot of open space between us and it. Open space is where we're going to be the most vulnerable to attack. How are we gonna cross it?"

"Only one way I can think of—as quickly as possible."

Ryan turned to the others and said, "Did you hear that? When we leave here we move on the dead run until I say stop. If we come under attack again or get ourselves cornered by one of these critters, put your backs to the wall and stay close together. Now let's find that stairwell."

After they returned to the main corridor, they continued in the same direction as before, running in long, even strides. The corridor echoed with their footfalls. Under the circumstances, speed was more important than stealth. The longer they remained in the kill zone, the worse the odds got. Though they brought up the rear, Wicklaw and the gren-wounded man seemed to have found their second wind. Perhaps the close call with a demon had something to do with it.

Ryan signaled for a halt as they neared the hole the demon had exploded from. The caution was necessary. It was always possible that where there was one demon, there were more.

With J.B. covering his back, Ryan crossed the hall, avoiding the yellow slime. He put his ear to the concrete wall, listening for signs of life. There was nothing. If another demon lay in wait deep inside the hole, it was still as the grave.

When Ryan looked up, J.B. had the Llama braced in two hands, sights trained on the gash. He waved him off and waved the others onward, aiming the Galil into the opening, finger resting lightly on the trigger. When they were well past, he ran to overtake them.

"One monster per hole, looks like," J.B. said as he caught up.

"Territorial bastards," Ryan commented.

"Lone hunters," J.B. said. "I'd hate to think what they'd be like if they worked in a pack."

"We'd already be dead."

In search of the stairwell, and a way down to the bottom of the dam, Ryan and J.B. started checking the hallway's few and widely spaced doors. They all opened onto interior rooms. Some were lined with metal-cased control panels studded with switches and toggles and dark indicator lights. The gauges and dials all read zero. Some held banks of computer consoles, all dead. There was also a storeroom with rows of metal shelves bearing spare parts—pipes, fittings, gaskets, sealed bearings, fasteners, housings, replacement motors and electronic components. Ryan and J.B. only looked inside long enough to verify that there were no stairs. And no Bob and Enid-era weapons cache.

Beyond the storeroom they came upon another cluster of eroded corpses, little piles of human remains soaking in yellow muck. Ryan and J.B. used their gun barrels to poke through the mounds of rags strewed against the bottom of the wall. In the middle of one of the mounds, Ryan found a third handblaster and a few spent shell casings. This one was an Astra copy of a Walther PPK, in .380 semiauto. Short on stopping power, it was primarily a belly gun, meant to be used at close range. The action was partially open, an empty cartridge had jammed sideways as it was ejected. Ryan racked the slide, clearing the jam. The semiauto pistol had four hollowpoint rounds in its mag.

"Bob and Enid sure brought a strange collection of blasters down here," J.B. said to Wicklaw. "Milspec full auto assault rifles. Black-powder wheelguns. And now an Astra .380. Be hard pressed to chill a full-grown mutie jackrabbit with that little thing."

"No one knows what they brought," Wicklaw said. "Must've been whatever they had on hand."

"Yeah, well, no wonder they got their butts kicked."

Ryan pocketed the pistol, and they quickly moved on.

In the dimness ahead, they could see the end of the hallway coming up. They had reached the far side of the dam. Scattered around on the floor up there were many more bodies and burned out torches.

"We have to be closing in on the stairwell, if it's here," Ryan said. "We're running out of room fast."

"Look at all those corpses," J.B. said. "Mebbe a demon has been setting a trap, knowing they'd have to try to use the stairs to get out, picking them off as they passed."

"Or mebbe it just got lucky once," Ryan said, "and decided to make this end of the hallway its home. We can't be giving this creature any more credit than it's due, like Wicklaw, there. It doesn't have to be triple smart to do what it does."

"Just instinct, then?"

"Instinct is plenty when you're that fast and that mean," Ryan said.

With the corridor's end in plain sight, they could no longer travel in a straight line. They had to weave around and between the litter of bodies and puddles. The odor made Jubilee moan and gag softly into her hand.

On the right was a single, closed door. It had a small window reinforced with wire mesh. The torchlight wouldn't penetrate to the other side.

"Could be it," Ryan said.

J.B. took hold of the knob, and as he opened the door, Ryan swept in with torch in one fist and Galil in the other. The stairwell landing was clear of demons, but the stench of death was even more oppressive than in the hall. It had substance, and it had weight.

The weight of numbers.

"I think we've got ourselves a chilling ground," J.B. said, wrinkling his nose. "There's got to be a whole lot of bodies below us. That thing wasn't waiting to ambush victims out in the hall. It was getting the lion's share of them in here. The ones that made it to the corridor it probably chased down from behind."

"If there's just the one," Ryan said, "and we can get past it, or through it, we might get to the bottom."

"Based on that stink, the odds aren't very good."

"At least it's a tighter space than the hallway," Ryan said. "That gives it less room to use its speed to maneuver and us a better chance to hit it and chill it."

"What do you say, Wicklaw?" J.B. said. "Ready to go for two?"

It was the pilgrim's turn not to laugh. The sight and smell of the corpses and pools of acid had turned his face pale under the beard. He covered his nose and mouth with his free hand. His eyes were watering.

"What's wrong, big man?" J.B. asked. "Don't care for the perfume? You're responsible for some of it."

"And now he's on the verge of becoming perfume, himself," Ryan said.

"Funny how things turn out."

"Jubilee, take hold of my shirt," Ryan told the girl. "Let's do this."

Ryan and J.B. started down, side by side, filling the stairway from rail to wall. They held their torches as high as they could, and aimed their drawn weapons down the stairs in front of them. The lower they descended the stronger the stench became. By the time they reached the next landing they had to breathe through their mouths to keep from puking.

On the stairs behind them, Wicklaw wasn't so fortunate. The sounds of his wretching, and the wet splatter that followed, echoed in the passage. The gren-wounded man caught the vomit bug from Wicklaw and abruptly followed suit. Clutching the stair rail, he leaned over and hurled last night's dinner into space.

"Could you two triple stupes make any more noise if you tried?" J.B. snarled over his shoulder.

"It doesn't matter, J.B.," Ryan said. "We're not going to sneak up on this bastard, anyway. It already knows we're coming. This is its prime hunting ground."

Evidence of what it hunted appeared below them, at the flickering verge of the torchlight. Stripped human skeletons lay stretched out along the stairs. At least a half-dozen of them. Some lay belly down, some belly up. Their clothing had been torn off and hurled aside. Some were missing one or both legs. As Ryan and J.B. stepped between the ruined bodies, the air had a heat to it, the abrasive heat of decay.

"Wait," the Armorer said. "Another blaster."

He bent, and using the muzzle of the Llama, nudged a pistol butt from the edge of the slime. From the shape of the grip, it looked like a heavy caliber semiauto. And it was. But the Beretta 92's action was fully locked back. Looking into the breech, he could see the magazine's floor plate. The last round had been fired. "Shit!" J.B. kicked the empty blaster aside. It wasn't worth wiping the slime off.

They continued down to the next landing, where the bodies were so thick it was difficult to step around them and the pools of slime. The skeletons lay one on top of the other. Most were facedown. Caught from behind as they tried to crawl away.

Based on the weapons and capabilities he'd seen, Ryan figured the demon's first pass was a hit and run, intended to blindside and incapacitate its victims, then it followed up at its leisure.

"It's still below us," he said. "Not far, now."

He held his torch out as far as he could reach. He couldn't see down to the plane of the next landing. He could see bodies on the stairs, though. Slower runners than the ones up above.

"These things can leap, remember," Ryan said to J.B. "It probably won't come running up the steps at us. Chances are it'll jump high, maybe along the ceiling, and drop down on top of us."

"Gotcha," J.B. said.

They descended more slowly, step by step in unison, pausing, listening. There were no clicks. No scraping noises. Gradually their torchlight illluminated the landing. The bodies were piled high there, too, but there was no sign of the demon. They couldn't see around the turn in the staircase until they stepped off onto the landing. This one had a door in it.

J.B. opened it, and Ryan stuck his head, torch and assault rifle through. Before him was a dank, dark corridor like the one they had just left. Like the hallway above, it was decorated with human remains. He listened for sounds of movement, but all he could hear was his heart pounding in his throat.

"Just another access corridor," he said as he drew back. "Still too high up."

"No sign of the damned thing?" J.B. asked.

"Guess it's lower," Ryan said.

Wicklaw and the gren-wounded man tiptoed around the bodies on the landing, keeping their backs to the stairwell wall.

"We have to keep going," Ryan told them.

Jubilee took hold of his shirt. As he stepped down onto the next flight of stairs, the clicking started. Not a repeated cycle of sounds this time. This time it was a solid stream of mad chatter.

And it was loud.

It seemed to be right on top of them.

"Where is it?" J.B. cried over the racket, raising his torch, scanning the stairs above and the stairs below.

With the echo in the stairwell, it was impossible to

vector in on the source of the noise. It came from everywhere at once.

Everyone was looking around frantically, and no one was seeing the obvious.

It was right under their noses.

Ryan saw it first. A darker area in the landing wall, to the right of where Wicklaw and the other man were standing. Elliptical in shape, in its center was a wet spot.

Seeping yellow.

"Look out!" Ryan cried, swinging Jubilee around behind him. "It's in the wall!"

Wicklaw immediately jumped for the stairs above, but the gren-wounded man made the mistake of turning and looking at the dark spot not four feet away. He froze, eyes wide with fear.

The clicking stopped.

Then the center of the wet spot exploded outward, sending softened concrete and yellow slime flying.

Ryan averted his eye and shielded his face with a forearm. He already had the Galil up, muzzle pointing in the direction of the hole. But things were happening faster than he could react. As he lowered his arm, he glimpsed a sleek brown shape vaulting, long legs extended, from the gash. It hit the landing and jumped to the stairs above before Ryan could fire.

The gren-wounded man slammed against the rear wall as if sideswiped by a runaway wag, his arms flung wide and loose.

Even though Ryan knew what was coming next, he still couldn't track the beast. And he didn't dare fire the

Galil blind into a wall ten feet away. The full-auto ricochets would have cut him and J.B. to pieces.

J.B. had his pistol up, too. But when the time came,
he couldn't fire, either.

It was over too quickly.

In a seamless, fluid move, the brown shape pivoted
on the steps and bounded back to the landing. As it hit
the floor, it snatched the stunned man around the waist
with one of its middle legs, folding him over like a
lawn chair, and leaped again, carrying him into the
wall.

No hesitation.

Clean grab.

Clean reentry.

Start to finish, it took maybe three seconds.

No one said anything for a long moment; they were
too astonished by the turn of events. J.B. used his gun
hand to thumb his glasses back up the bridge of his
nose, and let out the breath of air he had been holding.

Then the captured man had to have come to in the
grasp of the demon. From the depths of the wall came
a long terrible scream, growing fainter and fainter.

"Bob and Enid protect us!" Wicklaw moaned. The
acid spatter had burned holes in the back of his robe and
in his skanky, felted mass of hair. "We are doomed!"

Chapter Twenty-Four

Mildred, Krysty, Jak and Doc abandoned the redoubt's elevator and ran for the stairs, back the way they had come. When they reached the aboveground floor, Jak led them through the security checkpoint to the inner air lock door, where the clanging was the loudest.

He put his hand to the metal, then pulled it back. "Feel," Jak said to Krysty.

When she touched the door, she could feel the shock of the impacts through her fingertips. "Are they trying to break down the outer door?" she said. "Are they using a battering ram?"

"That would be a waste of effort," Mildred said. "Vanadium steel can turn back a direct hit from a cannon shell."

"There are too many impacts, too erratically spaced," Doc said. "It cannot be a battering ram."

"Then they must be rolling the boulders down onto the door," Krysty said. "They're barricading us in."

"It appears we won't be using that exit in the near future," Doc said.

"The pilgrims don't want to have to bother guarding the entrance," Mildred said. "This solves the problem for them."

"And makes our situation that much worse," Krysty said. "Even if the redoubt's mat-trans unit is in working order, we can't go back to rescue Ryan and J.B., now."

"Not the way we came in, at any rate," Mildred said.

"Stick to plan," Jak said.

"Jak's right," Doc said. "We have to address and solve one problem at a time, and in the order we have already agreed upon. This regrettable turn of events has not altered our priorities. We have to know whether we are in fact trapped here. And once we have determined that to our satisfaction, we can explore our options."

The resonant clangs continued as the boulders piled up outside.

"At least this means they won't be coming in after us," Krysty said.

"We have all the time in the world," Doc said. "Unfortunately the same cannot be said for our dear friends."

They hurriedly returned to the floor below and the service elevator. After brushing aside the dense mat of cobwebs that draped from the ceiling, they climbed in. When Krysty pushed the buttons for floor numbers ten and eighteen, the doors slid shut. Then the interior lights flickered, the car jerked, a motor above them whirred, and they began a descent so sickeningly rapid that they had to steady themselves on the walls.

When the elevator stopped with a lurch on floor ten and the doors opened, Krysty said, "Come on, Jak, let's find that mat-trans unit."

The albino nodded assent.

"Doc and I will be down on eighteen," Mildred told them as they stepped out of the car. "When you're done up here, come down and find us."

"Good luck," Krysty said.

"Same back," Mildred pushed the close button, and the doors shut. The elevator car jerked and began to drop once more.

She looked over at the old man and said, "What do you really think about our chances, Doc?"

"My honest opinion?"

"That's what I asked for."

"At this point, I am afraid it looks dire for all of us, my dear. Dire, indeed."

"What we need is a break," she said. "Ever since we mat-transed, things have gone from bad to worse."

"Yes, a turn of luck would be most welcome."

On floor eighteen, the doors opened onto another security checkpoint. It was the mirror image of the set-up at the redoubt entrance. There was a holding cell. And the firing ports in the armored glass of the sec station faced the elevator and the hallway on the other side of the cell—designed to prevent both break-ins and break-outs.

As they cleared the holding cell, through the open sliding window of the security installation, they could see more evidence of a sudden departure. There were paper coffee cups on the desk, the brown liquid they had contained had long since evaporated. Beside the cups were four paper plates that had once held food. Whatever the sec crew's last meal had been, it had turned to pillowy mounds of bluish mold, which had spread as far as it could across the desktop before dying, many decades past. As Mildred and Doc walked by the window, the faint currents of air they stirred up caused the fragile mounds to collapse in on themselves, raising clouds of gray-blue dust.

On either side of the corridor were red-and-yellow signs. Caution Biohazard. Caution Radiation Area.

Set in the wall of the intersecting hallway directly ahead was a long, heavily gasketed window. On the other side of it, banks of fluorescent lights blinked erratically, illuminating the corridor beyond and another gasketed window. On the far side of the second window, there appeared to be another hallway, and another after that, and perhaps another still, although the glare bouncing back and forth between the windows made it difficult to be sure of the actual number.

"What, pray tell, is all this for?"

"It looks like a bioengineering facility," Mildred said. "Prenuke state-of-the-art. Ultrasecure quarantine. Each of the barriers we're looking at is a biohazard containment level. The sealed enclosures are boxes inside of boxes. From the gaskets on the windows, they're probably reverse pressurized, which acts as a fail-safe against accidental release of dangerous material. If one box breaks, the atmosphere flows in instead of out, and there are still four more enclosures to contain the spill."

"A very complex quarantine regimen," Doc said. "What was the dangerous material that required such care?"

"Mead and Shumer's published work was on the use

of nonliving vectors to transfer specific snippets of genetic material. They would insert the new DNA sequences into viruses which when they infected the target cells, would splice in the desired instructional code."

"If these viruses got loose, they could accidently infect whitecoats and redoubt personnel?" Doc said.

"That's right," Mildred said. "And through the process of infection, the virus would transfer the new section of DNA code to every cell in victims' bodies. In an isolated, secure structure like this, dependent upon recycled air and a ventilation system, the escape of viral research material would mean an epidemic of unforeseen consequences. I'm guessing that's the kind of bioengineering operation that was going on here. It's the same application of technology that got them into trouble initially."

They followed the signs on the wall to the directors' suite of offices. On the other side of a glass barrier, through automatic glass doors, was an anteroom, Berber-carpeted, with a row of administrative assistant's desks blocking direct access to a pair of mahogany, floor-to-ceiling doors.

Bob's and Enid's spacious adjoining offices were on the other side of the massive doors, separated from each other by a wall of glass. The U. S. government had spared no expense on the lab directors' furnishings. Mead and Shumer, international outcasts of science, had cut themselves a very sweet deal. Not just leather upholstered couches and vast executive desks. They had their own wet bars. Private bathrooms. A connecting exercise suite, complete with sauna and whirlpool.

Mildred scanned the spines of the books that tightly

packed a wall of shelves. She recognized the standard chemical and medical reference works. There were also tomes on veterinary medicine, cellular biology, cellular pathology and virology.

She waved Doc over to the suite's computer workstation. Thumbtacked to the bulletin board alongside the drive tower were a series of snapshots, greeting cards and little notes.

The photos were of Mead and Shumer, together and individually, with different background scenes. One looked like a European capital. Another was somewhere in the Far East. There was a mountain-top ski resort. Holiday photographs.

Doc opened one of the greeting cards and read the inscription. "This would be Dr. Shumer's office, then," he said.

Mildred looked over his shoulder. The card's corny, gushy, romantic sentiment was underscored by the cover's painting of a fluffy kitten with enormous eyes.

It was signed, To my dear one, All my love, Enid.

The other cards' printed sentiments were even gushier. They offered vows of love eternal. Praised a perfect match of souls. Proclaimed stolen hearts. And there were little personal notes, very affectionate, written in a tight, controlled, microminiature hand. All were from Enid Mead.

"Here's a different sort of greeting," Doc said.

It was a new baby card, addressed to Bob. Inside the word "boy" had been crossed out, and the sentence altered to read, "Congratulations, it's an It! And it's ours!" It was signed, Love forever, Enid.

Mildred didn't bother trying to start up the computer. The drive tower housing had melted into itself and the monitor screen had blown out onto the hardwood parquet floor. Brushing aside a thick coat of dust, she looked through the assembled, bound and unbound spreadsheets, then the drawers beneath the counter.

"There are no research notes," she said. "They were probably all on the hard drive. And that's fried."

"Shall we try the other office?"

They left Bob's digs and moved on to Enid's. Her expansive bookcase had similar reference works on biochemistry and human and animal medicine. But additionally, there were shelves of books on prehistoric Native American culture in the southwest United States and northern Mexico. The walls were decorated with framed photos of Little Pueblo canyon, before, during and after the reservoir was filled in. And there were detailed photos of the cliff dwellings, the caves, and symbols their occupants had carved into the soft stone.

Pinned to Enid's workstation bulletin board were duplicates of the snapshots they'd seen in Bob's office. And a set of greeting cards. All addressed to Enid from Bob, with love.

One showed a tall, statuesque, masked woman in a black latex catsuit, complete with ears and a tail. She stood on towering high heels, brandishing a bullwhip.

A kitten of a different stripe.

There were others in the same vein. Heels. Whips. Latex. Cat-ear masks. Amazons.

"Mead and Shumer must have had an interesting relationship," Mildred said.

Doc nodded. "It went well beyond the confines of pure research, so it seems."

"This machine looks functional," Mildred said of Enid's computer. Apparently, it had been shut off before the redoubt was abandoned. When she hit the on button, the thing started to whine and boot up the operating system. The CRT screen flashed on. Mildred said, "Now, we're getting somewhere."

After a few seconds, the password prompt came up. Mildred typed in a word. It was rejected.

"Let's try this, then," she said, typing a longer word. After a pause, the system gave her access.

"What password did you use?" Doc said.

"Sexkitten, of course."

"I find it hard to reconcile the late Ms. Mead's physical appearance with the proclivities revealed by these missives," he said. "She reminds me more of an underfed, myopic chicken than an amorous cat."

"Still waters run deep."

Mildred had already keystroked the computer's search function to locate the main research protocol files. After some preliminary chittering, the screen filled with a list of code names and file numbers. The most repeated code name was TAB. Mildred opened the largest document with that designation. It was an image file.

A head appeared on the twenty-four-inch screen.

Three-dimensionally rendered, and slowly rotating.

The features of the brown face looked vaguely human, but melted, flattened and smeared. The mouth was extremely broad and the bump of the nose as wide as the mouth. Between heavy ridges of brow and cheek, the eyes were huge and all black. Inhuman. The face's covering didn't look like skin; it looked like a jigsaw puzzle of rigid plates of various sizes and shapes, held together by fine blacks seams of more flexible material. The skull was flat, and its top bore a crest of three-inch-long, black spikes that could have been monumentally thick hairs. There were no ears or earholes on the sides of the head. As the rear of the skull rotated into view, Mildred noted the fine stipling on its armored plates.

They watched as the animation loop repeated again and again. And every time it turned to face forward, its mouth opened wide, exposing multiple rows of black-edged, pointed teeth.

"What exactly are we looking at?" Doc asked Mildred. "Is it a bizarre insect of some kind, highly magnified?"

"Let's see," she said. She pulled the scroll tab to the bottom of the image frame, where she found a specifications table. The TAB acronym was spelled out in the table's legend.

Transgenic Autonymous Bioweapon.

"We still don't know what it is," she said, "but at least we know what it was designed to do. It's a killing machine."

Doc read through the table, then said, "From those specifications, it cannot possibly be an insect. It weighs 110 pounds and measures five feet in length. It's three and a half feet tall at the shoulder."

"It's not *all* insect, anyway," Mildred said. "That's what the transgenic designation means. That creature is a DNA construct, a composite of different gene sources."

"This is all quite baffling, I must admit."

"We need a component list of the donor gene sequences Bob and Enid drew from," Mildred said. She backstepped to the screen of code names and started opening other TAB folders until she found what she was looking for. "Here we go," she said as another list of files popped up. "Looks like Bob and Enid took sections of DNA from a wide variety of creatures."

Doc stared at the screen as she scrolled down the list. "That cannot be correct," he protested. "They borrowed genetic material from a bullfrog? From a flea?"

"For its size," Mildred said, "the bullfrog is a fearsome predator. It will attempt to kill and eat anything it can fit into its bucket of a mouth. Birds. Fish. Snakes. And a flea's fast twitch muscle fibers react hundreds of times faster than a human being's. Put that ability in a hundred-pound body, with the right hard wiring, and thirty-foot, standing leaps are a piece of cake."

Doc continued to read from the list. "And a scorpion? What are the implications of that?"

Mildred flipped back to the image file, scrolling up until the creature's short arms came into view. As the image turned, a six-inch, black thorn uncurled from a pod on the back of its wrist.

"There's the stinger," Mildred said. "The poison sacs are probably under the pod, protected by the meat of the muscle, and compressed by voluntary contractions." She returned to the spec table. "It's armed with a powerful neurotoxin. It produces immobilizing paralysis of the central nervous system within twenty seconds."

"I counted six appendages," Doc said. "The short upper pair, and four longer ones."

They scanned the row of nasty-looking horns that backed each of the lower legs.

"All its weapons seemed designed for close-quarters combat," Doc remarked.

Mildred used the cursor to point out a series of holes along both sides of its torso, or abdomen. "I think those are its ears," she said "Look at the way the side plates overlap. That body is capable of extreme cross-sectional flattening. And discounting the long rear legs, it's a fairly compact target, from back to belly."

"Not only fast, but hard to see."

"The contributions of these other gene donors aren't obvious from the external physiology," Mildred said. "The digestive system. Endocrine system. Instinctive drives. Things like that."

"I thought I saw something else," Doc said. "Return to the component list for a moment, please." When she did, he said, "Scroll down. More. More. There. Stop. Fifth line."

"Good Lord, it has human genes in it, too," Mildred said. When she double-clicked the file name, more information came up. Perhaps more than she wanted to know.

"Bob and Enid gave of themselves to create that thing," Doc said. "Their own substance."

"That's what it looks like," Mildred said. "The Transgenic Autonomous Bioweapon is their love child.

They mingled their genetic material with that of literally dozens of other species."

"'Congratulations, it's an It!'" Doc quoted.

"There's got to be more data here on the bioweapon's capabilities," Mildred said. She found what she was looking for in a text file. The document was addressed to a covert, government military funding source, and intended as confirmation of the research program's progress to date. In this document, the Transgenic Autonomous Bioweapon was also referred to with a more touchy-feely nickname—trannie.

"I was right about the fast twitch muscle fibers," Mildred said, looking up from the screen. "That's where the trannie gets its explosive power and speed. And it has a neural net to match."

"It appears to also have a propensity to dig tunnels and burrows," Doc said.

"Look at those enzymatic secretions."

Though the long biochemical names meant little to Doc, he could make sense of the graph affixed to the document. It showed the corrosive effects of the trannie's various secretions on hardened concrete over time.

"What it secretes and excretes," Mildred said, "lubricates passage through its burrows and breaks down the chemical bonds of the concrete matrix, reducing it to the consistency of wet sand."

Doc resumed reading. "It's highly territorial. It seeks out and destroys anything living within its range."

"And it's parthenogenic," Mildred said. "It self-replicates. It doesn't need a mate to start building an army of genetically identical offspring."

"What part of this thing is human?"

"That could take weeks to figure out," Mildred said. "But now we know why the project had to be buried in the bottom of the reservoir. This is a new predatory life form. Autonomous. Top of the food chain. It makes its own command decisions, based on its instinctive drives. Predictions about its behavior based on the sum of its genetics would be unreliable. The true nature of this beast would have to be observed. There's no other way to assess the interplay of new genes, body structures and instincts.

"How would such a weapon be deployed?" Doc said. "And how would it be controlled it once it's released in the field?"

"Some operational controls are built in, genetically hardwired," Mildred said. "Look here. This says it's photophobic. It avoids sunlight. Its preferred hunt and home locations are in the dark. That characteristic would keep it below ground, at least during the day. Bob and Enid had to have included that feature for a reason. I'd say it was so the trannie concentrates exclusively on its assigned targets, which are most likely in hardened, subsurface positions."

"How would they turn it off?"

"That would require a termination gene," Mildred said. "There's no other way to decommission something like this."

"You have lost me again, I am afraid."

"Every living cell contains a DNA sequence that starts the death process. An automatic self-destruct that kicks in at some point, either a function of age or of external conditions. A bioengineered creature made up of a little of this and a little of that would contain conflicting and potentially disastrous self-destruct commands. The flea code would tell all the cells to die too soon. The human cells would tell cells to live too long. The death codes would have to be removed from all cells, and replaced with something uniform."

"A serious complication, no doubt."

"If you read this document, it was the major sticking point of the entire program. The success of the project hinged on the ability to pull the plug on this weapon once its mission was accomplished. Because of its autonomy, because of its capabilities, termination had be built in. In terms of men and materiél, the cost of cleaning out an infestation of trannies after a successful mission would have been staggering. And maybe even impossible.

"Deciding on an appropriate life span for the weapon would have required elaborate and extensive computer modeling. From this, it doesn't look like they got that far. On the day the world ended, Bob and Enid hadn't come up with a way to kill their baby."

WHEN KRYSTY AND JAK found the entrance to a long, windowless corridor on the tenth floor, they figured they were on the right track. As a rule, mat-trans units were separated from the cores of the redoubts. Perhaps for safety reasons. There was always the danger of radiation leakage. Or power pulse interference with electronic and computer systems. Perhaps the isolation was for security reasons. In this case, the long hallway was the tip of the security iceberg. Barring their path, and completely blocking the corridor, was another holding cell-security checkpoint.

They walked through the unlocked cell and out the other side.

The tile floor vibrated steadily, minutely, underfoot. And there was a faint background hum.

"Sounds like the system is up and online," Krysty said.

On the other side of a pair of heavy swing doors was the redoubt's mat-trans terminus. Its banks of computers merrily chattered, tape and hard drives whirring as they collected and processed current pre-trans data from other stations along the wireless, invisible grid. On the far wall were two portholed steel doors, about ten feet apart.

"Two mat-trans," Jak said.

"That is strange," Krysty said. Normally, each redoubt was supplied with a single unit.

When they looked through the porthole on the left, they saw the usual armaglass walls and floor plates. This particular set was black, flecked with crimson.

"Looks like standard redoubt issue to me," Krysty said.

"Other one."

"That definitely isn't standard issue."

The door to the second chamber had an additional—and unique—element. Two feet from the floor, in its middle was a massively overbuilt, circular docking apparatus. Alongside the door was a wheeled cart that had been constructed around a windowless, vanadium steel box. At either end of the compartment were docking hatches that matched the apparatus in the chamber door.

Krysty peered through the porthole window and blinked in amazement at what she saw. The inside of the second mat-trans unit looked like an instrument of medieval torture, an Iron Maiden. It was lined with thousands upon thousands of needle sharp steel spikes. Three inches apart, they jutted from the cobalt-colored armaglass floor, ceiling and walls.

She opened the door. Right behind it was the only spike-free section of the chamber. A space of about a cubic yard.

Roughly the same size as the interior of the wheeled cart's box.

Krysty stepped around to the handle end of the cart. Attached to it was a hand-operated brake lever that locked all four wheels. On the top of the box in front of the handle was a red toggle switch with a caution notice. Next to that was a bulleted safety checklist.

"Stranger and stranger," she said.

The cart's hatches weren't locked. When Krysty looked inside, the first thing she noticed was the bad smell. It was so vile she jerked her head back. She held her breath to continue the examination. Around the middle of the interior walls was a line of quarter-inch steel tubing, perforated with evenly spaced pinholes. They looked like burner jets.

She flipped the red switch.

After a series of rapid clicks, there was a whoosh, and a yard of flame shot out the front hatch.

"What for?" Jak said.

"I'm pretty sure the flame makes what's inside want to leave," Krysty said. "Makes it want to go into the chamber."

"What's inside?"

"Good question. Whatever it is, those spikes keep it from moving away from the back of the chamber door."

Jak closed the door and looked through the window. "Blind spot," he said "Cannot see space unless door open."

"This unit has transport presets," Krysty said as she examined the chamber's wall-mounted control panel. "The redoubt locations are locked in. It can't be used for any other destinations."

Jak checked the control settings. The destination lat-lons were coded, A through V. "Where go?" he said.

Krysty found the answer on a large, framed wall map, five feet away. The code letters were marked in red in various locations.

Siberia. Ukraine. Urals.

Even Jak, whose ability to read was limited, under-stood the implication of the landmass shown on the map.

"Not use this one," he said.

"Definitely not," Krysty agreed.

If the map wasn't some kind of twisted whitecoat joke, it implied an ability to penetrate and splice into the mat-trans grid of the Soviet Union's predark redoubt system. To materialize some kind of cargo deep inside the most vital and protected enclaves of the enemy.

They took a swivel chair from the adjoining room and put it in the unspiked mat-trans chamber. Jak closed the door.

The faint hum grew louder and louder, building to an ear-spliting whine. Then the room lights dimmed for an instant. When they came back on, Krysty and Jak looked through the porthole. The chair had vanished and the jump mist was already dissipating.

Krysty unslung Ryan's rifle and set it down on the cart. Jak did the same with J.B.'s M-4000.

"We're good to go," she said. "All we've got to do is find them."

WHEN KRYSTY AND JAK rejoined Doc and Mildred on the eighteenth subfloor they compared notes on what they had separately discovered, and the truth about Little Pueblo's demons started to become clear.

"So, the trannies were meant to be a Doomsday bioweapon," Krysty said. "Designed to penetrate and depopulate the chain of Soviet redoubts after Armageddon."

"And using the Soviet's own mat-trans system to get the weapons inside," Mildred said.

"Quite an interesting strategy, really," Doc said. "If successful, it eliminates the threat of future enemy attacks. And taking control of the Soviet redoubts effectively doubles the available resources of the American nukecaust survivors."

"There's an ironic twist to the siting of the project in this location," Mildred said. She pointed to Enid Mead's shelves of books on Native American prehistory. "Enid certainly knew about the existence of the Little Pueblo Canyon demon legend from her extensive reading on the subject. A demon that hates the light.

That eats humans. That is spawned out of thin air, like a ghost. That is unkillable, like a ghost. From all the photographs she collected, I'd say she had a particular fascination with the vanished cliff people's culture. She and Bob had the power—and the funding—to make the canyon's ancient legend come to life."

"We still don't know what happened here after nuke-day," Krysty said. "We know the reservoir drained away, and the trannie, or trannies, got loose, but we don't know how. Or why they ended up in the dam."

"It had to be an accident," Mildred said. "Bob and Enid knew what their baby could do."

"I agree that the whitecoats had to understand the danger they were in, once their creature was free," Doc said. "But why did they not just abandon the place? That would have been the simplest solution."

"For the same reason the ville folk are still here, today," Krysty said. "The desert is hell to cross. Odds of making it to the other side are slim. This canyon is an oasis. If the demons are kept under control, and iso-lated in the dam, the chances of survival are pretty good."

"Bob and Enid kept their lab subjects on the bottom floor of the redoubt," Mildred said. "We need to go down and have a look at whatever's been left behind. With any luck, it'll give us an idea of how to fight the trannies."

Had the companions not taken a different route back to the elevator, had it not been for the sound of the huge pumps kicking in, they would have missed the hydro control station. As it was, through the closed door, they could hear a steady loud churning.

"That's mechanical," Mildred said.

"Let's have a look," Krysty said.

Inside, they found a fully automated system running through a hundred-year-old program. Steel boxed computers and slave units covered an entire wall. They were decorated with flow meters, and depth and pressure gauges. There was also a complicated, illuminated system schematic, with side channels, cutoffs, overflow pipes. Water flow direction was indicated by tiny, blinking blue lights. If the scale was accurate, the underground structure extended all the way to the foot of the dam.

"I think this may have something to do with maintaining the level of the lake," Mildred said. "The water source is obviously the river, which is running below ground, somewhere between this floor and the surface."

"Or perhaps the system of channels and pumps keeps the underground river diverted around this facility," Doc suggested. "It certainly was installed at the same time."

As they continued on to the elevator, they double-checked their weapons, making sure chambers held live rounds and mags were full, on the offchance the lab section was still occupied by the spawn of Bob and Enid.

Mildred pushed the button for floor nineteen. The doors slid shut, and the car jerked and dropped. After falling no more than ten feet, it stopped short, slamming to such an abrupt halt that it sent the four companions crashing to the floor.

Even before they regained their feet, a torrent of water began to pour through the seam between the closed doors.

Chapter Twenty-Five

J.B. poked the burning end of his torch and the muzzle of the cocked Llama pistol into the gaping new hole, careful not to get any of the yellow slime on himself. When he drew back he said, "The demon must've been waiting just behind the wall, ready to jump out when the next victim came past. I've never seen anything reverse direction like that. Pivot turn caught me flatfooted, I couldn't get a bead on it."

"The stairwell isn't any safer for us than the hallways," Ryan said. "Not when the bastards can bust through the walls and take us by surprise. That extra split-second advantage is all they need."

"And all we need is enough time to get a message from brain to trigger finger."

"Yeah, but buying enough time for us to get shots off is going to be triple tough," Ryan said. "This is the demons' stronghold, not ours. The fight is by their rules, not ours. And we don't know enough about either one to tip things in our favor."

"They can be chilled, though," J.B. said, glaring at Pilgrim Wicklaw. "At least we know that."

Wicklaw didn't argue the point. He was too busy squirming and scratching, his face flushed red and screwed up into a squinty-eyed grimace. The spray of demon goo had eaten lacey holes through the back of his robe, and some of it had gotten onto his skin. From the way he was acting, it had to have burned like hell-fire.

"We've got to move on," Ryan said. With Jubilee in tow, he and J.B. continued down the stairs.

Wicklaw brought up the rear, shuffling on his bad foot, scratching at himself and whimpering.

It occurred to Ryan, and not for the first time, that every person dumped into the top of the dam would do exactly what they were doing, trying to reach an exit at the bottom of the structure. That was the only hope for a safe escape. If the demons had a grain of sense, they would have most heavily colonized the lower portions of the dam; at least in the beginning, they would have let the food come to them.

As was the case with other predators, the oldest and strongest would control the best hunting ground. The younger, less experienced ones would be forced to prowl the edges of the prime turf, picking off strays and stragglers wherever they could.

Which probably meant the upper corridors.

Even the young, inexperienced demons had nothing to fear from their prey. Humans were slow to react, easy to panic and their weapons were ineffective. Ryan imagined the older ones fought the young ones to maintain their dominance. The demons could even be cannibalistic, he thought. Which would explain the absence of their corpses in the corridors.

Ryan knew he was making assumptions on slim evidence at this point. It was just as likely that the demons weren't concentrated on the floors below them. If the competition started taking victims higher and higher in the dam, it would force the older ones to abandon the lower floors, or starve to death. After a hundred years, with the dam walls honeycombed by their tunnels, they could be anywhere.

Everywhere.

He and J.B. were sorely under the blaster this time. Not faced with a learning curve, as Mildred would have described it, but a learning *cliff.* And they were both hanging on the same frayed rope a mile up.

As they reached the next landing, and its crop of acid-blackened human bones, there was a shrill creaking noise on the floor above them. Then a resounding bang.

"The door!" J.B. said, turning and pointing his weapon past Wicklaw, up the stairs. "That was the landing door slamming shut!"

"Shhh, listen," Ryan said over the sights of the Galil.

From above came soft clicking sounds. A steady stream of them. Like a cat purring. Only this was no cat.

"Nuking hell, it's in the stairwell," J.B. groaned.

"Down!" Ryan snarled at the girl. "Get down behind me!"

Wicklaw hurled himself, bad foot and all, between Ryan and J.B. Dropping his torch amid the yellow puddles and litter of bones, he lunged for the corner of the landing, and cowered there, covering the back of his head with his hands.

The pattern of the clicking suddenly changed. Instead of a steady stream, it started coming in short, rapid-fire bursts, separated by brief pauses. It almost sounded like the demon was talking to them. To its soon-to-be victims. Or perhaps it was communicating to the other demons that might be in earshot, announcing the pending kill, warning them off the spoils.

Then the sounds stopped.

Ryan tucked the Galil's tubular steel buttstock hard into his shoulder. His finger tightened down on the trigger, taking up the slack, bringing it almost to break point.

A shadow came down the stairwell, moving in great bounds, faster than the eye could follow.

Over the years, Ryan and J.B. had proved themselves expert marksmen, at close and long range, with every conceivable type of blaster to be found in the hellscape. Hitting what they aimed at was their stock-intrade; their lives had depended on that skill for years. They understood the limitations of the particular weapons they held, and their own physical limitations under the conditions of low, flickering light and speeding, oncoming target. They also knew the consequences if they didn't stop the demon in its tracks.

Saving ammo was the least of their worries.

Long seconds before the streaking shadow appeared, Ryan held his aim steady at the middle of the flight of stairs. Three heartbeats after the clicking stopped, an instant before the shadow appeared around the landing turn above, he opened fire with the assault rifle, full auto, six hundred rounds a minute, letting his target fall through the kill zone.

It either couldn't turn, or it didn't try.

The Galil roared in the enclosed space, spitting a yard of flame. The first three of its metal-jacketed .308s slammed into the step risers, cratering, shattering the concrete. The next five slugs hit something more resilient. Something that trapped and absorbed the destructive power of their mushrooming tips.

As the assault rifle locked back empty, J.B. squeezed off his fourth semiauto shot, firing as fast as he could pull the trigger. He, too, had taken a fixed lead on the target.

Which was still coming.

Instinctively, the comrades dived in opposite directions, J.B. lunged for the wall to his right, Ryan for the bend in the stairwell. The black shape shot between them, crashing headlong into the landing wall.

J.B. spun and tried to put his sights on the frenziedly thrashing and kicking demon.

The thing was no longer clicking; instead, mouth gaping enormously, it squealed. Shrill. Piercing. Nerve-grating. Like a pig whose slaughter had been bungled.

Trapped, crouching in the corner of the landing, his hands still protecting the back of his head, Pilgrim Wicklaw bleated, "Shoot it! For Bob's sake, shoot it!"

The wounded demon couldn't get to its legs, but it was still alive, and it was berserk. Thick white blood squirted through the .308-caliber entry holes in its chest as it snapped its torso, lashing out with its back legs, the serrated blades scoring grooves in the floor and wall. The demon moved so fast, hopping and jittering, flopping from one side to the other, spinning that in the torchlight it was difficult to even get a good look at it.

"Head!" Ryan shouted to J.B., pulling out the Astra .380. "Aim for the head."

J.B. leaned forward, and, timing the shots between the creature's violent jerks, fired twice in rapid succession.

The Parabellum rounds entered the side of its skull, just behind the huge black eye, and blew out the other side, point-blank through and through. A quart of pale beige paste splattered high and wide across the wall, and sharp fragments of whatever its skull was made of rattled around the landing, singing through the air like shrapnel.

"Uhh! Uhh!" Wicklaw moaned from the corner, frantically using the hem of his robe to try to wipe the creature's sticky brains and bits of its skull off his beard.

On the landing floor, the demon trembled, head to foot, in its death throes. The armored plates along the sides of its torso quivered, all six of its legs quaked. Its jaws snapped as more of the white gunk bubbled out of the ruin of its head. Slowly its back legs extended until they were stretched out straight behind it, and then it stopped moving.

"Radblast!" J.B. said, looking down at the locked back slide of the empty Llama. "That thing was hard to chill."

"It's dead, Jubilee," Ryan told the girl huddled behind him. "You can open your eyes."

She did so, clinging to the back of his shirt, peering around his arm to blink at the thing on the floor. She was goggle-eyed and speechless.

"I thought it would be much bigger," J.B. said, standing over the demon, and holding the torch close.

"It's big enough to snatch a full grown man off his feet and lug him away," Ryan said.

"Triple strong for its size," J.B. commented. "It can't weigh much more than a hundred pounds. Looks like a bug with all those legs."

"Yeah, but the teeth…" Ryan said. "No bug was ever born with teeth like that. They look like they could cut through sheet steel. And it's got rows and rows of them, one behind the other."

"Like a shark. Always growing new sets."

Ryan prodded a piece of the fragmented skull plate with the toe of his boot. It had a clump of black hairs, like thick steel wires, sprouting from it. The tips were cut or broken off on the diagonal, and looked needle sharp. "Radblasted ugly sucker, any way you look at it."

To Wicklaw J.B. said, "That's two down, pilgrim. Praise Bob, praise Enid."

"With who knows how many more to go?" Ryan asked. "We've got at least three floors to cross before we reach the bottom of the dam. How many more bullets have you got left? I've got four rounds in this predark pea shooter."

J.B. showed him the battered Smith Military Police .38. "Five shots is all I've got, assuming this blaster doesn't blow up in my face first."

"Keep the Llama," Ryan told him. "Maybe we'll find some more ammo for it." He slipped the Galil's web sling over his shoulder. "I'm keeping this, too. Just in case."

They found no unfired ammunition on the stairs below. No loaded blasters, either. There were lots more gashes in the walls, though, gaping holes where the demons had popped out or bored in. And more bodies on the steps. Bodies galore.

Ryan and J.B. had to boot the bones aside to clear a path.

It was as Ryan had guessed. The bulk of the demon sacrifices seemed to be concentrated at the base of the stairwell. And not because they had tumbled down there from above. These bodies lay where they had died, stretched out, crawling to get away.

From the fragile state of the bones, they were very old victims. maybe even from as far back as Bob and Enid's time. The skeletons lay two and three deep on the stairs. They appeared to be climbing over one another, as if still trying to escape. Though there were dozens upon dozens of them, the stench was much less horrible than higher up in the well.

Below, the bodies on the landing were mounded waist deep. A jumble of blackened bones that spilled up the staircase, covering the last four steps. There was a demon hole in the wall above them; its goo looked congealed or dried up. Ryan kept his weapon pointed at it, anyway.

"Looks like the end of the line," J.B. said as they stopped on the fifth step above the landing.

There were no more stairs to the right, just an exit door, half-blocked by bones.

"How are we going to get through all that?" Wicklaw said. "There's yellow slime everywhere."

It was true. The collection of stripped human remains dripped with the stuff. It had spread out in a vast pool beneath them.

"If you think we're going to carry you, pilgrim ," J.B. said, "you've got another think coming."

"There's worse things than a little acid," Ryan told Wicklaw. "But you already know that."

Covering the hole with their handblasters, Ryan and J.B. waded into the pile of eroded corpses. Ryan's boot heel came down on the side of a skull. Under his weight, it flattened to nothing, like he'd stepped on a pile of icy slush. It made the same wet squishing sound, too. The heaps of black bones fell away as they methodically kicked them aside, and crushed them to mush underfoot.

Before they got halfway across the landing, yellow slime coated their boots and spattered their trousers to midthigh, saturating the fabric. There were no wisps of smoke from acid eating denim, no lancing pain from acid eating into flesh. The demon juice had lost its punch over the passing decades. It was still nasty rank and sticky, but no longer powerfully corrosive. Ryan and J.B. slogged through a bog of ancient death, and when they reached the landing door, they cleared away the barrier with their boots.

The door opened onto a hallway like the ones they'd seen above, except the ceiling was lowered by the massive bundles of plastic pipe and galvanized electrical conduit that were strapped to it. The piles of bones that littered the floor were in similar condition to those in the stairwell—they squashed underfoot like rotten fruit.

"What's keeping this place up?" J.B. asked.

He had put his finger on the most remarkable feature of the corridor, the number of gashes in the walls. On both sides of the hall there was a hole every five yards or so.

Almost more holes than wall.

"Maybe the demons are holding hands," Ryan said.

J.B. poked at the lip of a gash with the butt of his torch. "They haven't been down here in a while. Gunk is all hardened."

They had covered seventy-five feet of corridor, searching in vain for a doorway, a chute, some kind of man-made passage that might lead to the outside, when a loud clunk shook the floor under their feet and brought down dust and grit from the pipes overhead.

The clunk was immediately followed by a roar—the roar of tons of rushing water somewhere beneath them.

"Sounds like someone just opened the floodgates," J.B. said. "Maybe the lake's draining away."

"What's going on?" Ryan demanded of Wicklaw. "Is it the pilgrims? What are they trying to do?"

"I don't know. I don't know what it is, I swear."

Over the noise of the flowing water, from the floor above them, came a now-familiar clicking.

"The demons are closing in," J.B. announced.

He and Ryan broke into a trot, trying to search as much ground as they could before company arrived. Jubilee kept pace, but Wicklaw fell back. If Ryan and J.B. hadn't stopped to examine a steel hatch set in the middle of the corridor floor, they would have lost him.

The hatch had a locking wheel, and was marked with a stenciled sign that read Turbine Channel Access #15a.

"It's for service access to the dam's turbines," Ryan said. "Water comes into the channel from the ville side, where the reservoir used to be. It runs down, drives the turbines and pours out the other side. That channel has to have an outlet downstream."

"But we're on the intake side of the turbines," J.B. reminded him. "To get to the outflow passage, we're going to have to go through them. There may not be a way to do that. The blades could be frozen. The intake screened. Ryan, it could be a dead end. Or worse, that rushing noise we hear might be the channel full of water."

Then the clicking from above was joined by clicking from the dark corridor ahead.

A second demon.

"We can't defend this hallway with nine bullets between us," Ryan said. "But if we duck down the channel at least we can put that hatch between them and us."

J.B. didn't waste precious time arguing. He grabbed hold of the hatch's wheel and started turning it. When the lock released, he flopped the hatch back on its hinges.

They held their torches down into the opening, half-expecting to see a torrent.

Twenty-five feet below, the flat concrete floor was dry.

But the sound of the water was much louder.

With Jubilee following, Ryan climbed through the

hatch and descended a steel access ladder that was lag-bolted to the wall. The one-eyed man stepped off the bottom of the ladder, set his torch down and helped Jubilee to the ground. Torch in one hand, Astra .380 in the other, he scanned the dark channel. It was square, twenty by twenty, and its floor was pitched. The slope steepened to the right, radically. Somewhere out of sight in that direction, it angled down to meet the turbine blades. The channel hadn't held water for a very long time. There were no puddles on the floor.

Ryan couldn't only hear the water's roar, he could feel the vibration of it flowing under his feet. It was traveling away from the ville, under the dam, and out the other side.

The hatch clanged shut above them. J.B. locked it from the inside before he started down the ladder. Wicklaw was already halfway down, moving carefully on his injured foot, which was bleeding again.

The attack came without a click of warning.

The demon had to have been crouching just out of sight to the left.

Ryan caught a glimpse of a shadow, flying through the air, maybe fifteen feet off the ground. It hit Wicklaw hard and low from behind and kept on going. The big man groaned as he was slammed facefirst into the ladder. He dropped his torch. Something else fell away as well, out from under his robe, landing on the floor with a thud, and Wicklaw dropped like a trapdoor had opened under him. He clung to the ladder with his hands, his arms fully outstretched, bearing his entire weight. One leg flailed to find the rungs.

Ryan blinked. The other leg was gone at the hip.

Wicklaw threw back his head and screamed. His blood rained down the ladder, rained down on the channel floor.

Ryan spun Jubilee out of the way and shouted to J.B., "Jump! Jump, now!"

J.B. didn't question, didn't hesitate. He pushed off from the ladder and fell past the mortally wounded pilgrim.

An instant after he hit the floor, the blur once again passed high overhead, this time from right to left. The second collision knocked Wicklaw from the ladder and sent him spinning through the air. As he did so, a slurry of blood and guts splattered the walls. Practically cut in two by the creature's leg horns, Wicklaw crashed to his side.

The demon fell on top of him at once, clicking up a storm, its sides puffing in and out. It opened its mouth impossibly wide, like it had unhinged its jaws, and leaning over his face, began to dry heave. Dry heaves that turned quickly wet. Yellow slime poured out of its throat.

Wicklaw shrieked, frantically clawing at the air, and kicking with his surviving leg.

The first gush was just a hint of what was to come. The demon bore down, puffing harder, and puked buckets.

Wicklaw went rigid, his back arching up from the floor. His face and beard covered in digestive slime, he blew yellow bubbles.

Ryan and J.B. took aim at the creature's back, but

neither fired. They remembered how many bullets it had taken to stop the last one. Wicklaw was a goner, and this demon was busy.

Tucking away their blasters, they snatched up Jubilee by the armpits and carried her between them as they ran down the intake channel. The light from their torches faded to gray thirty feet ahead; beyond that was black. The floor continued to tip until the angle was forty-five degrees; if it had been wet, they couldn't have kept their footing. As it was, it felt like they were half falling into dim oblivion, and never quite reaching it.

When the sound of the water stopped beneath them, they could hear the echoes of the demon wretching over its kill.

Ryan had seen some bastard hard things in the hell-scape, but the look in Wicklaw's eyes as the thing vomited acid onto his face was something he hoped he would live long enough to forget.

"There's the turbines," J.B. said.

The turbine assembly completely filled the channel, blocking their passage. The steel housing was mounted to huge anchor bolts set in the floor, walls, and ceiling. In the middle of the housing, a set of fan blades ten feet across was suspended on a central hub and axle. There was no screen or grate to impede the flow of water across the blades.

They set Jubilee down in front of the assembly. Then Ryan and J.B. poked their torches in the gaps between the fan blades. Right away, the nature of the problem was clear. The turbine had more than one set of blades, and each turned independently on the same axle. For them to crawl through the turbine, all the gaps would have to be lined up.

The two men tried to turn the first fan, pulling down on the edges of the blades. It wouldn't rotate. It wouldn't even budge. After a hundred years its grease had turned solid and its bearings were frozen.

Ryan wedged the barrel of the Galil between the lowermost blade and the turbine housing, and leaned all his weight on it. With a groan, the fan cracked free. It still wasn't easy to turn, but J.B. managed to move the blades far enough so Ryan could slip past.

Between the first and second sets of blades there was perhaps three feet of space.

Using the Galil again, Ryan pried the second fan into position and crawled forward to the third, which left enough room for Jubilee and J.B. to enter behind him.

"Can you move the first blade back?" Ryan said.

J.B. was already doing just that. He pulled down on the fan, rotating its blades to block the demon's path.

For the moment at least, they were enclosed in a steel housing.

"I don't think it can get in," J.B. said.

"We can't stay here," Ryan replied. "The longer we wait, the more of them are going to come. We've got to find the end of the channel. See if there's an opening to the outside."

He started attacking the last fan blade with the assault rifle. He bent the steel stock, but got the fan's frozen bearings to release. He crawled out the far side of the turbine and stood up. The end of the channel wasn't within the radius of his torch.

"I'm going check it out," he told J.B.

"Here, take the Smith," the Armorer said, squeezing his arm past the huddled girl. "It's got more wallop."

"No, you keep it."

Ryan left the Galil behind as well because he didn't want the extra weight to slow him down. With the .380 in one hand and the torch in the other, he sprinted away from the turbine. The grade continued downhill and steep. If he had something chasing him on the return trip, he was dead meat.

The outflow channel went on and on. He passed more demon holes in the walls. Nothing came out after him. He kept on running until he saw another hatch set in the floor. This one didn't have a wheel on top, and there was no stenciled sign indicating its function. He tried to open it, but couldn't. It was locked from the other side.

When he'd gone another fifty feet, he could see the channel's terminus ahead. It ended in a rusty red square. Not a spec of light showed through. It was like looking at the bottom of a mine shaft.

Ryan raced up to the floor-to-ceiling barrier. The gate was made of heavy steel, ribbed vertically and horizontally for strength, watertight or nearly so. Its hinges were on the other side, inaccessible. The gate was jammed closed. He tried kicking out one of the un-reinforced panels, hoping it had rusted through.

It hadn't.

And there was no budging the gate with any means at hand. It had to have weighed ten tons, easy.

"Fireblast!" he muttered, giving it another kick for good measure.

From the channel behind him came the sound of a terrible collision. And a squeal of bending metal. There was a pause. Then it sounded again. Collision. Squeal.

"Ryan!" J.B. shouted, his cry echoing down the channel.

Then the Smith boomed, and kept on booming.

Chapter Twenty-Six

Water poured between the elevator car doors, splashing over and swirling around the sprawled companions. As they pushed up from the floor, holding their weapons high to keep them dry, the elevator bobbed like a cork, tipping from side to side, and as it did so, banging into the shaft walls. Its control cables had gone slack when it hit bottom fifteen feet too soon.

"By the Three Kennedys!" Doc cried, pointing at the doors. "We are going under!"

"Hit the up switch!" Mildred shouted, bracing herself against the force of the incoming waterfall.

As Krysty was closest to the controls, she lunged for the button for floor eighteen. She punched it and kept on punching it.

The elevator's motor engaged, then labored mightily, but the car didn't lift.

Brown water lapped around their knees, its level rising quickly toward the elevator's control panel.

"It won't go!" Krysty said, still punching the button. "When the water hits the panel, it's going to short out!"

Mildred jumped for the trap door in the ceiling, but she couldn't reach it. "Get the escape hatch, Doc," she said.

As the old man pushed the trapdoor up and out of

the way, the bottom of the elevator broke free of the water.

Because of all the weight sloshing around inside it, the car struggled desperately to climb. The water drained out the way it had come in, through the seam between the doors, only much more slowly. It was still emptying when the car stopped at story eighteen. The doors opened and it poured out in a wave, sheeting across the floor.

Drenched to the waist, the companions stepped out of the car. They wrung the water from their coat tails and sleeves, and dumped quantities of it from their boots.

"Where water from?" Jak asked.

"Like Doc said before," Krysty replied, "the white-coats diverted the river underground so they could build the redoubt in the canyon floor. At some point the river broke free of its man-made channel and flooded the bottom story. It probably happened on nukeday, when the dam split open."

"That's certainly one explanation," Mildred said.

"You would argue something different?" Doc queried.

"We know the demons escaped to the dam, because that's where they are, today," Mildred said. "If the pilgrims' legends are true, we know when. We don't know how or why they ended up there. I think it's possible that Bob and Enid flooded the lab, themselves. That they did it on purpose, after their experimental subjects got loose."

"They flooded the entire floor in order to drown the demons?" Krysty said.

"That would be one way to eliminate the problem without risking their own safety, and the future of the redoubt and their research."

"What you are proposing could not have been a spur of the moment reaction to disaster," Doc said. "In order for the strategy to be effective, the flooding of the floor required an enormous amount of water, transferred in a matter of a few minutes. Otherwise the demons would have simply burrowed up through the concrete to avoid the deluge. And there's no evidence of their presence in the upper floors of this structure."

"So there had to be a system in place," Mildred said. "A failsafe built in to the lab floor. A last-ditch way to terminate their hellspawn."

"Only it failed," Krysty reminded her.

"That's true. The strategy didn't work. The demons survived the flooding of floor nineteen, and ended up in the dam. The question remains, how did they get there?"

"Started digging here," Jak suggested. "Kept digging. Not far dam."

"That's not possible," Mildred told him. "On Enid's computer, I saw the chemistry of the enzymes the trannies produce. These creatures were built from the ground up, and they were designed to burrow through redoubt-grade concrete after it had been softened by their natural secretions. Their secretions specifically attack the binding agents in the concrete. They won't work on the bedrock around here. It's one of the default controls Bob and Enid included in their design. It effectively cages the demons, limiting their movements and operations to the assigned target areas."

"So the only way the demons could have gotten to the dam is through concrete," Krysty said.

"Or an easier way…" Mildred said

"Which is?" Krysty prompted.

"A tunnel that leads out of floor nineteen and connects the redoubt with the dam."

"My dear Mildred, there is no way to verify if what you are suggesting is true," Doc said. "And even if there was confirmation, such a tunnel is of no use to us. That floor is under fifteen feet of water."

"If there was a way to flood floor nineteen in order to save themselves in an emergency," Mildred said, "there also had to be a way to empty it after the crisis had been averted. These are whitecoats. Thorough, thoughtful people who plan ahead. The development of transgenic bioweapons was the culmination of Bob and Enid's lifework. This redoubt was the key to their success. Everything they needed was here. Secrecy. Isolation. Technical support. Bottomless funding. They would make sure they didn't have to abandon the site if something unforeseen like this happened. They would correct their mistake by chilling it, drain the floor, and start over."

"We need to go back to that hydro control room," Krysty said. "If there's a way to drain the floor, it's probably there."

When they returned to the control station, the illuminated water flow schematic made a lot more sense.

They could identify the valve and T-junction symbols that directed the flow of water through various underground channels. The blue-colored lights, either on or off, indicated water's presence or absence in sections of the system.

Mildred pointed at the schematic and said, "Water was diverted from the river down through this passage and into the lab floor. The blue lights are lit all along floor nineteen, which probably indicates it's full of water. But they aren't blinking, like the ones in the river."

"So the trapped water remains static," Doc said. "There is no current moving, in or out."

"The lights continue on from the far end of the lab floor," Krysty said. "They go under the ville, the fields, even under the lake. It looks like they come up inside the dam."

"An underground passage," Doc said. "Just as Mildred hypothesized. Given its length and endpoint, I think it's safe to assume it had nothing to do with terminating the laboratory subjects."

"I think it's an emergency escape tunnel for the redoubt's whitecoats," Krysty said. "It's got to be. When there was five hundred feet of water overhead, the only ways in and out of Minotaur were via the mat-trans unit or in some kind of underwater wag that took people and supplies to and from the surface. If something went wrong with the transport vehicle, and the mat-trans unit failed, they'd be stuck down here. Bob and Enid wouldn't leave themselves without a backup."

"I think you're right," Mildred said. "And it's easy to see how the demons got to the dam."

"Pray do elaborate," Doc said.

"Bob and Enid tried to drown their offspring, but they didn't get all of them. Some made it out of the lab, down the emergency escape tunnel to the dam before the tunnel was flooded."

Krysty pointed at the line of unblinking lights between floor nineteen and the dam. "The water in that passage is all that's keeping the demons where they are."

"Yep," Mildred said. "And to rescue Ryan and J.B., we're going to have to pull the plug on it. With those stones back in front of the redoubt's entrance, it's our only way in."

"Because it follows a straight line to the dam, more or less, it appears to be a much shorter route than the roundabout path through the fields Ryan and J.B. were forced to take," Doc said.

After a quick survey of the station's simple control panels, Mildred located the remote switches she needed. Not only did she have to open the emergency escape passage's drain valve, which was on the far side of the dam, she had to close the water intake from the river, which kept the channel perpetually topped off. When she activated the water release valve, they heard the roar of rushing water from the floor below.

"How long are we going to have to wait for the water level to drop?" Krysty said.

"Better give it ten minutes," Mildred said.

Thinking about the danger Ryan and J.B were in, they gave it closer to five.

This time they braced themselves for the elevator car's splash landing, and managed to keep their feet. When the doors opened, a wave of brown water poured in, filling the car to the height of their shins. They faced a floor-to-ceiling, barred vanadium steel gate. The gate door had been left ajar, presumably a century ago by fleeing whitecoats.

The companions sloshed forward, into the still-flooded lab. A few of the recessed ceiling lamps had survived, and they threw pools of light onto the dirty water as it swirled away. The current was running strong toward the far end of the floor. The rips sucked away pieces of paper, styrofoam cups, even chair cushions. The banks of computers were dead; their cracked monitors full of brown water. As were the open desk drawers. The laboratory's countertops had been swept clean of glassware. A row of slime-streaked, bright yellow biohazard suits with helmets and self-contained breathing systems hung from a row of hooks along one wall. In the back eddies formed by the corners of the desks, clots of unidentifiable, shapeless things, all hairy green, or foamy brown, spun in endless circles.

Along the join of the walls and ceiling was a greasy black ring, the floor's high water mark. The lower walls were covered with mold slime, as was every exposed surface.

"It looks like a giant petri dish," Mildred remarked as she took it all in.

"Smells like a giant latrine," Krysty said.

They slogged on, toward another barred barrier that divided the lab floor in half. In front of the steel fence, a thick red line had been painted across the ceiling and walls, and presumably also under the water on the floor. A demarcation line. Riveted to the barrier's open door was a stenciled notice. Warning: Extreme Biohazard. Absolutely No Unprotected Personnel Beyond This Point.

The companions pushed through the gate, and into what had once been the lab-subject containment area. Along one wall were rows of screened stainless-steel cages, stacked three high. The critters inside them were a hundred years dead. As the retreating water had drained from the cages, it had peeled away their covering of slime.

Hairless, featherless, scaleless bags of gray skin lay on luxuriant beds of scum.

It was impossible to identify their species.

Or which end was up.

A quintet of much larger enclosures stood at the far end of the room. The cells were four feet by four feet by four feet, and separated by enough floor space so the lab attendants could wheel gurneys and supply carts around them—gurneys and carts that lay overturned near the back wall. These cages had vanadium bars, horizontally reinforced, like the room's security barriers, but inside the enclosures, covering sides and top, were sheets of clear plastisteel with neatly drilled rows of ventilation holes. The lab designers wanted no part of what was inside those cages to get out. The four of the five cells were half-filled with cloudy water, which still drained out the breathing holes. Above the water line, slime froth streaked the inside of the plastic.

On the wall beside the cages was a tall locker marked Emergency Response.

When Jak opened it, gallons of water rushed out of the bottom. Inside the compartment was a pair of flat, black metal tanks, joined in an aluminum backframe with webbed and padded shoulder straps. A corrugated steel hose led from the inverted tanks to the butt of a pistol grip device, complete with trigger, trigger guard, crossblock safety switch and an unmarked red plastic button. Atop the pistol grip was a pipe that ended in a fat nozzle. Directly under the nozzle was second, slightly longer length of metal tubing, bent upward at the tip. It was the diameter of a soda straw. An igniter. The weapon system's pilot light.

"Good grief, that's a flamethrower," Mildred said.

"A devastating weapon in close confines," Doc said. "And an excellent way to contain a disaster within these four walls. It combines lethality with sterilization."

"Tanks full," Jak said, looking at the fuel pressure gauge.

"It looks like Bob and Enid never got the chance to use it," Krysty said. "Whatever happened down here, it happened damn quick."

They sloshed closer to the line of large cages. The retreating water on the floor was now shoe-top deep.

In the closest cage, something big and white was drifting low in the water, fluttering weakly as it continued to drain away.

The trapped liquid was dark, murky, the lighting was bad, and the object was far from the inside of the plasti-steel wall. They couldn't make out exactly what it was. Not until more of the water oozed away, revealing a much larger skin bag on the cage's floor.

A skin bag wearing a white labcoat.

The bones of the man's skull and neck were visible through the sags and rips in the loose gray skin.

"There's another corpse in the cage over here," Doc said to the others. "It is also wearing a white coat. It is in rather remarkable condition, all things considered."

"That's got to be due to the water temperature," Mildred said. "It's been nice and cool down here for a hundred years. It was a fairly sterile environment to begin with, and thanks to the flooding there was no aerobic bacteria to deal with."

"Were these people experimenting on each other?" Krysty asked.

"Hardly seems likely," Mildred said.

"Why are they in the cages?"

"Maybe they climbed in to get away from the trannies," Mildred said. "Those cages could have been their only hope. It's obvious they couldn't reach the flamethrower in time. And the elevator was even farther away. I think they ducked in the cages and shut the doors behind them. I think that's all the time they had."

"And Bob and Enid drowned them, too," Krysty said.

"They were cutting their losses," Mildred said. "Under the circumstances, they couldn't try to rescue their people down here. They had no way of knowing whether they were still alive. They wouldn't risk letting the trannies reach the upper floors. If that happened, every person in the redoubt was going to die. So they sealed off this section and flooded it."

"Ghastly," Doc said.

"They died like rats in a trap," Krysty said.

There were three more of the large cages at the end of the room. Beyond them, in the light of flickering lamps the companions could see the entrance to the emergency escape tunnel. The heavy steel door stood half-open; above it was a red warning beacon-siren unit, an alarm system that alerted the redoubt when the corridor had been accessed. Water still flowed out that way, but in inches now, instead of feet.

"Mebbe one of the whitecoats tried to get out through the tunnel," Krysty said.

"Or the demons somehow managed to get the door open," Mildred said. "Or Bob and Enid sprung the door themselves to flush the demons out of the lab and force them into the tunnel."

"Some demons not make it," Jak said.

The falling water level exposed the bottoms of two of the remaining cages. Thick coatings of scum covered the lower limbs, but the heads, backs and torsos of curled-up forms were visible.

The trannies' hard external skeletons showed no evidence of decay, but their soft parts hadn't fared so well. The eyesockets were huge, empty craters. Their bellies had rotted, as had the bands of tough connective tissue between their armor plates. The full force of gravity, which now bore down them, was pulling their torso plates apart, exposing the voids between.

"Behold, the mighty minotaur brought low," Doc said.

"Bob and Enid's babies, you mean," Krysty said. "They managed to chill two of them."

"At least this affords us solid proof that the beasts are not immortal," Doc commented.

"Yeah," Mildred said, "but it took upward of seventy-five thousand gallons of water to do the deed."

Krysty approached the lab's last cage. The water had already run out. "This one is empty," she said, "and the cage door is open. It looks like one of them got away."

"A single escapee set all these destructive countermeasures in motion?" Doc said.

"One of these things is all it takes," Mildred said. "Remember, they don't need a mate in order to reproduce. Once just one of them gets into the walls of a large structure like this, it'd be almost impossible to eradicate. Trannies can't be pursued into their burrows because of the powerful acids they secrete, and because of the danger presented by their other weaponry in close-quarters combat. To clear a redoubt of these invaders, you'd have to tear the place down, inch by inch."

"Be easier, and safe, to just walk away," Krysty said.

"The data I scanned indicated a rapid breeding cycle and a short time from birth to sexual maturity. Bob and Enid designed the trannies to double their population size every two weeks. If they had ever been deployed, in a few months the demons would have outnumbered the Soviets. Assuming there were any were left by then."

"How many could there be a hundred years after one escaped?" Krysty said.

"Hard to guess on that. The population probably spiked early on, and then fell back and leveled off. A sustained population would depend on the number of offerings they were given. And on the room for colonization inside the dam. Trannies are extremely territorial. They'd fight each other for control of the available turf."

"Why did the redoubt survivors decide to feed these ungodly brutes?" Doc said. "Once they were in the dam, why not just seal them in and starve them to death?"

"Sealing them in isn't possible," Mildred said. "They could come through dam walls anywhere."

"But you said they have an aversion to sunlight."

"That's right. They hate it. And they'd avoid coming in contact with it at all costs. They don't like open spaces above ground, either. But they'd forego their instinctive preferences to hunt in the open at night if they got hungry enough. The ville folk are no match for them, and they know it. Their only option is to keep the demons content to remain where they are."

"Why feed them people?" Jak said.

"After nukeday there weren't any other large animals left in the canyon," Mildred said. "Besides, the trannies were bred to chill people. We are their meat and potatoes. Their sensory array is tuned to locate and track down human beings. Their gut enzymes are constructed to digest us. Again, this is primary weapons control. Bob and Enid couldn't have their demons running around chasing after Ukrainian sheep."

"Trannie chill-time," Jak said as he shrugged into the flamethrower's straps.

"Have you ever used one of those before?" Mildred asked.

Jak didn't answer her question.

"Test, first," is what the albino mutie said. He flipped off the pistol grip's safety switch, aimed the nozzle at one of the cages about fifteen feet away and pressed the red igniter button. With a hiss, a fine blue flame shot out of the tube beneath the nozzle. Then he pulled the trigger.

High pressure, aerosolized fuel shot out of the nozzle and burst into flame with a continuous roar.

Instantaneous inferno.

Jak was standing a bit close to his target as it turned out. The two-foot-wide stream of liquid fire hit it and split in two, spraying wide to either side, hissing and steaming as it landed on the wet floor.

Shielding their faces from the withering blast of heat, the companions shouted for him to turn the thing off.

When he released the trigger, the torrent of fire shut off and the igniter flame winked out.

Luckily, everything was still so waterlogged that nothing in the room caught fire. The plasti-steel walls of the target cage had blackened and partially melted; the ceiling above it was badly scorched and blistered. Jak had to check out the weapon, though. It was their best hope against the trannies.

Maybe their only hope.

Mildred tried to push back the door to the escape tunnel. It wouldn't open any farther because of all the debris. The lab's lighter material had been sucked down the tunnel. Doc helped her clear the door and shove it hard against the wall.

There were no operational lights in the escape passage. Visibility ended about twenty feet down it.

Hurriedly, the companions scrounged through the lab for materials to make torches from. Krysty found a water-filled drawer packed with surgical supplies. She and Mildred quickly stripped the wads of sterile bandages and dressings from their sealed foil pouches. Doc broke the legs off a tall stool, and they wrapped the ends with the bandages, creating a torch for each of them. A liberal dousing with rubbing alcohol made the material catch fire at once.

The redoubt's escape passage was very narrow, with a low ceiling. Doc had to bend over to keep from bumping the top of his head. The tunnel's featureless walls stretched off into the darkness at a slight down-angle, which helped with drainage. The heavier lab debris had been deposited on the floor as the water level dropped. The litter included computer diskettes, CDs, plastic labware, pipettes, hoses, test tube racks and pieces of broken glass.

The companions advanced with weapons drawn and safeties off. With the exception of Jak, they all carried shoulder-slung canvas bags with extra ammunition, speedloaders and grens. The albino walked in front with the flamethrower's business end in one hand and a blazing torch in the other. With a flick of the wrist, he could fill the passage from wall to wall with fire. Whether that would be enough to chill or turn back an attacking demon had yet to be proved.

There was really no room to maneuver in the escape tunnel. It was so narrow they were forced to walk single file. Their customary procedure in a situation like this was for the point man to kneel left and fire when they met opposition. The second gun knelt right, and the third and fourth guns stood and fired over their heads. The kneeling pair didn't rise to their feet until the shooters behind gave the clear signal.

Jak abruptly stopped the column and held his torch near the wall to the left.

In the dancing light, they could all see a narrow, vertical depression in the surface, about six inches deep and three feet in length, where the acid-softened concrete had been scraped away. The depression was cross hatched with talon marks.

"Trannie work," Jak said.

"It tried to tunnel out," Krysty said.

"I wonder what made it stop?" Doc queried.

"Maybe it realized that direction was a dead end, that it couldn't burrow any farther," Mildred said. "It probably has some way to sense the depth of the concrete. It could be something like sonar. Or maybe it can taste the difference."

"Or the water started pouring in, and it had to run," Krysty said.

"I don't think it would have made it, if that was the case. Bob and Enid were trying to kill it. They would have closed the passage at the other end before they opened the floodgates. They wouldn't want to risk it getting past the barrier and into the dam."

"But it did, anyway."

"Could have gotten spooked by something and taken off. Got by the door at the far end before it closed."

"Things move that fast?" Jak asked.

"Fast isn't the word for it," Mildred said.

The companions continued down the tunnel at a careful trot. They found no other evidence of demons at work on the walls. They found a lot more debris though, some of it slippery underfoot.

The passage ended in what at first appeared to be a blank wall. As they closed in on it, they could see the mouth of a three-foot-wide drain pipe set at ground level.

Doc got down on his knees and peered in, the torch and the cocked Le Mat thrust in front of him. "I cannot see any light," he said. "But there has to be an opening at the other end. This is the drain line. It could also be a continuation of the escape tunnel."

On the wall to the left of the open pipe were a series of steel rungs leading up to a dark, circular opening in the tunnel's ceiling. The top three rungs were bowed as if by a tremendous weight.

"That way into dam," Jak said.

Holding her torch high, Mildred said, "There used to be a locking hatch up there. I can see the lip of the sealing ring."

Jak passed his torch to Doc and climbed the rungs first. With the flamethrower pointed above his head, he hit the igniter button and used its flame to see by.

Mildred came after him, her Czech ZKR ready to rip.

She scrambled out onto the horizontal passage and Doc tossed up their torches. This tunnel had been filled with water, too, because the floor was still wet. There had indeed once been a locking hatch that secured this end of the passage. Its lid was flopped back on twisted hinges. There were dents and score marks along its outside edge where it had been wrenched and pried out of its frame.

Bob and Enid had managed to close the hatch in time. Perhaps it was even an automatic response when the lab emergency exit door was breached. Not that it had done any good.

"The trannie used the rungs below for leverage," Mildred said. "That's why they're bent like that. It battered and pushed at the inside of the hatch until it could get it open."

"Triple strong," Jak said.

"And triple desperate."

Krysty and Doc passed their torches up, then joined them.

"By the Three Kennedys!" Doc exclaimed, clapping a hand over his nose. "What a putrescent pall!"

"It smells like a bonfire of thirty-thousand unplucked turkeys," Mildred said.

There were gashes in the walls of the upper passage. They were spaced every few feet.

These were big ones.

Deep ones.

"Are those what I think they are?" Krysty said.

"Light 'em up, Jak," Mildred said.

The albino stuck the flamethrower's nozzle into the nearest hole and touched off a blast of fire. It howled into the ragged cleft in the wall. The congealed secretions at its base melted into spitting, smoking goo that streamed across the floor in yellow rivulets.

"Short bursts, Jak," Mildred said. "And whatever you do, don't breathe in that smoke. It'll eat your lungs to rags."

Jak gave each of the gashes the same treatment as they advanced, working both sides of the corridor, cooking the first five yards of burrow in two-thousand-degree heat.

The companions listened hard after each blast of the flamethrower, but nothing moved in the dam walls, nothing scrabbled to escape the horrific onslaught, nothing died in screams of agony.

"Apparently no one is home," Doc said.

"At least for the moment," Krysty said.

Ahead of them, the tunnel began to neck down even farther, the walls narrowing, the ceiling dropping. And at the edges of the light they could see more demon holes on either side.

"The tighter the space, the bigger the trannies' advantage," Mildred warned them.

She wasn't suggesting that they change course. There was no other course open to them. They had to proceed.

As the companions continued to advance into the darkness, from almost directly above their heads came a muffled shout followed by a rapid string of gunshots.

"That's Ryan and J.B.!" Krysty cried over the racket. "That has to be them. And they're under attack." The redhead shouted up at the ceiling, "Hang on, Ryan! We're coming!"

"Krysty, he can't hear you," Mildred said. "We've got to reach them, and fast. This tunnel has to come out somewhere."

They rushed forward, and as they did so, a shape appeared out of the inky blackness ahead. It slipped out of the wall to the right and dropped into the middle of the corridor, blocking their path. It crouched there, low to the ground, its shape compressed and difficult to distinguish from the floor.

The trannie made a clicking sound.

Like purring.

It cocked its flat head this way and that, its huge black eyes taking them in. Unafraid.

It was so far away.

Mebbe thirty-five feet separated Bob and Enid's demon from the companions.

It was hard for any of them to believe that the time to react had already long passed.

But it had.

Before Jak could unleash the flamethrower's destructive power, the trannie launched itself at them. It was all Jak, Doc, Mildred and Krysty could do to dive and fall out of the way, and flatten themselves against the floor.

The wind of its passing buffeted them. Its horn points screeched across the concrete.

The trannie was traveling so fast it couldn't change its trajectory. It was twenty feet down the corridor beyond them before it could land, brake on the wet floor with its back legs, turn and jump again.

Mildred rolled up with her revolver, leaving her torch on the ground where she'd dropped it. Diving away, the others had let their torches fall, too, and the resulting low angle of light cut visibility by a third.

She knew it was coming, and she knew she might not be able to see it before it was on top of her. From a solid, kneeling position, she held the ZKR raised and braced with her free hand. She had no plan; all she had were her reflexes and skill, both honed to Olympic silver-medal caliber. Mildred didn't see the onrushing target as much as she sensed it, flying high and tight along the ceiling. The custom wheelgun bucked in her hands as she got off a single snapshot. A finger of flame bloomed from the muzzle and an earsplitting thunderclap exploded in the tight space.

The shadow zipped past.

Over her shoulder, in the dim light, she saw Doc knocked backward, off his feet, and slammed to the floor, his prized Le Mat skittering away into the dark.

Doc clutched at his stomach with both hands, moaning.

Chapter Twenty-Seven

J.B. watched Ryan's bobbing torchlight fade, becoming fainter and fainter until it vanished down the slope below. His own torch was propped up against the inside of the turbine housing, casting stark, leaping shadows over the huge blades and their supporting axle.

There wasn't much room to move. The available space consisted of a scant triangle of open area, its apex at the axle, and sides drawn by the edges of the fan blades. To fit inside, J.B. had to kneel, bent over, with his shoulders twisted sideways, parallel to the channel.

Jubilee was a lot smaller, but she had a baby in her belly, which limited her mobility. Hunched over, holding on to her knees in the narrow space, she was no more comfortable than he was. In the light of the torch, she looked even younger than her thirteen years.

The sounds of violent, strangled wretching echoed from the intake side of the turbine. Back there in the dark, it sounded like the demon was turning its stomach inside out over its helpless victim.

Jubilee shed no tears for Pilgrim Wicklaw, her ex-husband and the father of her baby. Why should she cry over that blackheart bastard? J.B. thought. He noted there were no tears on her part, period. Not for herself, or for her unborn child. The girl sat on the floor of the housing, her eyes closed tight. From her pallor, she was in deep shock. Her former husband's blood had drizzled onto her face and down the front of her robe. She breathed raggedly through her mouth, her hands shaking uncontrollably.

The girl was in a bad way.

J.B. tried to see between the fan blades that were all that stood between him the creature still noisily puking buckets of acid. The glare of light from his torch made it impossible; he could see only pitch-blackness. He shifted the Smith to his left hand, shaking a cramp out of his right, surprised to discover that he was squeezing the pistol butt that hard.

At extreme close range, the .38 caliber wheelgun packed plenty of knockdown power. Even against a demon. Because it was going to have to crawl into the turbine to attack them, J.B. figured he had a pretty good chance of doing it some serious, brain-splattering damage. No matter how fast and dangerous the thing was in the channel, it was going to have to stick its head between the blades.

J.B. didn't like the idea of Ryan doing the channel recce alone, and going so lightly armed. He would have preferred to do the scouting, himself. If he had gone through the turbines first, instead of Ryan, the job would have fallen to him. And he wouldn't have been left behind, protecting the girl. Even though the toughest survived in Deathlands, he wouldn't have left the girl behind.

With a long, guttural moan, the demon stopped its wretching over Pilgrim Wicklaw.

Except for the hissing of the torch and the wheeze of Jubilee's breathing, there was silence. Horrible silence.

J.B. strained to hear what he knew he would hear— scraping sounds, followed by silence.

Then more scraping. Much closer.

Razor-sharp claws grated on smooth concrete. Something was bounding through the dark, in great, distance-devouring leaps.

"Wh-what n-now?" Jubilee whispered to him.

"Shh," he said.

J.B. didn't know "What now?" because he couldn't be sure what the demon was going to do next. Whether it would give up the hunt because of the fan that stood in its way, and the close quarters it was going to have to negotiate, or whether it would try to climb over the steel barrier, or push it out of the way; in either case, J.B. was going to have room to aim and fire. And either way the girl was in position to get out of the housing and survive, at least in the short term.

When the scraping stopped, the clicking began. Sharp. Metallic. It was very close, and very loud. Its vibrations penetrated the housing floor and, J.B. had no doubt, the channel walls as well. Not human, definitely not human, but intelligent just the same. The clicking was a code understood only by other demons. A code repeating its message of territory and blood over and over again.

Jubilee reached out and caught hold of his arm, squeezing it hard and digging in with her nails.

"It's going to be okay," he told her. "I want you to stay as still as you can, now. Understand?"

She nodded.

He pointed to the far side of the turbine, the side that Ryan had exited through. "Can you get out that way in a hurry if I tell you to?"

Jubilee looked at the triangular gap between the blades in front of her. "Uh-huh, I think so."

"Don't move until I say so," he told her. "But when I give you the word, I want you to get out of here quick and run. I want you run as fast as you can until you meet up with Ryan. Everything's going to be all right if you just do what I say."

Despite his assurances to the girl, J.B. didn't really know that everything was going to be okay if she bolted from cover when they came under attack. But he was damned sure that things were going to go very badly in the turbine if the demon climbed inside.

J.B. turned back toward the clicking. The gaps between the fan blades that faced him were all black. All but one.

It was reddish brown.

A demon face looked in at him.

J.B. brought up the Smith & Wesson in a blur, but before he could fire double-action, his target was gone.

Just like that.

Its after-image swam before his eyes—spiky clumped hairs on an obscenely flat head; black, gleaming eyes as big as his balled fists; rows of black-edged teeth dripping with yellow bile.

The acrid stench of fresh vomit wafted into the housing.

The demon was on the other side of the turbine fan,

calmly considering its options. Whether to jump in after them or not.

"What is it?" Jubilee said to J.B.'s back.

"Get ready."

The clicking shut off and there was another scraping sound. Talons on concrete. The demon had made a jump. After a few seconds of silence, J.B. heard another scrape, much farther away.

He knew from the greedy, hungry look he'd seen in the demon's eyes that it wasn't giving up on them. Whatever the radblazes it was doing, it wasn't giving up.

J.B. held the Smith's sights on the gap where the creature had last appeared, thumbed back the hammer and let his finger curl tightly around the trigger. "Come on, you ugly puking bastard," he said to the darkness. "Time to eat some lead."

When the demon came, it came hard and head-on.

The turbine housing jolted from the tremendous, battering-ram impact. The jarring shock and clanging noise stunned J.B. right down to the soles of his feet. He felt like he was the one who'd hit a wall.

His propped-up torch fell over and rolled away. He fumbled for it and picking it up, held it in front of him, low to the ground.

He couldn't believe his eyes.

The bottom edge of the fan blade was bent in a good foot. It was the blade's weakest spot, and the demon had hit it dead center, hurtling out of the dark like a rocket. To twist the forged steel out of shape required awesome power, and even more awesome determination. The shock mounting of the demon's brain allowed it to with-stand full force, head-on collisions.

And come back for more.

Outside the turbine, claws scraped as the demon jumped away, preparing for another ramming.

The Armorer braced himself with both hands this time.

The impact shook the housing and its occupants to the core. It made the fan blade groan as it was driven in yet another foot.

The demon wasn't trying to turn the blade on its axle, either because its body wasn't built to perform that kind of task, or because it knew better than to expose any part of itself to blasterfire from within. It didn't need to turn the blade if it could bend it far enough out of the way.

There was no guarantee that it would bash out its brains before that happened.

"Run!" J.B. told the girl. When she didn't move, he grabbed her by the arm and shook her. "Run!"

Jubilee cleared the housing an instant before the demon gave the fan yet another full-out slam.

This time the blade bent from higher up, from closer to the axle. On the next collision, J.B. knew the beast was going to be under its curled edge and in his lap.

"Ryan!" he shouted down the channel, as the demon jumped away, readying itself for another go. It wasn't a cry for help. J.B. knew there was no help to be had, not from anywhere. He was inches, maybe seconds away from a most terrible death. It was a cry of warning to his friend that something bad was coming his way.

Something triple bad.

When the demon hit the blade again, its head and shoulders popped through the gap it had created. Snarling, snapping, slashing with its claws, it thrust itself forward.

J.B. backed away on his knees, twisting sideways and off balance, firing the Smith again and again.

As THE SOUND OF GUNSHOTS rang out, Ryan dashed from the channel's end, and sprinted up the long, steep slope. No way would he leave his oldest friend and battle companion to die alone. Not while he still had bullets, blade and breath. As he vaulted over the locked hatch in the floor, something moved thirty feet in front of him, fast and low to the ground.

He skidded to a stop. Bracing the Astra's butt against the heel of his left hand that held the torch, he took aim at the shadowy form.

The demon pulled its trigger before Ryan could pull his. Leaping flat against the wall and springing off it in a blur, it landed ten feet closer to him and on his weak side, the torch side.

It was the size of a large dog.

Thinking he had caught it flatfooted, Ryan swung his sights around.

And it vanished again.

He whirled, following the scraping noise its claws made on the concrete, and picked up sight of it at once. It had landed closer to him still, in his blind spot on the left.

Blind spot no more.

Ryan squared off with the crouching demon, holding the muzzle of his weapon pointed slightly down, and not aimed directly at the thing. The creature gave him a full-frontal view, offering up its narrowest silhouette and the smallest possible target.

It didn't jump away from him. Instead, it raised itself up to its full height, which was about four feet from the floor. Its back was rounded, appearing almost hunched, and it was made up of interlocking armor plates. Standing on its rear legs, it used the edges of their horns to strop the matching rows of prongs along its middle legs.

Quick, precise strokes.

Not the act of a creature that felt it was in any danger.

Ryan backed up, figuring that every step added a fraction of a second to the time he had to react.

The demon gave him a sidelong look, cocking its head. Curious. Contemptuous. Then it followed after Ryan, moving one leg at a time, with exaggerated, even palsied slowness.

Was it mocking him?

Ryan sensed the hatch in the floor before his foot hit it and detoured around it.

The creature stalked him like he was something soft, toying with him, teasing him.

Ryan swung up the .380, trying to take advantage of the larger target being offered.

The demon jumped away, bouncing off the wall, hitting the floor and jumping again.

No way could Ryan track it, let alone hold a lead on it as it zigzagged around the dark channel. Giving something that fast 360 degrees of attack was a tinhorn mistake. And Ryan was no tinhorn. He started backing up toward the wall behind him.

The creature stopped its elaborate jumping-bean act. It alighted beside the hatch, watching him retreat.

Arrogant.

Supremely confident.

Ryan pressed his back to the concrete wall. Whatever stand he was going to make, he'd make it here, and now. He let the torch drop from his hand. It rolled against the foot of the wall. Keeping track of the demon over the Astra's sights, he quickly reached down and drew his panga from its leg sheath.

As the long blade scraped free of the leather scabbard, Ryan heard another gunshot. This one a muffled, flat crack through the floor. It sounded like a .38, but it wasn't J.B.

The demon didn't flinch at the sudden noise. It was too hard-focused on its prey. Head lowered, body lowered, it began to close in, preparing to spring.

From the turbine end of the passage came an explosion of rattling noise. Like buzz saws slicing into unanchored sheet steel. Then the buzz saws clashed together. Blades screaming. Grating. Shattering apart.

Whatever the racket was, it made the demon pause in its attack. And held its attention for a fraction of a second longer than it did Ryan's.

Ryan recognized the opportunity he'd been waiting for and without hesitation seized it. With the Astra aimed at the creature's left eye, he fired his first shot and rode the sharp little buck of its recoil back onto the target. The hollowpoint round struck well behind the huge eye because by the time the bullet arrived, the demon was already moving to the right. The bullet entered the back of its head and clipped off a saucer-sized chunk of skull.

The impact must have stunned the demon, because though it continued to glide to the right, it did so almost lazily, carelessly, and best of all, it didn't jump, which allowed Ryan to put three more quick rounds into it before the little pistol's slide locked back. He placed the bullets in a line down its neck and along its side, hoping to hit arteries and vital organs.

Something skittered, spinning across the channel floor, hitting the toe of his boot.

It was a piece of brown skull plate. Upside down. There was a big gob of white goo cupped inside.

Brains.

Demon brains.

The racket back at the turbine continued unabated, but Ryan's demon no longer seemed interested in it.

Goo as thick and clotted as buttermilk leaked from the small holes in its torso, dripping and splattering on the floor.

Goo leaked from the hole in the back of its skull, running down either side of its neck.

It was still alive.

It was still standing.

From its body language, it wasn't happy.

Ryan dropped the empty .380 and shifted the panga to his strong hand, figure-eighting its heavy blade in the air in front of him.

The demon rolled its head on its shoulders as if testing its injuries. Then it snapped its jaws together and thrust out its stumpy little arms. As it closed in on Ryan, it did so in a straight line, no longer evading because his blaster was on the floor, no longer playing with him because the fun and games were over. It showed him its twin stingers, curved black thorns extending from the top of its wrists.

Then it jumped.

HER EARS STILL RINGING, her head still reeling from the battering of the turbine, Jubilee crawled out between the fan blades and into the channel. As her knees hit the concrete, there was another collision behind her, and the shriek of metal, yielding.

It was coming.

The demon was coming through the blades.

Scrambling to her feet, she started to run down the grade. The weight and position of her baby made it impossible for her to muster any real speed. In front of her was a fuzzy wall of blackness. The only light came from behind, from the torch inside the turbine. Passing through the fan blades, it threw crazy, angled shadows across the ceiling and walls.

She had just reached the edge of the light when the final collision came, a clanging crash, and a squeal of steel bending back.

If the one-eyed man was somewhere ahead of her, she couldn't see his torch.

The man she'd left in the turbine let out a shout, and then opened fire with his handblaster.

Supporting her bouncing stomach with a hand and arm, she veered closer and closer to the channel's wall, until she was running alongside it. It was so dark ahead that she felt she was running blind. Downhill. Jubilee put out her free hand and let her fingers intermittently brush the wall. The grazing contact made her feel a little better. At least she knew she was headed in the right direction.

Three more strides, and the guiding wall abruptly fell away from her fingertips. A half step more and her fingers slapped against a hard edge, then smooth wall again. She knew what it was.

A hole, Jubilee thought as she ran. Oh, dear Enid, a hole.

She could see nothing, not in front of her or to the side. It was as if a black hood had been pulled over her head. She could only run and pray that nothing followed after her.

A prayer that went unanswered.

From behind, she heard and felt a concussive blast of air. The demon had jumped from its burrow.

Jubilee let go of her belly and sprinted, pumping her arms, driving with her legs, ignoring the pain in her lungs and her stomach. She knew what came next.

Even though she thought she was prepared for it, the terrible force of the impact stunned her.

The demon sideswiped her from behind, low and with such power that it knocked both of her legs out from under her, making her twist in the air and slam facefirst into the wall. She hit her forehead squarely and flashes of white light exploded inside her skull.

Jubilee didn't feel herself bounce off the wall. She didn't feel herself crash to the floor. For a few merciful moments she lay unconscious on her back, aware of nothing. It was the feel of hot air rushing down onto her face and the sound of gagging that awoke her.

That and the evil smell, so thick she could taste it.

She opened her eyes and saw only blackness.

All her other senses told her she was about to die.

J.B. THOUGHT HE WAS PREPARED, too. In position. Pistol steady. Ready to fire, single action. His target only a few feet away. And well lit by the torch. But everything happened much faster than he had anticipated. The demon's head was there, in his sights, all right, but when he fired, there was no head to hit. In the time it took for him to squeeze the trigger, the creature had jerked back, and rolled out of the way. The hammer fell, the primer ignited, and his bullet whined harmlessly off the turbine housing's floor and skipped under the bent fan blade.

It lunged again, almost at once, squirming its head under the fan blade and snapping its teeth.

He fired again, double action this time. With the same result. Loud bang, way late, clean miss.

The scale of the problem sank home to him.

The demon could react a hundred times faster than he could.

He had three bullets left. If the demon could taunt him into emptying his blaster into thin air, he would be trapped inside the housing, with nothing but fists and feet to fight with.

J.B. had a choice to make, and he made it. Firing another quick shot at the gap beneath the bent blade, he grabbed his torch and started backing up on his knees.

He fired again and again in the general direction of his attacker, spacing the blasterfire so he still had one shot left as he squirmed out of the other side of the housing. Once outside, he couldn't see into the turbine, but he could hear the demon scrabbling around the first two fan blades. He fired his fourth shot blind, then threw his weight against the last fan. He turned the blades to block the creature's path, then jumped back.

Claws screeched on steel.

Razor-sharp teeth clacked together.

And the demon clicked its side plates so fast it sounded like a mutie rattlesnake coiled to strike. In this case, a hundred pounder.

The fan didn't rotate on its axle. And the edge of the blocking blade didn't bend.

Which was what J.B. was counting on. He figured that with the confined space in the housing, and the obstacles it held, the demon wouldn't be able to get up enough steam to ram the barrier out of the way.

There came a soft moan from the darkness behind him.

J.B. turned and called out, "Jubilee? Ryan?"

No one answered.

Torch in hand, empty pistol tucked in his waistband, he ran down the slope. Right away, he saw a pair of dark forms on the channel floor. One lay on its back, the other crouched over it. Only one was moving, but he couldn't see that until he got closer.

The demon's sides rapidly heaved in and out as it

began to gag. It hadn't vomited acid on the girl, yet. It was working itself up to it.

Out of bullets, with no other weapons at hand, J.B. yelled curses at the creature and swung the torch around, trying to divert its attention.

The demon ignored him. It didn't even turn its head to look his way. Mouth gaping wide, it continued to dry heave in Jubilee's upturned face.

J.B. couldn't tell if she was alive or dead. There was no pool of blood beneath her. But her chest wasn't rising or falling. If she was alive she was holding her breath.

In desperation, he grabbed the Smith & Wesson from his waistband. Holding the gun by its five-inch barrel, he wound up and threw it at the demon as hard as he could. Four pounds of handblaster spun through the air and hit the creature in the side of the head with a solid thwack!

That got its attention.

As it turned to face J.B., he began to retreat, holding the torch out in front of him to keep it back. If it had jumped, it would have had him, then and there. But it didn't jump. Instead, it stepped lightly over Jubilee and followed him purposefully, slowly, as if it knew or sensed he had nowhere to run. It even let him turn and dash back to the turbine, which was as far as he could go.

J.B. knew it was a dead end, but he was trying to buy a little time for the girl, hoping that she would regain consciousness and join Ryan, or that he would come to her rescue while the demon was otherwise occupied.

Though he really had no plan going in, a plan occurred to him as he heard the renewed frenzy of the creature fighting and clawing to get out of the housing. And to get at him.

It was desperation time.

There was nothing to lose.

If the idea didn't work, his and Jubilee's chillings would just come a few seconds sooner.

Hurling his full weight against the top blade of the fan, J.B. turned it on the axle and set the trapped demon free.

Scrambling all six legs on the metal floor, the creature shot out of the housing. It stopped at once, confronting its fellow demon by raising itself up to its full height, arching its back and snapping its side plates.

As J.B. flattened himself against the wall, the thing looked at him, then at the competition, then back at him.

The other demon clicked a furious warning as it honed the horns on its back legs.

Turf war.

J.B. didn't actually see them jump. The movement was too fast for his eyes to follow. He saw them clearly for only an instant as they came together, colliding in midair, heads clashing, bodies thrashing, whip-sawing each other with their serrated legs. They locked limbs, sank in multiple rows of teeth and hit the floor rolling. Intertwined, they jumped, hurling themselves against ceiling and floor, all the while slashing with their horns.

There was no give and take to the battle. Only take. Each demon frantic to dispose of the other, to chill and mark the human prey with vomit before more challengers showed up.

The grating, screeching noise of their combat was like a dozen wag engines, all blowing their crankshafts at once. And doing it over and over again.

Afraid the death-locked creatures might roll over him, J.B. backed away from them, along the wall. Over the din of the fighting, he heard blasterfire down the channel. Four rapid shots. Light caliber.

No ricochets.

It was Ryan. It had to be. And now he was out of bullets, too.

J.B. ran to Jubilee's side and knelt over her, relieved to see that she was breathing. He made her sit up. She was conscious but still woozy. There was no blood; she didn't appear to be wounded. He quickly helped her to her feet, then pulled her by the hand.

"We got to find Ryan," he said. "We've got to do it fast."

As they hurried down the channel's slope, the ear-splitting chaos from behind got suddenly louder, then in a black blur, it overtook them. A twisting, churning, multilegged shape scraped across the ceiling and hit the floor twenty feet in front of them, blocking their path.

Chapter Twenty-Eight

As her gunshot echoed down the narrow corridor, Mildred pivoted from the hip, automatically tracking her target with the ZKR's sights, past the crumpled and doubled over Doc. Ten feet from where the old man lay groaning, the transgenetic bioweapon had come to its final rest. A quivering heap of armored plates, its six legs splayed out beneath it, the thing threw long shadows across the floor.

"Nice bit of shooting," Krysty said, holding her own weapon trained on the slumping form.

Mildred recovered her torch from the floor and stepped closer to the trannie. She had put the single .38 slug through both of its enormous eyes. In one and out the other. The mushrooming hollowpoint bullet's impact had blown away not just the eyeballs, but the entire front of its face. At the edges of the massive wound, Mildred could see the skull's armor plate in cross section; it was a sandwich, an outer layer of brown, a middle layer of white, then brown again on the inner surface. In the yawning gap where the backs of the eye sockets and the bridge of its nose had once been, a pale and wrinkled brain weeped thick white tears.

The trannie had lost its entire upper jaw, but the

lower one remained, exposing triple rows of triangular-shaped, razor teeth, and a black-edged tongue whose pointed tip moved reflexively as shocked and dying nerves continued to fire, reaching up to touch the palate that was no longer there.

Jak nudged the creature in the side with the toe of his boot, keeping the nozzle of the flamethrower aimed at what was left of its head. "Chilled," was his solemn verdict.

Mildred quickly turned her attention to Doc. "Are you hurt?" she asked Tanner.

It took a long moment for him to answer. And when he did, his voice came out in a breathless wheeze. "Only my dignity, my dear Mildred," Doc said. He pushed up into a sitting position, still tenderly clutching his stomach. "Thank the stars that hellish creature grazed me in passing. Oof, it was like being kicked by a mule."

"You're lucky it didn't kick you," Mildred said. "It would have laid you open, end to end."

As the two women helped Doc to his feet, Jak continued down the narrowing hall. He was still in sight when he turned and waved for them to join him.

As they hurried over, he pointed at the circular installation in the ceiling and said, "Hatch."

It was dogged from their side.

"Go on, open it!" Krysty said to him. She, Mildred and Doc took up covering positions, their weapons aimed at the hatch, and at whatever might decide to come through it.

The ceiling was so low that standing on tiptoes even Jak could reach the locking wheel. It hadn't been turned in a very long time. Throwing his weight against the wheel, he cracked it loose, and it spun easily. As he un-dogged the hatch, two things happened in rapid succession. First, a clattering, crashing, screeching din broke out above them, then came a flurry of tightly spaced gunshots.

SEEING THE TWIN, curving stingers extended and dripping poison, seeing the wounded demon drop into a crouch, Ryan knew the thing was going to jump for him. And that when it did, wounded or not, he was way undergunned.

Every nerve tingling, he concentrated on the timing. Its timing. His timing.

When the demon crouched a little lower, preparing to drive with its long back legs, Ryan turned and bolted upslope. One stride was all he took. He didn't wait to hear the scrape of the claws on concrete; if he'd waited it would have been too late. He turned a 180 and jumped.

The predator fell for the feint.

Unable to correct its course in midflight, the demon vaulted past him, whipping wind across his back. It skittered on the concrete, trying to stop, and ended up bouncing off the base of the wall. It never lost its balance. Standing up to its full height, it slashed at the air with its stingers, sending droplets of poison flying.

Ryan backed away.

Now it was mad.

And the same trick wouldn't work twice.

The demon circled deliberately, making Ryan put

the wall to his back. The one-eyed warrior whipped his blade back and forth as the thing closed in and crouched for the kill.

Ryan had already picked out his target, the join of head and shoulders, when the hatch in the floor crashed back and Jak Lauren scrambled through it. Ryan couldn't see the tanks strapped on his back, but he could see the fine blue flame coming from his hand.

The demon turned to look at the new meat, then back at Ryan, as if trying to decide which to chill first.

With an air-sucking whoosh, thirty feet of aerosolized fuel ignited, turning the inside of the channel as bright as day. The torrent of fire cascaded down on the suddenly immobile demon. Shielding his face from the terrible heat, Ryan retreated.

The demon let out a piercing shriek and jumped once, headfirst into the ceiling, a ball of fire. Jak kept the flamethrower's trigger pinned, hosing it in a steady stream. The demon's legs shriveled to nothing and it collapsed onto its side. Crackling. Spitting. Smoking.

Jak let the flamethrower wink out.

The channel reeked of high test fuel and flash-cooked grasshopper.

Krysty, Mildred and Doc climbed through the hatch. Krysty ran up to Ryan and hugged him. "Are you okay?"

"I'm fine."

"Where's J.B.?" Mildred said.

He pointed toward the awful sounds coming from the darkness upslope. "I left him up there, with Jubilee."

"What's that noise?" Krysty said.

"Don't know," Ryan said. "It doesn't sound good."

Over the racket, and its echoes, they heard a familiar voice shout, "Ryan! Ryan! Hurry!"

"That is John Barrymore," Doc said.

"He must have seen the light from the flamethrower," Ryan said. He took the ammo bag from Krysty and opened it.

"Your SIG's in there," she told him.

Ryan pulled out his predark semiauto pistol, shouldered the bag, then led the way as they ran uphill to find J.B.

They didn't have far to go. By the light of their torches they could see their friend's predicament and the source of the clattering din.

A pair of demons locked in mortal combat thrashed in the middle of the floor. Thrashed and jumped, bouncing off the walls and ceiling, tearing at each other with teeth and claw. Every impact sent white blood flying from their wounds. There were demon legs on the floor. Severed legs.

J.B. and Jubilee stood pinned against the right-hand wall, unable to move for fear of being crushed.

The companions lined up and took aim at the jumping combatants.

"Wait!" Ryan said. "Don't shoot unless they stop fighting. Save the ammo. You can make it, J.B. Run along the wall. They're too busy to notice. We've got you covered. Run J.B.!"

Dragging the pregnant girl behind him, the Armorer did just that. When they had joined the others, Ryan waved them all back to the open hatch.

"Leave 'em or finish 'em?" Jak said to Ryan.

"Finish them while we can. Down the hatch, Jak."

Ryan took a frag gren from the satchel and primed it. Letting the grip safety flip off, he counted to three, then bowled the gren toward the fighting pair. He wasn't looking for a ten-ring.

It only had to be close, like horseshoes.

A second after he hit the floor behind the hatch, the air was split by a mind-numbing thundercrack that rained concrete dust down on Ryan's head. He felt the heat of the blast roll over him, then demon bodies and body parts, blown to bite-size fragments whistled through the channel, clattering as they skipped off the floor and ricocheted off the walls.

They were still clattering as he ducked through the hatch and pulled it closed. Ryan spun the locking wheel, redogging it.

"Locking the hatch was probably a wasted effort, my dear Ryan," Doc told him. "We had some contact with Bob and Enid's pets in this corridor, as well. They've extensively tunneled it."

"How did you get to us?" Ryan said, watching as Mildred worked on Jubilee, checking her for injuries.

Krysty explained about the redoubt's emergency escape tunnel, how it had been flooded in an attempt to chill the trannies, how she and the others had drained it to get access to the dam.

"Is the redoubt's mat-trans unit working?" he asked her.

"We ran a jump test on it. It's warmed up and ready to go."

"I don't know about the rest of you," Ryan said, "but I wouldn't mind putting a few hundred miles between us and this radblasted place."

He got no argument there.

The companions advanced down the passage, which got wider and wider as they retraced their steps. Ryan and J.B. took note of the gashes in walls and their blackened edges.

"Jak fried them on the way in," Krysty said. "To keep the trannies off us."

"Better give them another dose," Ryan told the albino.

Jak moved ahead of the others, quickly with the flamethrower, shooting a burst of fire into each hole. He paused before hosing down a gash on the right. His body language made the hair on the back of Ryan's neck stand up.

"Hold it, everybody," he said, raising the SIG and aiming it at the hole.

Standing well to the side of the opening, Jak pointed at a trickle of bright yellow dripping from the bottom of the gash and pooling on the floor.

Everybody took aim.

His back to wall, Jak angled the flamethrower's nozzle around the edge of the gash, and unleashed a terrific blast of heat. A high-pitched scream harmonized with the roar of burning fuel. In the next instant, the scorched demon jumped from the wall and past him, a sizzling fireball. It hit the floor and leaped into the gash in the opposite wall.

Inside the burrow, the fire light winked out, extinguished by the tight fit and by slime.

Ryan already had the pin out of another gren. "Fire in the hole!" he yelled, pitching the fragger deep into the gash and jumping out of the way.

Like a cannon maw, the hole bellowed and belched ten feet of flame. Debris exploded from the wall, sending a plume of white guts and shattered armor spraying over the ceiling and floor. Mildred twisted Jubilee out of the way and shielded her with her body.

When the smoke cleared, Mildred said, "The ladder down to the emergency tunnel is just ahead. From there on we're moving away from the dam. We should be safe."

Ryan saw the open hatch in the floor. "You didn't close it?"

"We couldn't close it," Krysty told him. "The trannies ripped it off its hinges."

"That might mean some of them got down ahead of us," J.B. said.

"We've got to act like that's what's happened," Ryan told them. "And hope it didn't."

Jak climbed down the bent rungs first, then Ryan followed. The others stayed in the upper corridor, watching their backs with drawn blasters.

On the lower tunnel floor, nothing moved. It was dead quiet except for the steady hiss of the flame-thrower's igniter, dead dark except for its blue flame. Krysty tossed them down a torch.

Ryan picked it up and immediately pointed at the drain pipe set low in the wall. "Keep an eye on that," he told Jak.

Then he called up to the others, "Come on down."

No sooner had they all reached the floor than something started moving way back in the drain pipe. Something big. Claws scrabbled at the slippery surface, unable to get good purchase.

Jak knelt down and fired a blast of flame into the mouth of the pipe, then he hit it again.

"Everybody get moving," Ryan said as Jak stood up. "Go on, run!" Priming another gren, he pitched it down the pipe, giving it a rolling spin, making it clunk and bang its way deep down the pipe.

The hard crack of the explosion was muffled by the pipe, the concrete and the distance. Gray smoke curled up from the lip.

Nothing came flying out in chunks.

"At least that'll give the bastards something to think about," J.B. said as Ryan joined him, stride for stride.

They didn't think about it for long.

Behind the companions in the darkness, over the slap of their own footfalls on the concrete, they could hear the demons coming.

Scraping.

Clicking.

Snarling.

Crashing into the walls as they fought one another to be first at the fresh meat.

"They can follow our scent," Mildred said as she ran. "The wind currents will have carried it all through the dam. They'll come after us like sharks up a chum line."

"Sounds like there's hundreds of them," Krysty said.

"Could just be the echoes," Mildred said.

"Could also be that's how many there are," Ryan said.

He and Jak fell back, taking up a rear-guard position. And just in time to see a blur bounding out of the darkness, springing high in the air.

Jak held down the flamethrower's trigger, filling the corridor with a sheet of fire, angled at the ceiling. The demon was coming so fast that it blasted through the seething wall of flame. It sailed over their heads like a comet, trailing a fiery tail, its curved stingers fully extended, trying and failing to make contact.

As it skidded down in front of them, Doc's Le Mat bellowed and spit a yard of flame from its barrel. The impact of tightly packed metal odds and ends, screws, nuts, bits of scrap steel, made the demon's head vanish all the way to its neck. Burning bits of skull skipped down the hall ahead of them, creating a thousand points of light in the blackness.

The companions jumped the still kicking, still flaming corpse.

From behind them came a rhythmic, scraping sound. Another demon had broken free of the pack. And was closing.

As they ran, Ryan turned and bowled a gren down the corridor. It thudded into the dark, then exploded. The hard whack of detonation was followed, a split second later, by the juicy splatter of a demon flying apart.

That didn't end the threat. As the blast echoes faded, Ryan could hear a dull roar over his shoulder. It sounded like a tidal wave bearing down.

And it was going to overtake them.

Shouting "Go!" to the others, Ryan grabbed Jak's

arm and pulled him to a stop. No explanation was necessary. The albino could hear what was coming, too. They had to fight a delaying action, to give the others a chance to escape.

Ryan pitched another gren, and, as it bounced into the dark, swung up his SIG, holding it steady with both hands. The wave's roar got louder and louder, and then the frag blew, sending forth a hard gust of wind and a boiling cloud of cordite smoke. Segments of leg and torso rolled down the corridor toward them.

Firing the semiauto pistol as fast as he could, Ryan swept his aimpoint back and forth between the hallway's walls, creating a narrow zone of death beyond the edge of the light. The 9 mm slugs ricocheted off the concrete, and made solid, meaty thwacks as they slammed into demon flesh.

If one went down in the darkness, there were many more close behind to take its place.

Shoulder to shoulder, jostling for position as they burst through the cloud of gren smoke, two demons bore down on the stationary targets.

Jak cooked them both in the same withering blast, a sweep of fire that melted their eyes, burned off their spiky topknot, and cooked their soft white guts to the consistency of hard boiled egg. The twin flaming corpses screeched along the ceiling, slid down the walls and crashed to the floor in side-by-side heaps.

Ryan heard the scrape and the pause that meant another demon was incoming and airborne. He held the SIG low and opened fire, again as fast as he could pull the trigger. Out of the darkness the demon flew, its body fully extended. Ryan's Parabellum rounds stitched it from abdomen to throat, the bullets slapping into and coring the armored plates.

It hit the floor and jumped one more time, right into the aerial bonfire Jak made. The lead in its belly melted along with it eyes, topknot and guts.

Ryan dumped the empty mag on the floor and slapped a fresh one home. Acrid smoke from all the burning corpses was starting to fill the corridor, making their eyes sting and tear. Through the pall came a horrible clashing and the shrill screech of horn on concrete.

A trio of demons appeared, leapfrogging one another. The second one in line timed its leap so it came down on the first. Using its hind leg, it slashed before the competitor could jump away. The head of the demon in the lead jumped from its torso. As the body crashed to the floor, the skull caromed off the wall, its jaws still snapping.

The third demon landed on the back of second, and the battle was joined. They fought face-to-face in the middle of the corridor, almost faster than the eye could follow. With savage downward slashes of their rear legs, they raked open each other's bellies, spilling white guts onto the floor. And still they fought, biting, clawing, dying in each other's grasp, with the taste of each other's blood in their mouths.

In that moment, Ryan realized that it wasn't just the companions' scent that was luring the creatures on. It was the promise of new real estate. The dam had been fully tunneled, fully occupied, for many decades. The reopened escape tunnel offered them access to the redoubt for the first time in a century. It was the demon equivalent of the Oklahoma land rush.

First come, first to stake a claim.

Before the next wave could strike, Ryan and Jak turned and raced to close ground with the others.

"There's a heavy door at the entrance to the lab," Mildred shouted to them as they caught up. "If we can make it there, I think it'll keep them out."

Ryan could already see the light at the end of the tunnel, about seventy-five feet ahead. Behind him, the tidal wave roared. As he ran, he dipped a hand into the ammo bag and fished out another gren.

He was last to reach the lab entrance door, but before he slipped past it, he lobbed the gren down the passage. As he threw it, he realized that he'd grabbed a stunner instead of a frag.

Ryan slammed the door shut as the flash bang lit up the corridor in absolute white light. The shock wave slammed the far side of the door, rattling it in its frame. When he peeked out, he saw smoke and chaos. Demons blinded, deafened, disoriented, hurling themselves headfirst into the walls, the ceiling, into one another, spinning wildly on the floor. Those closest to the blast were chilled dead, their brains scrambled to mush.

From the roar and the clatter, there were others behind, and they were coming in droves.

Ryan slammed the exit door shut and dropped the locking bar into its latch.

No sooner had he secured the door than the clicking started up behind them.

Ryan spun to face the lab. The noise wasn't coming from the section of the room they were in. The large cages on the floor and the tiers of smaller ones along the wall hadn't held anything alive for a century. The clicking was coming from the other side of the barrier that divided this section of the lab from the next. Something was moving beyond the half-open gate. Ryan saw the spiky tops of the demons' heads between the steel bars.

"Dark night!" J.B. exclaimed. He had a gren in his hand but didn't try to toss it through the gate. The room was too small, and there was no cover. The frag shrap would have cut the companions to pieces.

Krysty and Mildred opened fire with their .38s, popping off rounds at the dark shapes. Their slugs whined and sparked off the bars.

"Hold it, hold it!" Ryan said. "We've got to get control of the gate. The gate's the key. We can't let them get through it. Jak, beat them back."

The albino laid down a smothering blanket of flame, sending it splashing between the bars, onto the desktops and floor. The demons jumped away from the heat, to the far side of the room.

As the blast of fire dissipated, leaving behind scorched ceiling and floor tiles, the companions rushed forward to claim ground.

J.B. pulled the barrier gate closed, but there was no key in its lock and no way to secure it.

On the other side of the bars, spread out along the matching barrier in front of the elevator, was a trio of demons. They weren't fighting one another; there was plenty of prey to go around.

All three launched themselves at the bars. It was a synchronized attack, and it was met with a synchronized response.

The companions unleashed all-out fusillade, firing point blank through the bars, into the gaping mouths, into the exposed bellies. As a demon lunged, trying to plant its stinger in Doc's forehead, he shot straight into its face. Before it could pull back, lead balls had shattered its skull into confetti, blasting white gunk all over the floor.

It was a slaughter, pure and simple. Joyous slaughter. They blew the demons apart and filled the lab with clouds of blaster smoke.

When their ears stopped ringing, the companions could hear loud banging from behind them. Turning, they saw the escape passage door jumping in its frame as trannies battered it from the other side.

"That door isn't going to hold!" Ryan said.

J.B. opened the gate and they all rushed through it, leaping over the shattered corpses, to the second line of floor-to-ceiling bars. Ryan was the last one through the gate in front of the elevator. He pulled it closed, but again, there was no way to turn the lock. The key was gone.

"Get the elevator open," Mildred said, taking aim between the bars at the jolting emergency door.

Doc pressed the lone button beside the elevator doors. With a clunk, they slid open.

"Our chariot awaits," he said.

As he spoke, there was a tremendous thud. The emergency door buckled in the middle and broke free of its hinges, slamming flat to the floor. Demons poured in through the opening, scrambling shoulder to shoulder and over one another's backs.

Ryan and Mildred fired their weapons, covering the companions' rush to the elevator. The hail of bullets did little to slow the oncoming wave. The trannies crashed against the first barrier. One of them hit the gate and it swung open. A second later the rest were streaming in after it.

As Ryan and Mildred raced into the car, she said, "We can reflood the bottom floor and chill them all. Hit eighteen, J.B."

The Armorer pressed the button for floor eighteen.

"Fry them up, Jak," Ryan said.

The albino stepped forward, the flamethrower's igniter hissing. As the trannies slammed the final barrier, he sent a torrent of liquid fire arching onto them.

The elevator doors didn't close.

"Hit the button, J.B.," Mildred said.

"I am hitting it."

Jak fired again as fresh demons clambered over their burning kin and the open gate. Flame surged across the gap and through the bars, then the flamethrower sputtered and died. The igniter still burned blue and bright, but the tanks were out of fuel.

The doors started to close, but in extreme slow motion.

"Radblast!" J.B. shouted as three demons cleared the gate and launched themselves at the open car.

The combined impact of their bodies buckled in the sheet steel. The trannie in the middle managed to get a forearm between the doors just as they slid shut.

In front of the companions' faces, the claw hand flexed, the long stinger uncoiled.

"It's going to make the doors open!" Mildred cried.

Ryan already had his panga out and was swinging it down in a tight arc. The lopping slice cut the arm off flush with the doors, which clanked shut, and then the car started to creep upward. The severed claw lay still at their feet but the stinger squirted drops of poison.

The car rocked as the demons threw themselves, full force, at the doors and wall.

Jak ditched the empty set of tanks and drew his .357 Magnum Colt Python. The others checked their weapons' ammo, and quickly reloaded.

When they reached floor eighteen, an electronic bell dinged. The doors clunked and again slid apart in slow motion. Through the widening split they saw the hallway lights were on. And they saw the demon crouched in the corridor, preparing to jump into the elevator with them.

The companions flattened against the car's back wall and opened fire through the gap and into the edges of the doors, hitting the creature dozens of times as it leaped.

Knocked sideways by the multiple impacts, the demon crashed into the wall and bounced onto its back.

The doors opened all the way.

The electronic bell chimed.

Nobody got out of the car.

"If they've already escaped the lab floor, they could be anywhere in the redoubt," J.B. said. "We can't stop them by flooding nineteen."

"Time to jump, while we still can," Ryan said.

"Punch ten," Krysty told J.B.

The doors closed on the demon corpse and littered hallway. The elevator moved upward. When the doors opened again, the companions were braced and ready for anything. But there was no welcoming committee waiting for them this time.

Krysty and Jak led them on a dead run through the security gates and the heavy double doors to the redoubt's mat-trans section. As they entered, they could feel the idling unit's steady vibration through the floor. The banks of chattering computers indicated that the system was online and ready to process. They headed for the two portholed steel doors on the far wall.

Ryan smiled broadly when he saw the scoped Steyr waiting for him atop the steel cart in front of the doors. As he picked it up he said, "Glad I didn't lose this." After shouldering its sling, he passed J.B. his Smith & Wesson scattergun.

Then he peered into the half-open door of the nearest mat-trans unit. Surprisingly, it was furnished in steel spikes. "Doesn't look too comfortable," he said.

"That's for the trannies," Krysty told him.

"Advanced bioweapon deployment technology," Mildred said. "To Russia with love, from Bob and Enid."

"The other one's for us," Krysty said.

Jak opened the portholed door, and the companions started filing into the little room.

Jubilee held back, looking very scared.

"There's nothing to worry about," Mildred assured her. "The machinery works just fine."

"There's more to worry about if you stay," J.B. told the girl.

The reminder didn't help matters. Jubilee was petrified. Mildred shot J.B. a why-don't-you-shut-up-and-let-me-handle-it look.

"The six of us have jumped dozens of times," Mildred said, "without any lasting ill effects. Jumping just this once won't hurt you and it won't hurt your baby. You'll just fall asleep and wake up someplace else. Someplace safe."

At Ryan's urging, and with a firm push from behind, Jubilee got into the chamber with the others. Ryan stepped in last. All around them, the armaglass was midnight black shot through with crimson.

Like sprays of blood.

As he closed and secured the chamber door, through the porthole window, he saw demons. They burst through the swing doors, fighting one another to be first into the room, hot on the scent trail of their intended victims.

One of them looked at the mat-trans door and saw Ryan's face framed in the glass. From the far side of the room, it launched itself and crashed headfirst into the door.

But it was too late. The mat-trans cycle had began and the room was starting to fill with mist. As the mist grew thicker, its tendrils lengthened, stretching down to curl around the heads and shoulders of the travelers.

"It's going to be all right," Ryan told the trembling girl. "Just sit down, close your eyes and it'll be over before you know it."

As they took their places on the floor, he reached out a battle-scarred fist and took hold of Jubilee's small hand. Krysty smiled at him, her emerald eyes flashing pure love, and took hold of the girl's other hand.

Blackness felled them.

RYAN AWOKE on the floor of the chamber, his head spinning. For a second, as he struggled to regain his senses, and to control the dry heaves that racked his throat and cramped his belly, he thought it all had been a dream. Little Pueblo. The dam. The pilgrims. The demons. Just another in the long chain of horrible nightmares that chased them every time they mat-transed and rematerialized.

When he pushed up and saw the Jubilee sprawled across his leg, he knew it hadn't been a dream.

Mildred had already recovered and was taking Jubilee's pulse.

The woman noted the concern on his face and said, "She's going to be okay, Ryan."

Even as she spoke, the girl began to moan and stir.

When the effects of the jump had passed and they had all regained their strength, they exited the chamber and found their way out of the new redoubt.

The complex's hidden entrance opened onto a much different landscape than the one they had left. It was lush and it was high. Surrounding them were steep, densely forested slopes of evergreens. And above them, blue skies.

"Could be Canada," J.B. suggested.

"Or Montana," Mildred said.

Jubilee stared at the vista in amazement and delight. She had never seen so much green in all her life.

The sweet scent of wildflowers drew them away from the entrance and to the meadow below. It was dappled with pale blues, pinks, yellows. A crystal-clear brook ran through the tall grass. The jump had made them all thirsty, and they lay down on their bellies and drank their fill.

Across the narrow valley, at the base of the mountain on the other side, a line of large, four-legged creatures browsed the edge of the forest.

"Plenty game here," Jak observed.

"That's what I was thinking, too," J.B. said. "We shouldn't have any trouble finding dinner."

"Look at your new wife," Krysty said to Ryan.

The girl was sitting cross-legged in the grass, putting the finishing touches on a flower bracelet to match the brightly colored blossoms that she had woven into her hair.

"Forced marriages don't count," he said. "You know that."

"I don't see any sign of a settlement," Mildred said. "No buildings. No smoke. No nothing. This is wild country. We can't leave her here. We're going to have to take her with us."

"That's fine," Ryan said. "She can come along until we find some good folks who'll take in her and the baby. There must be someone, somewhere in some ville who will provide room and board in exchange for work."

"What about Little Pueblo?" Krysty asked. "What's going to become of it, now?"

"The trannies are loose in the middle of the ville," Mildred said. "There's no way to contain them. I'd say Little Pueblo is done for."

"Justice comes, a hundred years late," Ryan stated grimly.

Epilogue

From the edge of the canyon rim, Pilgrim Plavik surveyed Paradise for the last time. To his back the sun was
setting, casting rays of soft orange light across the
spread of cultivated fields and tiny, clustered settlement of Little Pueblo.

Looking down from that distance at what had happened in a single, terrible night was almost impossible
to believe. A night of blood-curdling screams and vol-
leys of blasterfire. And afterward, the sounds of wretching.

A chorus of wretching that swelled and faded,
swelled and faded until nearly dawn.

No one alive had dreamed that such a thing could
happen. Certainly not Pilgrim Plavik.

The offerings to the demons had been more than
ample and made on schedule, he had seen to that. On
his orders, the only door to Bob and Enid's tomb had
been piled high with boulders.

The demons hadn't used the door, of course. They
had burrowed out through the face of the tomb and
through the roof. Too many holes to count. And once
free, they moved too quickly to see.

The hour was late.

The whole ville had been asleep.

Everyone but Plavik. He had awakened after an hour or so, restless, energized in the aftermath of his victory over the one-eyed man and his companions. Sex with any one or combination of his wives hadn't interested him. He had put on his boots and left city hall. In the dark, he had climbed the familiar path to the top of the dam, and there watched the moon dance on the surface of the placid lake. He took stock of his kingdom and marveled anew at his fountain of luck.

It was from the dam crest road that he heard the agonies of Little Pueblo begin. He had no idea what was happening below, but he was unarmed and there was nothing he could do.

Blasterfire and screams echoed in the canyon for hours, followed by the wretching.

Then as the sun came up everything became still. Natural sounds, comforting sounds took over. Birds tweeted. Bugs chirped. A soft breeze rustled in the corn.

Plavik waited until well after sunrise before descending the dam and returning to the city center.

He found an open air charnel house. Bodies lay in the streets, some torn limb from limb, all of them sat in rank yellow pools. At first glance, and first smell, he knew that it wasn't the work of human beings.

Bodies lay inside the buildings, too. The rooms of city hall were choked with corpses. The other pilgrims, their wives, and their children had been butchered in their sleep.

Little Pueblo's field hands had fared no better. Some had made it out of the low buildings that circled the square; most had not. The chillers had come in through the doors and windows. Sealing off the exits, they had trapped and slaughtered the men amid the debris of their household furnishings, broken beds and spilled mattress stuffing. And that done, they had drenched everything in yellow slime.

Fearing the worst, Plavik had stood on the curb and shouted at the top of his lungs. Shouted for someone. Anyone. His cries echoed off the canyon walls and faded. He shouted himself hoarse. No one came. They were all dead.

His was a kingdom of one.

From the trees that lined the edge of the park, he could see the holes that riddled the tomb. If there had been any doubt in his mind what had happened, it vanished in that moment.

The demons had broken out.

In the cover of night they had laid a table for themselves. In darkness they would come back again to feast.

Plavik had spent his final night in Little Pueblo.

It was hard for him to decide what to take. He remembered the ordeal he'd endured to reach Paradise. He knew he couldn't carry enough water to last the entire journey, and that every extra ounce on his back reduced the chance of his surviving the crossing.

He had been much younger then. Stronger. His flesh tempered from fighting. But even more important than that, the young, hot-tempered Plavik hadn't known what he was getting into when he set off. The pain that would come. The suffering. The nearness of death. He no longer had the luxury of that ignorance. He knew precisely what he faced, and how slim the odds were.

Plavik looked up into the still-bright sky. High overhead, riding the towering thermals created by the canyon's walls, the buzzards of Deathlands slowly wheeled and circled.

A long-lost sword.

A willing heroine.

A quest to protect humanity's
sacred secrets from falling
into the wrong hands.

Her destiny will be revealed.

July 2006.

GOLD
EAGLE ®

James Axler
Outlanders®

Reborn as neogods, an anient race begins its final conquest in…

RIM OF THE WORLD
Outlanders #37

An ancient artifact claimed to unlock secrets hidden for two thousand years and restore the control of a ruthless Sumerian god has the Cerebus warriors battling blood-thirsty rebels in their determination to prevent such a destiny.

Available May 2006 at your favorite retail outlet.

GOLD EAGLE®

GOUT37

THE DESTROYER™

#143

America's health system is going to the dogs...

BAD DOG

In an effort to prevent skyrocketing health premiums, the president of the Institute of Nationalized Humane Health Care has started using trained dogs to snuff out costly, disease-carrying people. Remo must stop the dog attacks at the source—by eliminating the elusive, mysterious dog handler himself.

Available April 2006 at your favorite retail outlet.

GOLD EAGLE®

GDEST143